A
COMMON
DEATH

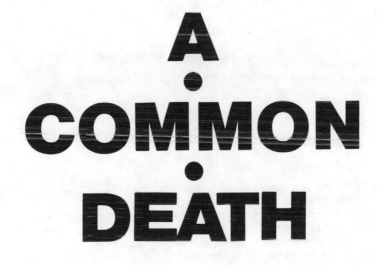

A COMMON DEATH

NATASHA COOPER

Crown Publishers, Inc.
New York

For Gerald
with love and many thanks for the scam

Copyright © 1990 by Daphne Wright

Published by Crown Publishers, Inc., 201 East 50th Street.
New York, New York 10022. A Member of the Crown Publishing Group.
Originally published in Great Britain by Simon & Schuster Ltd. in 1990.

CROWN is a trademark of Crown Publishers, Inc.
Manufactured in the United States of America.
Library of Congress Cataloging-in-Publication Data
Cooper, Natasha.
   A common death / by Natasha Cooper.
     p.   cm.
   I. Title.
PS3553.06215F47   1990   90-2249
813'.54—dc20   CIP

ISBN 0-517-576651
10 9 8 7 6 5 4 3 2 1
First American Edition

Author's Note

As everyone knows there is no such government department as DOAP – the Department of Old Age Pensions. It and all the characters who take part in the following story are wholly imaginary and have no counterparts in the real world.

XCIV

They that have power to hurt and will do none,
That do not do the thing they most do show,
Who, moving others, are themselves as stone,
Unmoved, cold, and to temptation slow;
They rightly do inherit heaven's graces,
And husband nature's riches from expense;
They are the lords and owners of their faces,
Others but stewards of their excellence.
The summer's flower is to the summer sweet,
Though to itself it only live and die,
But if that flower with base infection meet,
The basest weed outbraves his dignity:
For sweetest things turn sourest by their deeds;
Lilies that fester smell far worse than weeds.

William Shakespeare

1

WILLOW KING learned to lie in 1983. Her first attempt being successful, she started to work at her new talent for deceit, refining and polishing it until it had brought her most of the things she had ever wanted – and a lot of other things she had never even suspected herself of wanting. As the years passed, her talent also brought her amusement and no small degree of happiness. By the end of the decade she believed that it had made her impregnable to misery or disaster. But then chance, and someone else's tragedy, showed her how wrong she was.

When she arrived for work one icy morning in November, quite unaware of the storm that was about to break over her head, she was pulled up short by the sight of the office forecourt. Instead of the usual trickle of Civil Servants parking their cars or chaining bicycles to the railings, there was a positive phalanx of policemen drawn up ahead of her. Six white police cars, the first with its blue warning light still flashing, were parked in front of them. Willow's first sanguine thought was that there must have been a bomb scare, or perhaps some threatened riot. But even as the thought formed in her mind, she knew that those crises could not have drawn so many – and such senior – policemen to the Department of Old Age Pensions.

Willow was shocked by the instinctive fear induced in her by the sight of such immense police strength. Reminding herself that despite her facility for deception she had done nothing actually criminal and therefore had no need to fear any policeman in the world (and particularly not in London), she walked firmly towards the constable who stood nearest the main door. She was almost as tall as he, which helped her to control the instinct to cringe before him.

'Yes, Miss?' he said as she made to sweep past him.

'My name's King,' she answered crisply, flashing her pass at him, and waiting for him to open the door for her. 'Assistant secretary (finance).'

'Thank you, Miss,' he said, making no move to open the door. Instead he held out his hand for the pass.

Blinking a little, Willow handed it over and watched him as he carefully examined it. For the first time in years she found herself embarrassed by the dreadfulness of the photograph that had been embedded in the plastic rectangle. She knew that it made her look older than her thirty-eight years and even more dowdy than usual. The photograph being black-and-white, there was not even the colour of her dark-red hair to give any kind of distinction, and her spectacles had caught the camera's flash, reflecting it so that her eyes looked like liquid egg white.

'Miss Wil-hel-mina King?' asked the young officer, pronouncing her impossible name as though it were three separate words. It must have been about thirty years since anyone had used anything but her nickname and Willow was disconcerted for a moment. Then she nodded, she hoped with the requisite dignity and coldness.

'Report to the officer inside, Miss King,' said the policeman.

Willow did as she was told, asked fruitlessly what was going on, and then made her way to the lifts. For one absurd moment she wondered whether this police operation could be some frightful new economy drive, designed to frighten the Civil Servants into working harder, arriving on time, or ceasing to use the photocopying facilities for their own private affairs. But even as she allowed her imagination to quicken, she knew that she was being unsuitably frivolous. There was an air of drama and even of suppressed violence about the place that morning, which did not square with any government-inspired efficiency drive.

Working on her self-control and reminding herself that her part-time job at DOAP required a degree of seriousness foreign to the other side of her life, Willow took the lift up to the eighth floor. The lift was old and inefficient and so Willow was accustomed to read something during its jerky ascent to stop herself exploding at the waste of time. On that particular morning she took from her briefcase a minute from the under secretary about an esoteric pensions problem. As the lift arrived with a bump on the eighth floor and the doors swished open, Willow walked forward still immersed in her memorandum and almost collided with the heavy blue-clad figure of one of the department's drivers. Raising her head in order to deliver a nicely judged apology, she saw the ugly face and angry brown eyes of Albert Dagnan, the minister's personal chauffeur.

'What are you doing up here, Albert?' she asked genuinely surprised. He might perhaps have legitimate business on the tenth floor, where the minister's offices were, but otherwise his place was in the canteen, the garage or the drivers' room on the ground floor.

'I didn't know I was answerable to you, Miss King,' he said with all the truculence for which he was notorious in the offices of DOAP and shouldered his way past her into the lift.

Willow blinked and made a mental note to have a quiet word with the establishments officer next time she ran into him. Lack of polish was one thing but gratuitous rudeness to a senior Civil Servant was another and could not be allowed to pass uncensured.

Righteously indignant, she walked briskly into the anteroom of her office to find her administration trainee, Barbara, and her typist, Roger, both working hard.

Pleased by the unusual industry, she bade them good morning and was surprised that even then they did no more than look up briefly and acknowledge her greeting. Willow let her pale-green eyes narrow as she looked at Roger, virtuously pounding away at the electric typewriter and occasionally sniffing and blowing his nose with all the theatricality he used to signal his frequent ailments.

'You're very industrious this morning, Roger,' she said, allowing the approval to sound more obviously than usual in her chilly voice. 'What's up?'

He turned his head so that she could see the whole of his face and she tried to suppress a gasp as she saw two long scratches down his right cheek and painful-looking bruising around his right eye. Poor Roger had suffered several times from thugs who pretended to take exception to his undoubted campness as an excuse to beat him up on late-night tubes, in dark streets and wherever else his nocturnal life took him.

'Haven't you heard, Miss King?' he said hoarsely, as though his throat hurt him too. Despite his ailments, he smiled like someone faced with an unexpected treat. Willow shook her head vigorously, confident that the 'Extra-firm' hairpins that skewered her long chestnut hair in place would stay in, whatever she did to them. Roger's expression changed to one of mingled excitement and sympathy, and for one dreadful moment Willow wondered whether the secrets that underpinned her life had been found out. No, she told herself, that was absurd; the atmosphere in her outer office must have something to do with all the police downstairs. Looking far more censorious than she realised, she said:

4

'Heard what? Barbara, what on earth has been going on?'

'The minister has been killed, Willow,' answered the black-haired Scottish girl with an equally sympathetic expression on her round pink face.

'Poor Algy,' said Willow inadequately. She felt as though she had just been kicked – hard – in the solar plexus. 'What happened? Was it a car accident?'

'Oh no, Miss King,' broke in Roger, with the excitement fighting the sympathy all too successfully. He sneezed explosively, but for once he had a real drama on his hands and ignored the minor physical one. 'He's been murdered. They found his body on Clapham Common last night. He'd been beaten up and his head smashed in.'

'Roger!' Barbara's voice was full of reproach before she turned to the assistant secretary. 'Why not sit down, Willow, and let Roger get you a cup of tea? It must be a terrible shock.'

Willow shook her head slightly, but then relented.

'Yes, a cup of tea would be nice, Roger. A strong one, I think. Bring it into my room, will you? Barbara, come to my office in an hour, when I've had a chance to sort things out.'

'Yes, of course, Willow,' the girl answered, efficiently slapping a pile of papers into place. 'Oh and by the way, the PUS wants to see you as soon as possible.'

'All right,' said Willow, checking her watch and wondering whether she would be able to put all thoughts of Algy's death out of her mind for long enough to summon the patience necessary to deal with the permanent secretary. 'Find out if he can see me at, oh, say half-past eleven.'

She turned her back on the pair of them and went into her own room, badly wanting solitude in which to deal with the shock of what they had told her. Putting the briefcase down on a side table between the windows, Willow stood staring out over the grubby buildings of Clapham towards

5

the common where Algernon Endelsham had met his end. Still shuddering inside from the shock, Willow found it as hard to blame her staff for their suppressed excitement as it was easy to understand their sympathy. The lives they led were of stultifying boredom, lightened only by the dramas, shifting romances and sexual affairs of their colleagues. The murder of any minister, let alone one as spectacular and famous as Algy Endelsham, would have been the drama to end all dramas, and Willow could imagine how the entire population of DOAP must be longing to discuss it.

In a way it was hard on her own staff that they felt they had to disguise their interest because of their ineradicable conviction that she had been desperately in love with the minister. She was both touched and a little repelled by their apparent care for her sensibilities.

About eighteen months earlier, soon after he had been given DOAP (his first ministerial job), Algernon Endelsham, to the astonishment of the entire staff, had started to pursue Willow. The incoming minister was the handsomest thing that had been seen in either House of Parliament since Lord Palmerston, he was sensationally young for his position, well-known on television, apparently rich, famously athletic, brilliantly clever (some people thought he was even cleverer than Willow herself, though that was hotly debated in the office canteen at the time) and with a devilish reputation as far as women were concerned.

Despite herself, Willow had been half-flattered as well as half-amused by his advances, but she had had enough doubts about his sincerity and motives to ensure that she kept her own genuine admiration of him in check. Besides, she had secrets to keep and they meant that she was never tempted to succumb to the minister's undoubted charms. Her life was thoroughly satisfactory to her and she would no more have thought of complicating the Civil Service part of it with an affair with her minister than she would have joined an Everest attempt or a space flight to the moon.

6

The sound of her office door opening made her turn from her sightless contemplation of the trees of the common. She looked round to see Roger placing a cup of deep-orange-coloured tea on her desk with exaggerated care.

'Thank you, Roger,' she said in a dismissive tone. Ignoring it, he lingered by the door for long enough to say:

'I am sorry, Miss King. It's terrible enough for us all, but for you. . .' The dying fall on the last word was masterly and he could not quite resist waiting to see how she took it. Disconcertingly, she laughed.

'Yes, Roger. Thank you very much. Don't forget to find out from Barbara what the permanent secretary wants me for and get all the files I'm likely to need in here half an hour before I have to see him.' This time Roger accepted his dismissal and left her alone.

Willow took a sip of the tea, winced as the violence of the tannin hit her palate, but then drank thirstily. She had planned to get straight down to work, but found that she could not: the news she had just heard seemed to have driven all thoughts of work out of her mind. Sitting at her desk she tried to translate the physical shock she had felt at the news of Algy's death into appropriate emotion.

The thought of it made Willow feel sick; imagining his pain and terror dried out her mouth and made the palms of her hands sweat; and yet she could not find any tears for him. Throughout her austere childhood, crying had been forbidden, and she had always been encouraged to rationalise away or deeply bury any feelings that were strong enough to threaten her stability. As a result she had grown into a woman whose immense competence was never spoiled by recognisable anguish, passion or even anxiety.

It had been her parents' nightmare that the child they had brought into the world so late in their lives might be unable to look after herself when they died, or be dangerously unhappy without them. To preempt either

7

eventuality, they had struggled all her life to teach her to be self-sufficient emotionally as well as in every practical way. They had succeeded all too well, and when they did die within six months of each other, Willow was well able to live without them. She was also quite unable to grieve properly for them.

The shock of that inability had shown her what their wholly altruistic training had done to her. Willow was far too rational to blame her parents for it, and she had set about trying to learn to allow herself feelings. But not all the rationality and determination in the world could make good the lack of thirty years' natural experience of strong emotion. She was deeply shocked by the death of Algernon Endelsham. The horror of it would, she told herself, remain with her for a long long time. But she could not cry for him.

There was another horror, too, and perhaps a worse one: someone had hated or feared her old suitor enough to batter in his skull until he was dead. The thought of that hatred was stifling.

Without even realising what she was doing, Willow applied the old recipe for self-control and tried to find other ways of thinking about Algy's death in order to rationalise the horror she had felt.

Subconsciously searching her frugal northern mind for some distraction, she started to think about the waste his death represented. There were very few politicians of such talent, let alone such aesthetic appeal, on either side of the House. Algy had had a fine brain, and a quick wit that turned the dullest DOAP meeting into an entertainment for anyone who could keep up with him. Willow had been one of the few and had greatly enjoyed the sparks that their minds had struck off each other. The vivid memory of some of those meetings made her smile in the solitude of her office; DOAP had been a safe if dreary place before Algy's advent. He had done much to remove the complacency and the safety, but he had lightened the dreariness too.

Willow knew that she would miss his incisive intelligence and his sometimes cruel wit. She heard someone coming in to her outer office and made certain that her face showed no sign of the turmoil in her mind. Whatever her reservations about her tendency to rationalise away emotion, she had absolutely no desire for her staff and colleagues to see evidence of any of her feelings.

At that thought she even laughed a little bitterly. The news that she had seemed at all distressed at the announcement of Algy's death would have fled round DOAP in an instant and would have confirmed her colleagues, seniors and subordinates in the universal view that she had succumbed to Algy as soon as he had so inexplicably tried to seduce her.

Willow knew quite well that as a spinster in her late thirties, with apparently only an aunt to love, unbecomingly dressed in her neutral suits and low-heeled shoes, she was considered to be an object of half-pitying derision by a large section of the office. At the time of Algy's pursuit she had even overheard a conversation between two arrogant young principals from another division saying patronisingly how sensible it was of estabs to have put poor Willow into an innocuous department like DOAP instead of Defence or the FO where she'd have been easy meat for any Russian-lover trap.

The object of their scorn had laughed at the time, and she wished that she could not laugh any more. Algy, who had said that he loved her – although she had never been able to believe him – had been beaten to death. Willow put down her cup and rested her face in her hands. To know that any human being had suffered like that was horrible, but a man she had known and liked. . . . What could he have thought in that split second before unconsciousness, when he must have known that he would die? Her mind flinched at the thought.

In order to distract herself from it, she tried to imagine what sort of person could have killed him like that.

Willow was slightly appalled to discover that her mind was thoroughly intrigued by the identity and motivation of the killer and not at all interested in wreaking vengeance on him – or her.

The red telephone at her right elbow shrilled with illusory urgency. Willow started at the noise, sat up straighter, and picked up the receiver.

'Willow King,' she said in a voice that betrayed no agitation or sorrow at all.

'Willow, Bob Smith here,' came the voice of the permanent secretary's private secretary. 'The PUS can't make eleven-thirty, but since the finance committee meeting has been cancelled, would you come at three?'

'Cancelled,' repeated Willow blankly. 'Why?'

'Well, with the minister hardly cold and no replacement appointed, we can hardly. . .'

'Oh, no, of course not. Right, Bob. Three o'clock. I'll check with Barbara.'

'I already have. That's OK. I can tell the PUS then?'

'Yes, all right.'

Willow replaced the scarlet receiver and made herself look at the letter file in front of her. Speculating on the reasons for the death of her erstwhile friend and suitor would do no good at all, she told herself. But she found that the letters could have been written in Mongolian for all they meant to her as her mind began to rove over the probable or even possible enemies of Algy Endelsham.

Knowing that she really would have to achieve some self-control if she were to get any work done, she took a deep breath and started to read the letters in the file on her desk. Some she annotated, others she put aside to think about; and on the rest she scribbled notes for Barbara and the rest of her staff. At the bottom of the file, though, was a sad letter from one of the minister's constituents, a widow of eighty-two who could not understand the new pensions legislation and felt that she had been roughly treated at her local DOAP office. A familiar type of letter to politicians no doubt, it was not however the kind of thing that normally appeared on Willow's desk. Her business was with the financial implications of policy, not the nuts and bolts of the application of that policy. Wondering why the letter had reached her desk at all, she turned it over.

There, stuck to the back instead of the front, was an extravagantly large yellow Post-it with a scribbled note in Algy's elegant, if eccentric, handwriting:

Willow, I know this isn't your pidgin, but I'm a bit stuck. We've written endlessly, explained endlessly, and the local office has done everything they can. All we need now, I think, is the sort of letter you are so good at. Could you run one off? I know you're far too busy to be bothered, but no one can do that sort of thing better. Please, Willow?

He had signed it with a hieroglyph that she hoped none of her staff could interpret. It referred to the days of his courtship, when he had bombarded her with flowers and invitations and letters all signed 'Your devoted and despairing Algy'. At the time of his embarrassing pursuit she had taken his protestations with a giant's pinch of salt, but that morning, perhaps because he was dead, she began to wonder whether she had done him an injustice. Staring down at his handwriting, Willow found herself almost looking at him, so vivid was the picture in her mind. And in a moment that picture was subsumed in an equally vivid one of his handsome face, kicked and bloodied in the mud of Clapham Common.

Willow managed to regain her usual self-discipline in time to get through almost as much work as usual, and by the end of the day she was exceedingly thankful for it. The conversations that were broken off wherever she went in the building, the sly or pitying glances that were cast her way, not to speak of the more overt expressions of curiosity or sympathy, were enough to overset anyone with a less than rigid self-command. Never had she felt more distant from her colleagues – or more thankful for her separateness.

Curiously enough on that strange and difficult day it was the permanent secretary who came closest to breaking down Willow's control. They were old enemies: he had always resented her quickness and her immediate and easy understanding of statistics and finance; while she despised his slower brain and was deeply frustrated by the petty revenge he exacted from her whenever he could. As she walked down the grey corridors to his room just before three o'clock in the afternoon, inhaling the familiar smells of floor polish, disinfectant and a faint human staleness, she wondered what he would say about the minister. For if the PUS disliked Willow, he had positively hated Algy Endelsham.

Ministers, in the PUS's experience, were easy to manipulate, at least in the early days of their ministerial careers when their confidence was usually shaky. But Endelsham could have run rings round the PUS from his first minute in the department and had rarely tried to hide his own contempt for the man. Willow remembered one funny, if rather unkind, meeting of the finance committee when the PUS had made a complete clot of himself and afterwards Algy had asked her quietly how such a fool could ever have reached the middle echelons of the Home Civil Service, let alone achieved one of the highest appointments. Willow had shrugged and said, 'He's only such a fool about figures; really very sound on pensions policy. . . and faithful and long serving. Buggins' turn, I suppose, and the fact that he's never annoyed anyone senior to him by being too clever.'

'Not like us, you mean, Willsy,' Endelsham had said with an appealing gleam in his grey eyes.

That, she told herself as she arrived outside the PUS's office, must have been what attracted us to each other: neither of us had to struggle to understand the other and we always picked up all the implications of whatever was said,

12

unlike the rest of this lot. Bracing herself for the encounter to come, she pushed open the door.

Bob Smith looked up from his desk, ostentatiously checked his watch, and, having got its approval, smiled at Willow and stood up to announce her to his master. Resisting the temptation to ask him whether he was aping the PUS's absurd mannerisms with a view to achieving seniority, Willow walked past him and stood in front of the PUS's huge mahogany desk.

'It's a bad business, this,' he said by way of greeting.

'You could well say so, PUS,' she replied with a derisive twist of her lips.

'Oh, very sad as well, of course. But we had after all begun to get poor Endelsham into harness and the Lord knows who we'll be landed with next.'

Suddenly it seemed to Willow absolutely monstrous that this time-serving second-rater should talk of Algy Endelsham's death in such terms. She felt her pale face flushing and almost had to bite her tongue to stop herself telling him what she thought of him. He looked up at her as she stood in front of him and said as though he had only just thought of it:

'Oh, my dear Willow, I am so sorry. I had quite forgotten that this might be a personal bereavement for you. Are you all right? I'd suggest that you took a day or two off were it not for the difficulty of running the new pensions White Paper with only a part-time assistant secretary. That's what I wanted to talk to you about.'

Willow only just managed not to roll her eyes up to heaven. Like all the other inhabitants of DOAP, the permanent secretary made it clear that he believed that Willow King had given in to Algy's seductive charms and must therefore be heartbroken by his death. It was too predictable that the PUS should choose a day on which she might be expected to be vulnerable to needle her about her working arrangements. She listened to what he had to say and compounded her original lie, at last giving vent to a little of the spleen that was churning around inside her.

'Really, PUS, I must say that I am surprised at this attack. It is the policy of the Civil Service to allow part-time employment. I have family responsibilities that I cannot delegate: as you well know, after my mother's death there was no one but me to look after my Aunt Agatha, and she is far too old and frail to be left alone entirely. You know perfectly well that I have to spend half the week with her. And as far as I am aware I do all the work that is necessary in the other three days that I spend here. If you can tell me of anything that is being skimped or ignored, please do so and I shall attend to it.'

Shifting uncomfortably under her direct gaze, he muttered something vague about the inconvenience of not being able to consult her on Mondays and Fridays. But there was nothing specific about which he could reasonably complain. He merely resented the fact of her partial freedom from their shared treadmill and had chosen a moment when she was likely to be weak to exercise his bitterness. She left his office at last, despising him even more than usual.

When she got back to her own room, Roger greeted her with the pleasing intelligence that she would be required by the chief investigating policeman first thing the following morning.

'He's using the ground-floor conference room, Miss King, and they say he's a real tartar. But not to worry, the under secretary (estabs) is sitting in on all the interrogations to make sure of fair play.'

This latest manifestation of Roger's insatiable desire for drama helped to restore Willow's equilibrium and it was with a tolerant smile that she thanked him for the message, assured him that she would obey the police summons and recommended that he suck medicated pastilles for his sore throat and put witch hazel on his excoriated face. It was left to black-haired Barbara to plant a dart of anxiety in their cool boss.

'Come off it, Roger. Willow's got no need to fret herself: the poor min. is known to have died yesterday evening between seven and nine and Willow's got an alibi for all last night – unlike the rest of us.'

2

W ILLOW left the office soon after seven with a briefcase full of work and went home to the first-floor flat
in Abbeville Road that she had bought ten years earlier.
Opening her front door, she inhaled the familiar smell of
damp and mothballs and wondered whether she ought
not to increase her mortgage and get somewhere better,
or perhaps even have the whole flat properly decorated.
At first it had been all she could afford and then, just as
her income would have been increased on promotion, she
had taken her momentous decision to work part-time and
had had to adjust to a half salary.

Without the proceeds of her parents' exiguous life
insurance policy and the sale of their house in Newcastle,
she would not have been able to take the risk at all
and would never have discovered her peculiar talents.
Dumping her laden plastic briefcase on the sturdy but
ugly oak table in the middle of the living room, she took off
her overcoat and shivered in the dank coldness of the flat.
She quickly lit the sputtering gas fire and then retreated to
the kitchen to make herself a mug of instant coffee. A drink
might have been more calming, she thought, remembering

16

the bottles of supermarket whisky, gin, indifferent sherry, and Bulgarian Cabernet Sauvignon at the dining end of the room, but she craved warmth. She took the thick pottery mug of coffee to the sofa and sat down, avoiding the broken spring that could be so uncomfortable, and tried to pull herself together.

The knowledge of Algy's death lay like a spiked weight at the back of her mind and its possible ramifications filled the rest. Reminding herself once again that she had no reason to fear the police, that she was safe in her self-sufficiency and could deal with anything that cropped up, Willow still could not control her uncharacteristic nervousness. For the first time in years she felt young and vulnerable and actually wanted someone else to advise her. Despising her mood, telling herself to brace up, Willow finished her coffee, put on her spectacles again and went to the kitchen to cook four fish fingers and about half a pound of frozen broad beans. After supper she settled down to the work she had brought home and tried not to give another thought to the murder or her looming interview with the police.

The following morning, after an indifferent night's sleep broken by all kinds of unpleasant dreams that dissolved as soon as she woke, Willow walked into her interrogation with her chin up and her dark red hair tightly drawn away from her freckled white face. The first person she saw was the establishments officer, Michael Englewood, to whom she had told that first, crucial lie about her Aunt Agatha.

If only his sense of duty had not insisted that he support his colleagues during their interrogations, Willow would not have been faced with her horrible dilemma: to tell the truth at last and be unveiled in front of him and the whole of the department for what she was; or to lie once again. She would have had no hesitation in taking the second course if only the police had not been involved, but their presence would turn expedient untruth into a crime. Willow could feel waves of wholly unjust hostility to poor Mr Englewood rising in her mind as he stood up to greet her, a questioning look on his tired, pleasant face.

Knowing that her dilemma was not his fault, and that he deserved all her gratitude for having supported her against the PUS in her determination to work part-time, Willow made herself smile at him. He smiled back, with all the shy kindness she had grown to expect from him.

There were plenty of high flyers who despised Michael Englewood for his fussiness, his old-fashioned clothes and his apparent satisfaction with the uninfluential backwater into which his career had taken him; but he was well enough liked by the majority of the DOAP staff. Only his secretaries seemed neither to despise nor to like him, and Willow had occasionally wondered why so many demanded to be transferred after a few months.

'This is Miss Willow King,' he said to a man in plain clothes, who was seated at the large oval conference table, reading a file. Then Englewood turned back to smile at her again. 'Willow, Inspector Worth, who is in charge of the investigation into the minister's death.'

'Are you all right, Michael?' she asked, ignoring the police officer in a forlorn attempt to gain time in which to decide what line to take. 'You sound horribly hoarse. Is it this beastly cold that's been going the rounds?'

'Presumably. I'm almost beginning to believe in that journalistic fantasy of sick-building syndrome. We never seem to be free of bugs and viruses here,' he answered, fingering the paisley silk cravat that he occasionally affected in winter instead of a tie.

The policeman coughed irritably, as though impatient at the waste of time, and Willow turned towards him at last. She was struck by the lively intelligence in his dark eyes. In a moment's frivolity, she even admired his rugged handsomeness and exotically broken nose, but was quickly sobered as he said:

"Morning, Miss King. Now I haven't much time, and so I'd be grateful if you'd tell me exactly where you were the day before yesterday between the end of the working day and, say, ten-thirty.'

Carefully avoiding any anxious glances at Englewood, Willow braced herself. Before she could even speak, she heard his voice warm with indignation, or even anger. Taking a quick look at him, she was surprised to see his face reddening and his mouth stretched tight over his teeth.

'As I've already told you, Inspector, Miss King does not work on Mondays or Fridays and has spent every single Monday night for the past eight years in Suffolk caring for an invalid relative,' he said, coughed and took a tin of blackcurrant suckers from his jacket pocket.

'I'd rather Miss King answered for herself, Sir,' said the policeman coldly in a voice that seemed to have had every nuance of accent or colour scoured away from it, 'and I'm sure it would be better for your throat if you talked as little as possible.'

Englewood's furious intervention put an end to the last of Willow's doubts and she spoke with as little hesitation as she had when she first invented her aunt.

'Mr Englewood is quite right, Inspector Worth. I was in Suffolk, with my aunt, Miss Agatha Carlyle. She was my mother's sister.'

Inspector Worth's head snapped up at that piece of elaboration and Willow realised that she had made an idiotic mistake. That was just the kind of extra detail that would sound false and might lead him to check-up on her alibi. She had decided to bank on the fact that with two thousand or more people working at DOAP, the police were highly unlikely to test anyone's whereabouts until they were a little further into their investigation. And she was quite confident that when that had happened they would have no suspicions of her and therefore no need to test her story.

'I see,' he said coldly. 'Telephone number?'

'I'm afraid she's not on the telephone,' said Willow, relieved to have something truthful to say.

'Right. Thank you, Miss King. Leave the address with my sergeant please. He's in the next-door office.'

Willow just managed to stop herself asking 'Is that all?', substituted, 'Not at all', and left the room, wondering whether she had made an almighty fool of herself. She also carefully forgot to find the sergeant.

The idea of running into any interested colleagues bothered her and so she made for the stairs that no one used except during fire practices or when the lifts were out of order. As she walked slowly up the stairs, idly disliking the grey-green lino that covered them, she comforted herself with the fact that she could always come clean about her real alibi if the police turned tiresome and forced her to throw away her carefully designed and preserved disguise.

It was not until she had reached the sixth floor and was already panting a little that she remembered that there was a crime called 'wasting police time'. There was no doubt that, if he were a vindictive man, the inspector could have her prosecuted for that – if for nothing worse – if he bothered to check her alibi. This is where lying gets you, she said to herself grimly as she realised that having the entire story coming out in court would be fifty times worse than confessing it at the first possible opportunity, even in front of the establishments officer. She would be disgraced; she would probably have to resign from DOAP in any case. But infinitely worse, she would look the greatest fool of all time.

By the time she had climbed the next two flights of stairs she had cudgelled her mind back into rationality and decided that she would just have to work out for herself who had murdered Algernon Endelsham. Then if the police were absurd enough to want to prosecute her, she could try to buy them off with the solution to their mystery.

Willow had infinite faith in her own brains – for her childhood and much of her early adulthood, they were all she had had to give her any sense of identity or self-worth – and, after all, she had known Algy as well as anyone in the department, and far better than any of the police. It also occurred to her that to concentrate on the intellectual problem of who it was who had beaten Algy's brains out might distract her from the miserable reality of his death.

Besides, it would be rather interesting, she thought. With the finance committee under control, her staff reasonably well trained and the rest of her life working beautifully, Willow had been feeling rather short of challenge. To go about the department ferreting out secrets and finding the truth about the murdered minister might give her mind some much-needed testing, and the results could be useful. That the challenge she had chosen might become dangerous or distasteful never occurred to her.

There was a slight smile on her unpainted lips when she walked up to Roger's desk and the crispness was back in her voice as she inquired of him whether he had finished typing out the redrafted version of her part of the new White Paper or whether his cold was so bad that he was still unable to produce a full day's work.

'Er, no, no I haven't quite finished actually, Miss King. It's really been so upsetting, what with the minister's death and the police and all the things everyone's saying,' he said, blushing slightly. 'I got waylaid downstairs when I took your photocopying down, and had to listen to all the latest theories.'

The scars on his right cheek were turning crusty as they healed and looked fiercely itchy. Willow almost said something sympathetic about them, but then decided not to embarrass either herself or Roger. She was also tempted to comment on his infuriating dilatoriness, but, not wishing to provoke one of his all-too-frequent outbursts of personality, she merely asked him to do his best and walked into her own office, calling Barbara to follow her.

They got through the piles of work on Willow's desk in record time and Barbara raised various problems that had arisen during her chief's absence. Willow dealt with them with all her customary efficiency and Barbara was moved to say:

'I am glad that you're all right, Willow. . . . Not letting it all get to you.'

It was the first really personal remark the girl had ever dared to address to her assistant secretary, and Willow was a little repelled by the hint of intimacy between them.

'Thank you, Barbara,' she said, trying to concentrate on her assistant's efficiency and ignore her distaste. 'But what is "it all"? The minister's death is horribly distressing, but everyone here has to deal with that.'

The 22-year-old trainee flushed and scraped the carpet with her shoe like a child in her headmistress's study. Willow was amused to find her so much less sophisticated than she had always appeared. 'Come on, Barbara, out with it. You've started, so I really think you ought to finish.'

They both laughed at that and the momentary amusement seemed to give Barbara the courage to amplify her earlier remarks.

'Well, it's just that everyone seems to think. . . They all know about you and the minister, you see, and they're saying. . .'

'That he threw me over and I killed him, you mean?' said Willow, who had never even considered the possibility that anyone might suspect her until that moment. Her tone of dry amusement made Barbara look at her directly for the first time since they had stopped working.

'Well, yes actually. But don't you mind?'

Willow, who normally thought about her own emotions as little as it was possible to do, considered for a moment or two.

'Yes, in fact I do. It's such an insult, for one thing, and not only to me.'

'The minister, too, you mean?' Barbara suggested doubtfully.

'No, Barbara,' said Willow more coldly. 'It suggests that they think that all single women in this office – or for that matter in the whole of the Civil Service – are hanging about hoping for some man to dignify them by selecting them for his own pleasure. Idiotic! I can imagine – just – some men thinking it, or the sort of idle women who spend all day in hairdressers' shops reading selfishness-inducing magazines, but intelligent women like the ones who work here? It makes me feel ashamed of them.'

'I thought you were going to say that the insult lay in their assumption that you would ever allow your emotions to overrule your judgment,' said Barbara, blushing because she, too, was guilty of pining for a particular man to dignify her existence by so selecting her.

'That too. But Barbara, since we're wasting time gossiping, tell me: am I the only suspect they've dug up? Or are there other victims of their overheated fantasy?'

'It did occur to someone in the canteen yesterday that perhaps the permanent secretary had been sneered at once too often and decided to act instead of sulking for once, but that only raised a laugh. Everyone knows he's far too much of a physical coward to hit anyone, let alone a man six inches taller than himself,' answered Barbara.

Willow got out of her chair and prowled about her office, trying to excise the sudden, unexpected sympathy that had sprung into her mind. She had never expected to feel remotely sympathetic towards the PUS, but she did experience a sickening lurch of fellow-feeling as she realised that the pair of them must be equally despised and talked over by the denizens of DOAP. Reminding herself of the maxim 'It's all good copy', which had got her through the embarrassing days of Algy's blatant courtship, Willow turned back to her subordinate.

'I overheard something in the canteen, too, last week,' she said. Barbara, clearly bothered about what Willow was going to say, fiddled with the red combs that held her dark hair in place. One fell out and, slipping from her fingers, dropped on the floor. The girl grovelled after it and when she stood up again made an enormous fuss about putting it back. Willow watched with a hint of amusement in her eyes.

'A bunch of messengers were talking their usual smut and making jokes about the minister's, er. . . sexual preferences. Was it true, do you know?' she asked.

Barbara, with the relief showing so obviously in her stance and expression that Willow wondered what they had been saying in the canteen about her, answered slowly:

'Well, I suppose it could be, Willow, but a man like that. . . I mean, with the kind of womanising reputation that Algy Endelsham had: do you really think it's likely?'

'Not very perhaps,' answered Willow, as though carefully considering, 'but anyone who displays his conquests so flagrantly might well be hiding something, don't you think? And despite Wolfenden and all that, I imagine a politician could still be blackmailed. . . .'

'But hardly murdered. In any case, I'd have thought you of all people had ample evidence to refute such a suggestion.' Barbara's almost cheeky tone pulled Willow up short, and she realised how sensible had been her previously constant determination never to gossip with her staff or take any interest in the extra-curricular goings-on of the department. Retreating into the personality she had heard described more than once as 'the terrifying Willow King', she dismissed her AT and settled down to work.

By the end of the day Willow had allowed herself to hear a lot more gossip about the minister and his relations with innumerable other members of DOAP and she no longer

24

wondered why it was that some of her staff got through so little work in their entire weeks in the office. She had talked to most of the people she had ever worked with, and heard views ranging from the least uncomfortable one that the minister had been mugged by a stranger to perhaps the most horrible: that he was being blackmailed, had gone to hand over the money to his blackmailer, decided to take the 'publish and be damned' line and been beaten to death.

Willow heard that unpleasant idea from a long-serving higher executive officer in the registration department, whom she had met coming out of the canteen after lunch.

'Really, Thomas,' she said, 'you can't believe that. It's about as likely as believing the min. to have been a blackmailer himself.'

'Don't be absurd,' said Thomas. 'Admirable Algy needing to blackmail anyone? It's a risible idea.'

'Oh, I don't know,' said Willow, quickly trying to imagine a situation – however absurd – in which a minister might have been in a position to blackmail one of his Civil Servants. 'Think,' she went on in an exaggerated story-teller's voice, 'the minister discovered that a group of you lot in Registry were getting up to something quite frightful and he tried to extort money out of you as the price of his silence.'

'All right, all right, Willow,' said the HEO almost laughing, despite his patent astonishment at her unlikely flippancy. 'I agree that the whole idea of blackmail is absurd. Hello, Albert,' he went on in a voice in which surprise had quite displaced amusement. 'Did you want to speak to me or to Miss King?'

Once more Willow found herself faced with the looming hostility of the minister's driver.

'Neither, Sir,' said the chauffeur, stepping reluctantly out of their path and directing at Willow a look of such contempt that she almost took a step backwards.

Having parted from the executive officer, Willow went slowly back to her own office, wondering whether Albert's obvious loathing had been caused by her apparent trivialising of the minister's death. The driver had clearly overheard every word of her sarcastically intended scenario. She could think of nothing else that could have elicited such contempt from him. Shrugging off the uncomfortable feeling, she settled down to work again and did not relax her concentration until the end of the day.

Sitting back in her chair a little after six o'clock, she examined all the theories she had heard that day and decided that none was completely convincing, although several had elements of plausibility. Thinking over the day, she was slightly appalled to realise how much time she had wasted in chatter and speculation. For Willow, unlike many of her colleagues and subordinates, the office had always been a place for work rather than entertainment and substitute life, and consequently she had done almost as much work in her three-day week as they had done in five.

It occurred to her as she was locking away her confidential papers and facing another solitary evening's work in Abbeville Road that it might be useful to see the place where Algy had actually died. She was not silly enough to expect to find any physical clues that the police might have missed, but she did think that following the steps of aggressor and victim might give her some useful ideas.

Collecting her grey mackintosh from the curly bentwood coatstand by the door, Willow left her office. As usual she was among the last to go, apart from the few young high-flyers who believed that the field-marshal's batons they carried in their knapsacks would be more obvious to their superiors the longer they spent in the office. But just as she reached the front door, she encountered the establishments officer buttoning up his reversible coat with the mackintosh side outwards.

'Evening, Willow,' he said, looking slightly startled at the sight of her. He tucked the ends of a thick scarf into the neck of his coat. 'Bitterly cold, isn't it?'

'Good evening, Michael. Yes, isn't it foul? You're leaving rather late, aren't you?'

'It'll be the first time for ages that I haven't caught the six-fifteen from Waterloo,' he agreed, adding in what she thought quite unnecessary detail, 'I've taken that train every evening for nearly twenty years. But I've been sitting in with the inspector, listening to apparently irrelevant alibis all day. He's an impressive worker, I can tell you – and incredibly patient.'

'Poor you,' said Willow. 'But why patient?'

Englewood's face twisted into a curious self-deprecating grimace.

'He never even sounded sharp, let alone lost his temper, despite having to listen to hours of the most idiotic, giggly excuses, alibis and coy questions,' he said with an impatience she had never heard from him before.

'Goodness, Michael,' said Willow, rather entertained to hear him sounding quite different from the weary, kindly man she had always thought him, 'you sound positively vitriolic.'

To her surprise, his face reddened once more and his hard-looking moustache quivered. With a visible effort, he controlled himself and spoke in a voice that was almost as mild as usual:

'Oh, but surely you've heard of my appalling temper.'

'Certainly not,' said Willow, shivering a little in the bitter cold, but too interested to cut the encounter short. 'But as you know, I never encourage my staff to gossip to me.'

'I know, and that's one of the many things I've always admired in you, my dear Willow,' he said, sounding quite normal again. 'But I have very little tolerance for the kind of giggling stupidity and malicious tittle tattle in which the department's typists seem to specialise. But never mind that: as I was saying, Inspector Worth put up with it all admirably. Although,' he added with a sly smile, 'I could see how much he appreciated your incisiveness and good sense.'

'I noticed that it was abominably stuffy in that room even when I was there this morning; you must have the most frightful headache as well as your cold,' said Willow, changing the subject. For some reason she did not want to talk about the policeman's possible reaction to her and her alibi, and she was beginning to find Michael Englewood's unprecedented compliments rather repellent.

He smiled ruefully: 'In fact, I have; but you're the first person to have noticed, Willow. You are an extraordinarily perceptive woman.'

'Well I dare say the walk to the tube will clear it,' she answered hastily. Algy's death seemed to have plunged her into more personal contact than she had ever allowed before. She did not like it at all and had no intention of letting herself get on to intimate – or even personal – terms with Michael Englewood.

'Are you going that way, too?' asked Englewood.

'No, I have to go to Peter Jones – late night shopping tonight,' she said in ill-considered excuse. 'I thought I'd walk across the Common and pick up a 137 at the top of Cedar's Road.'

For a moment she thought that he was going to protest and remind her that the bus also stopped outside Clapham Common tube station, but after a second or two he shrugged, wished her good night and strode away. Willow stood, looking after him and wondering what it was that he had so nearly said. Neither of them was very good at personal contact and he had probably just been as uncomfortable with their unusual intimacy as she had been. Perhaps that was why his compliments had been so unpleasant, she thought. Willow rather wished that she had brought up the subject of the minister's driver's violent rudeness to her and ensured that their conversation had been confined to matters of DOAP's personnel. She tightened the belt of her chain-store mackintosh and turned towards the common.

Walking past the rows of ethnic restaurants, sleazy-looking secondhand shops, and car breakers' yards, Willow found it harder and harder to imagine Algy Endelsham taking this walk, but when she reached the common itself and skirted the edge of the first pond, she began to wonder whether he had simply wanted to clear his head after a day of tiresome meetings.

The sound of the water, whipped up by the wind into slapping wavelets, the relative freshness of the air and the feeling of space all around were extraordinarily relaxing. The moon was nearly full and, whenever the clouds parted, its pale-grey light fought with the boiled-sweet glare of the orange street lights.

Willow walked quite briskly along the main path towards the bandstand, where she intended to turn right, almost enjoying herself. She was timing the expedition and reckoned that she would reach the place of Algy's death in about four minutes at the pace she had chosen. Passing the bandstand, she noticed various men standing about: some were alone, others chatting in pairs or groups. It seemed to Willow to be a curious place to hang about in the freezing dark of a November evening. The men ignored her completely and she them as she plunged off the path on to the soggy grass.

After two minutes' walk Willow found herself in thick darkness. She would never have imagined that the street lamps shed such a small area of light. She could still see the orange blocks of light, of course, but they did not affect the darkness that enveloped her. It dawned on her that she was not going to discover anything without light and she wondered why she had never thought to bring a torch. She thought of turning back, but since she had never left a task unfinished in her life she walked on, increasingly uncomfortable in both her mind and her cold, wet feet. The lights on the far side of the common glowed seductively, and Willow kept her eyes on them, determined not to give way to her absurd fears.

Clinging to rationality, she told herself that it was curious how a place, which only an instant before had seemed perfectly safe and even pleasant, should for so little cause have taken on an air of desperate menace. Sounds that she had not even noticed before seemed sinister: the rustling of shrubs, the creaking of the chains of swings in the distant playground, steps in the distance, all made her start. The only noise that seemed to carry any comfort with it was the steady throaty rumble of the traffic along the south and north sides of the common.

Willow quickened her pace and almost forgot the reason for her solitary ramble as she identified the soft slap of several pairs of trainers moving up behind her. Determined neither to look back nor to break into a run, she kept her own steps firm and her breathing as level as she could, but it did not help her. She became more and more afraid. The sound of the running feet was accompanied by hoarse, male panting, which made her think suddenly of all the rapes and cases of grievous bodily harm that the local free newspapers reported in such avid detail. The thought of all the young men she had seen hanging about the bandstand ceased to be curious and became rather threatening.

She fumbled in her handbag for the personal alarm she had carried unused for years. It had a tiny mirror in the top and she held it up, trying to see what was going on behind her. There was far too little light to see anything, even if the mirror had not been fogged with dust from the bottom of her bag. Letting her arm drop, she held her thumb over the cap, ready to press it down at the slightest need.

At last she could bear the suspense no longer and turned in her tracks to face whomever was behind her. The clouds blew away from the moon at that moment and Willow found herself face to face with three young men dressed in shorts and sweatshirts. Their faces contorted with effort,

30

sweat dripping from their ears and noses, they ran past her into the night.

'It is extraordinary how unpleasant even quite baseless fear can be,' Willow said aloud in an attempt to steady her wayward nerves.

'Who's there?' An angry male voice demanded out of the darkness. Without a second's thought, quite instinctively, Willow pressed down her thumb. An eldritch shriek wailed out across the dark common, surprising Willow just as much as the man who had called out to her, and made her drop her handbag on to the soggy ground. The man who had shouted had a powerful torch and switched it on, dazzling Willow as she stood in the centre of its white beam.

'Miss King, isn't it?' came a tantalisingly familiar voice, which she could not immediately identify. It sent an extraordinary shiver through her, partly pleasant but threatening too.

'Who are you?' she asked, hating the almost hysterical note in her own voice. The torch was moved and in its light Willow recognised the inspector who had interviewed her that morning. Bitterly angry with herself for exposing her folly to him of all people, she fumbled with the red cap of her alarm to turn it off. At last the hideous noise was silenced. It seemed extraordinary that the policeman should have recognised her, given how many of her colleagues he must have interviewed. She wished very much that he had not. There was something about him that made her uncomfortable, and she felt horribly exposed by his identification of her.

'And just what do you think you're doing? Revisiting the scene of the crime?' The inspector's hitherto colourless voice was tinged with sarcasm and that helped Willow to get a grip on herself.

'Don't be ridiculous,' she answered, bending down to pick up her bag and pushing it shut with a decisive snap. 'I was merely trying to get across the common to catch a bus to Sloane Square and I was disconcerted by a party of joggers running up behind me out of the dark.'

'Well that's a damned silly thing to do,' he said, and she felt her blood beginning to beat faster again at his tone. 'If women like you kept to well-frequented, well-lit streets and took ordinary precautions there would be far fewer. . .'

'And if people with cars left them in garages all the time there would be far fewer road accidents,' retorted Willow, suffering both from reaction and the rage that indiscriminate woman-blaming always produced in her.

To her surprise, the inspector laughed.

'True enough, and sometimes when I'm in a hurry, I wish to God they would. I apologise for swearing at you. And it is true that as a woman you are probably safer on this bit of the common than any other. But you startled me, appearing out of the night like that talking to yourself.'

'Not half as much as the joggers frightened me,' she retorted, startled into a kind of friendliness. This she realised would be the ideal moment to explain to him about her alibi for the murder and her reasons for hiding it in front of the under secretary (estabs). She opened her mouth, but the policeman started to speak before she could get out any words at all.

'Well and so they should have. They might not have been as innocent. Be a bit more careful in future and you won't get into trouble again,' he said and she stiffened at the patronage in his voice. 'Ah, here come my men. Off with you.' He turned his broad back without waiting for her to say anything and retraced his steps.

Willow was left to pick her way across the cold boggy ground to the well-lit firmness of the path. As she walked she thought about what might have happened to her and its bearing on Algy's death. Could he have been molested by a bunch of mindless louts on the scrounge for easy money? Had it been simply chance that he had walked into trouble? If that were the case, then she would have no chance of discovering what had happened to him. Shaking a little in reaction to the shock of her unwonted terror, she tried to apply her mind to the problem and decided that she could not leave her investigation there.

Under the orange lights of one of the main paths, she stood still, looking all round her in an attempt to imagine why anyone should want to walk across the common. The traffic still roared by on all sides; a dog barked, rather a large dog by the sound of it, and its owner shouted. A train hooted in the distance, like some strange mechanical animal howling at the moon.

Trains! Willow thought at last of one reasonable excuse for crossing the common. It would be the most sensible way of getting from the DOAP tower to Clapham Junction railway station – if one had the time. Not that Algy himself would have been aiming for the Junction; it must have been several years since he had had to rely on public transport. But it might well have been the destination of his murderer. No longer feeling the humiliation of her encounter with the policeman or the icy dampness of her feet, she tightened the belt of her mackintosh once again and set off towards the station.

Willow took her time about the trek, using the back streets, and was surprised about how few people she passed. The walk took her nearly twenty minutes and when she reached the station she found herself at a loss. She could hardly cross-examine the station staff about whether they had found bloodstains on any of the platforms or any object that might have served as a weapon dumped in a dustbin or unfrequented corner; still less could she search for any physical evidence herself.

Nevertheless, she thought, having made the effort to get there, she was going to look around. Buying herself the cheapest ticket as a passport into the station, she went down into its depths. The place was quite unfamiliar to her and she was surprised by how busy it was. If the murderer had wanted to be somewhere where he could not be seen, this would not have been his choice. On the other hand, there were so many people – and some of them looked quite mad and violent enough to have done something pretty frightful – that he might not have stood out at all.

Walking along the sunken corridor beneath the platforms, trying to absorb some atmosphere or reach some useful conclusion about the place, Willow arrived outside the public lavatories, where she was accosted by a very dirty man in an old blue overcoat, tied at the waist with string.

'Give us the price of a cup of tea?' he asked. Trying not to turn her head away from the extraordinarily feral aroma that rose from his clothes and beard and hair, Willow fumbled in her bag for change. Even in the days of her early career, she had often given money to beggars, as a kind of prophylactic gesture. Her elderly parents had always been afraid of what might happen to their unplanned child if they died before she attained financial security. Throughout her childhood they had issued dire warnings of the consequences of failure, which had given her an unassuageable fear of ending up pensionless, destitute and sleeping rough in old age.

'God bless you,' said the tramp, pushing his face towards her. She caught the smell of alcohol on his breath and only just stopped herself from recoiling. In trying to atone for her disgust, she looked at the man directly and saw in his eyes a wholly unexpected flash of intelligence and sympathy. Grubbing in her bag for a fistful of pound coins, she handed them over, asking:

'Are you often here?'

'Always, lady,' he answered, but his eyes had dulled again.

'Last Monday night,' she was beginning when a member of the station staff came over to them and put a hand on the man's filthy coat.

'Come on, Dad, stop annoying the lady,' he said gently enough. The tramp turned and shuffled off in his cracked and string-tied shoes.

'I'm sorry, Miss,' said the uniformed man. 'He means no harm, but he gets a bit carried away at times. There's no need to be afraid.'

'Thank you,' she said. 'I wasn't really frightened. But, thank you. You let him sleep here, do you?'

'Not always. Sometimes he gets drunk and abusive; sometimes we get complaints. But if he's quiet and makes no trouble, most of the lads let him lay. And he has a wash sometimes in the gents'. Seems a bit hard if a bloke wants to wash and gets chased away.'

'Yes indeed. Thank you again,' said Willow, wishing that he would leave her alone so that she could go and question the tramp about what he might have seen on the night of Algy's death. But, kindly and helpful, the ticket collector (or whatever he was) stayed put and she had no alternative but to leave.

When she got out of the station she was faced with the prospect of getting home and realised that walking really would be the easiest way. There was no tube and to go by bus would entail several changes. A taxi passed by with his orange light shining in welcome and she succumbed to temptation.

By the time she was back in her flat and running herself a therapeutic hot bath, she had decided that she would have to go back to the Junction sooner or later. There was really nothing to suggest that the murderer had been there before her, but she could not get rid of a nagging suspicion that he might have been. Lying in the hot water, ignoring the chipped and stained enamel that made the old bath so unattractive, she decided that it was highly unlikely that the minister's murder was accidental or random, however comforting that would have been. If that were true, it would follow that whoever had done it had been on the common for that purpose alone and would have planned a safe retreat. If the retreat had been by car Willow knew that she would have no hope of finding it, but if not, then Clapham Junction – the busiest of all Britain's railway stations – was the likeliest possibility.

The immensity of the task she had taken on suddenly seemed daunting in her tiredness. How could she possibly ask the questions that needed to be asked, find the people who could bear witness to what might have happened? Reminding herself that she had long ago learned that the best way to tackle an apparently impossible task was to take it step by step and refuse to let anxiety sap her valuable energy, she put the mystery out of her mind, ate a frugal supper, did some work and went to bed. But she was neither happy nor confident, and she slept badly.

3

B Y THE END of the following day, Willow had had a superfluity of DOAP. She had heard at least four new versions of the enmities aroused by Algernon Endelsham, each one exaggerated by the sourness or jealousy of its inventor, she had a nagging headache and a tightness at the back of her throat, which suggested that she had caught the latest DOAP virus; she had nearly lost her temper with one of the senior members of the finance committee, who seemed to her to be deliberately misunderstanding the monetary implications of the new policy paper; and she had snapped unnecessarily at Barbara, who had made the mistake of assuming that she was now on a new and matier footing with her assistant secretary.

Willow found it a tremendous relief to know that she could leave the whole lot of them behind. She said good bye to her staff, accepted their good wishes for her dutiful stint with 'Aunt Agatha', took her usual route back to Abbeville Road, and changed her clothes. The noncommittal jeans and black crew-necked sweater she put on would have told no one anything. Only her shoes might have betrayed her to anyone who bothered to look at them, for they were handmade of the softest black leather, and superlatively comfortable. But Willow was confident that no one in Clapham would bother to look at her feet. She removed her glasses, put in contact lenses, blackened her eye lashes and found the plain-glass spectacles that provided the necessary camouflage.

Taking a small red nylon parachute bag from her wardrobe, she hastily packed night things and her sponge-bag, just in case she met any colleagues on the tube, and then walked to Clapham Common station. There she bought a ticket from the machine and proceeded by Northern and Victoria and Circle lines to Sloane Square. Standing on the escalator in amongst the crowd she removed the hairpins and rubber band that kept her hair off her face and took off the plain-glass spectacles. Having pushed her ticket through the automatic gate, she found a corner out of the crowd, where she applied lipstick and blusher to her pale face.

Suddenly she looked up, certain that someone was watching her. It was a most unpleasant sensation, and one she had never noticed before. Ignoring the small mirror in her left hand and the lipstick in her right, Willow searched the bustling, angry scene in front of her. The crowd was the usual mixture of the hurrying and loitering, but no one caught her eye or gave any sign of interest in her. Unconvinced by that, she shivered in her black crew-necked sweater and jacket, but there was nothing she could do and so she finished making up her face and went on her way.

Leaving the station, she crossed Sloane Square and entered the expensive portals of Gino's hairdressing salon. The warm, lush scentedness of the shop welcomed her back into her other life and provided instant gratification in its total contrast to the bleak ugliness of the DOAP tower and the mothball-and-damp smell of her flat.

For the moment, she put the knowledge of Algy's death out of her mind and let herself sink back into irresponsible comfort. Gino's receptionist took her bag and jacket and handed her a pink wrap, which shrieked at Willow's red hair, and ushered her through to the salon. Willow smiled at one or two other regular Thursday-evening clients, who were already sitting facing the tactfully bronzed mirrors, and then greeted Gino's chief apprentice. He sighed when he saw the condition of her hair and clicked his tongue as he ran his fingers through it. She grinned at him and patted his stalwart shoulder.

'Never mind, John. Do your best with it,' she said cheerfully.

'You'd better have conditioner, don't you think?'

'All right, John. Whatever you think best,' said Willow, settling her neck in the least uncomfortable position against the hard edge of the basin.

He bent forward to start ridding her hair of the accumulated grime and dryness, massaging her scalp with such thoroughness that she was about to protest when she became aware of a hardness against her left shoulder. The young man seemed to be pressing himself against her in a pulsating rhythm with a disturbing effect. Could he possibly, she asked herself, have seen Warren Beatty in *Shampoo* and be imitating him for amusement? There could be no other explanation. Mentally shrugging the offending shoulder, she closed her eyes again and let him wash, rinse and condition her hair. But when he had tenderly wrapped her head in pink towels, she did cast a sideways and downwards glance, only to burst into real laughter. There was an immensely long hairbrush stuck into his trouser pocket, handle down. 'Mae West, eat your heart out,' said Willow to herself as she was handed into Gino's chair.

'The writing must have gone well this week,' said Gino, massaging her neck.

'Why?' said Willow, amused by the new opening gambit.

'Because you look so happy – I've never seen you laugh out loud before. And because your hair is even more terrible than usual, Miss Woodruffe,' he said. As so often before, Willow was childishly pleased to hear her invented name; it seemed to be part of the ritual of switching from one life to the other. She glanced at the hairdresser in the mirror and smiled at him.

'Good one, Gino. But, no, I'm not going to come in twice a week. I've told you before that I make such a mess of my hair when I'm writing that it's not worth it. Just be thankful that I come every week, rain or shine, and do your best.'

He laughed, too, and seeing that for once she was in the mood to talk, he allowed his practised easy patter to flow out. Willow listened, occasionally asked a question and answered the few he asked her, and by the time he had started to blow-dry her hair, she had begun to relax properly. They could not talk comfortably while the dryer was roaring in their ears and so Willow amused herself by watching her fellow customers in the mirrors. There was the stringy old woman who was always there at that time on a Thursday, having her toenails painted. Who, Willow wondered, could possibly want to look at the old girl's feet? Next to her was a thin, dark woman, who always looked as though she were longing for a cigarette and picked at the slightly yellowed skin around her fingernails as her hair was teased into shape. Then there was one empty chair. Gino switched off the dryer just as Willow noticed that, and she said straight away:

'Gino, what's happened to the pretty blond woman who usually sits there?' She pointed rudely, looked at him in the mirror to make sure he knew what she meant and was surprised to see an expression of sympathetic excitement enliven his swarthy face.

'Mrs Gripper?' he said, flicking a long, thin comb through Willow's half-dried hair.

'Is that who she is? Not the wife of the *Daily Mercury* Gripper?' Gino nodded and looked sly. Willow waited, knowing that the hairdresser was a repository of gossip and secrets from almost every one of the women who came to him. At last he gave in a little.

'She probably feels she can't face anyone yet. It only happened on Monday,' he said. Willow's mind raced: Monday; Algy; seduction; jealousy and lust; revenge. A motive! But wouldn't it be too much of a coincidence?

'What happened on Monday?' she asked aloud.

'A very good friend of hers was killed. She rang today to ask if I could go to their house to do her hair, because she was not feeling strong enough to go out.'

'Perhaps she was just ill,' suggested Willow, thinking that the friend in question must be Algernon Endelsham, but that however close a friend he had been, there must have been something more than the fact of his death to make a grown woman unable to leave her house for an hour. Such an exaggerated reaction would be excessive in anyone, even if she were newly and passionately in love. Gino shook his head decisively.

'No. When I got to Graham Terrace, I saw that she must have been crying almost ever since Monday. She looked terrified, too,' said Gino, smoothing Willow's hair preparatory to finishing the drying.

'Perhaps she was just afraid that you would tell all your other customers that she was in a state,' said Willow drily and closed her eyes. 'Who was killed, and how do you know she had anything to do with him?' She knew that she had caught Gino on the raw, because she heard the snap as he put down the dryer.

Opening her eyes, she saw him riffling through a heap of dog-eared magazines. At last he found the one he was looking for, and brought it to her. Laying it open in front of her, he picked up the dryer again.

'There!' he said, dramatically as he pushed up the switch and the machine roared again. 'It's unmistakable,' he went on above the noise.

Willow looked at the row of four-inch-square photographs, searching for the pretty blonde. But it was Algy who caught her eye first, resplendent in white tie and tails. Suppressing a sigh of regret for the loss of such rare masculine beauty and talent, Willow looked at his companion. Sure enough, there was the pretty, slightly fragile-looking blonde who usually occupied the chair two down from Willow's. 'Mrs Eustace Gripper', as the caption called her, was wearing an off-the-shoulder ball dress and looked enchanting as she stood confidingly close to her tall escort.

'What makes you think that there was anything between them?' said Willow, as soon as Gino switched off the dryer. 'It would be madly indiscreet of them to be seen together like that if there had been.'

Gino shrugged and looked ineffably knowing.

'You can't mean that she told you,' said Willow, really surprised. 'Or was it someone else? Some terribly good friend of hers, who just couldn't keep her mouth shut?' She watched the Italian closely, but he was far too experienced to blush or wince. He merely laughed.

'That would be telling, wouldn't it, Miss Woodruffe,' he said, reaching for the hairspray to glue Willow's hair in place.

'Yes,' she said crisply. 'That's why I'm asking.'

'People tell me a lot of things,' he said quietly. 'And I never repeat them. Never!'

Remembering a song from HMS Pinafore, Willow smiled to herself and then said aloud:

'You just hint, don't you, Gino? My goodness, you must have fun with us all. I'm glad I've no secrets.'

'Everybody has things to hide, Miss Woodruffe,' he said, smoothing her newly curled hair. 'There, how do you like it?'

'Very much,' she answered, hoping devoutly that he knew nothing of her secrets.

As she examined her reflection, she thought with affectionate nostalgia of her first physical transformation from Willow King to 'Cressida Woodruffe'. It had taken place on the morning of her first meeting with Eve Greville, who was to become her literary agent.

Willow had sent Eve the typescript of her first, unpublishable, novel and Eve had suggested that they meet to discuss 'Cressida's' next attempt. Unwilling to present herself as a severe-looking Civil Servant, Willow had gambled some of her limited resources on an expensive, clinging black jersey dress to wear instead of one of her loose, ill-fitting, neutral suits, and had booked an appointment at a famous hair-and-beauty salon.

There she had given the staff a free hand and watched in amusement and some admiration as they recreated her. Excited by the length, thickness and good condition of her dark-red hair, the hairdresser had released it from its savagely controlling pins and washed and curled it into an artfully tousled mane. So framed, her white face lost its severity and took on a curiously convincing attraction. The cheekbones that seemed almost painfully sharp when her hair was dragged away from them looked dramatic in contrast to the luxuriance of her new curls; her nose seemed much less prominent and as she smiled her lips lost their pinched look.

Later, with subtly graded olive and brown eyeshadows brushed on to her lids and glossy mascara on her pale eyelashes, let alone the carefully chosen blusher warming her skin and coral lipstick emphasising her mouth, Willow was confronted with a reflection she had never expected to see even in her most extreme fantasies. She could not be described as classically beautiful, but the face she saw in the mirror that day looked modern instead of spinsterly, vividly alive and – she could not deny it – thoroughly attractive.

In order to protect the secret of her double identity, Willow had never returned to that particular hairdresser, but Gino had proved an efficient successor whenever Willow needed to appear anywhere as 'Cressida'. As the advances and royalties she earned built up into what seemed to her to be a fortune, she learned to enjoy the transformation process for its own sake rather than for the disguise it gave her. The spending of money on glamorous clothes and hairdressing gradually stopped seeming either wasteful or extravagant and, by the time the murder shocked her out of her easy security, it had become a positive pleasure.

'Thank you, Gino,' she said, smiling at his reflection as he held up a hand mirror so that she could judge his handiwork at the back of her head as well as the front.

'As always: a pleasure, Miss Woodruffe. I'll call the manicurist now, and I'll see you next Thursday.'

'Yes indeed. Good night, Gino.'

When the manicurist had finished and Willow's nails were as clean and gleaming as her hair, she paid the relatively enormous bill and walked slowly back towards Chesham Place, where she had her other flat, revelling in the contrasts of her existence. Now that she had left Willow King behind, and had become 'Cressida Woodruffe' once more, she felt less bothered about all the lies she had had to tell at DOAP.

After all, without that first one to Michael Englewood, she would never have discovered the pleasures and luxuries that 'Cressida Woodruffe' had brought her; she would still be frustrated, bored, and unhappily wedded to the department because of the index-linked pension that would come to her when she retired at the age of sixty. And she would still be lonely.

Reaching the house in which she owned the second floor, she let herself in and went upstairs, knowing that the flat would have been impeccably cleaned and supplied in her absence by Mrs Rusham, her daily housekeeper. When Willow walked into the drawing room she was greeted with the sweet fresh scent of about five dozen freesias, which Mrs Rusham had arranged in a pair of black Ming vases on the chimneypiece.

Heaving a sigh of relief, Willow took off her jacket, flung

it over the back of a sofa and poured herself a modest glass of Palo Cortado sherry, not even noticing that the ache in her throat had gone.

Glass in hand, she pottered about the large elegant room, taking renewed pleasure in the walnut bureau bookcase she had bought at Sotheby's four years earlier, in the Chinese embroideries that hung in the embrasures on either side of the fireplace, in the thick pale silk carpet that covered the polished parquet and the soft plumpness of the handmade sofas. When she had begun to write the first book, one of her ambitions had been to generate enough money for just such a room, in which she could try to create an atmosphere of peaceful luxury. Looking around on that Thursday evening, she considered that she had succeeded. There was space, there was warmth and there was a delicate concentration of colour and light.

The panelled walls had been painted in a pale duck-egg blue, which set off the golden wood of the furniture as well as the old French chintz curtains and flattered almost every kind of flower that was placed in front of it. The sofas were loose covered in thick twilled silk of a colour somewhere between silver-grey and pale olive-green, and the two Louis XV elbow chairs in a muted stripe that combined all the other blues and greens in the room. The chimneypiece was white marble and over it hung an oval Chippendale looking glass, which reflected the pride of her collection, a blazing Turner watercolour of sunrise over Durham Cathedral. Celadon lamps with cream-silk pleated shades cast an easy mellow light over the room, and the rose and violet colours on the cream background of the glazed chintz warmed it.

Relaxing into the pleasure of her ritual inventory of the ravishing things her novels had bought her, Willow wandered over to the Pembroke table on which Mrs Rusham always arranged her post and messages. There was the usual collection of bills, fan letters, letters from her publisher and agent, proofs of other people's novels with requests for comments, and a message written out in Mrs Rusham's laborious hand:

'Mr Lawrence-Crescent telephoned to say that he will be held up at his office this evening, and so he won't be able to arrive until about nine-thirty. Unless he hears from you to the contrary, he will still come to take you out to a new restaurant he has discovered.'

Willow smiled as she thought of the pleasure Mrs Rusham must have had in talking to Richard Crescent on the telephone. There must be something about his very restrained good looks and well-mannered Englishness that strongly appealed to the housekeeper, for she was devoted to him and obviously considered that Willow herself treated him with far too little care.

In fact Willow did care for Richard, who had become her first and only lover three years earlier. Despite the unparalleled physical intimacy she had achieved with him, Willow liked to keep a certain emotional detachment in their relationship, and she was fairly certain that Richard also felt safer with that than he would have with a more conventional love affair. He had let her know very early in their acquaintance that he loathed talking about his feelings and would have found it embarrassing to have to listen to hers.

Not too displeased to have an extra couple of hours in which to prowl about her kingdom, Willow collected a second glass of sherry and a copy of a new novel she badly wanted to read and took them both with her into the bathroom, where she ran herself an enormously deep, hot bath, scented with Chanel No.19 bath oil.

As she lay in the fragrant water, becoming more radiant by the minute, she ignored the book and bent her mind to the question of how on earth she was to pursue the only real lead she had into the mystery of who had killed Algernon Endelsham. She wondered what Gino could have meant by saying that Mrs Gripper had been 'terrified'? Terrified of what, or of whom? Unlike the fortunate police, Willow

46

could not ask direct questions of anyone she suspected. Instead, she would have to dig things out without help from anyone. Clearly she was going to have to get to know Mrs Gripper quickly.

Perhaps she could hang about outside the house in Graham Terrace Gino had talked about, and then faint across the doorstep just as the woman emerged. . . . Willow put that promising fantasy aside as she remembered that Mrs Gripper had not left the house even for her weekly hair appointment. For the first time in her life as Cressida, Willow thought it a pity that she had deliberately evaded all her agent's and publisher's attempts to introduce her to people. After all, if she had allowed them to do as they had wanted, she would probably have been able to badger a friend or acquaintance for an introduction to the apparently bereaved Mrs Gripper. Richard Crescent could have helped her to meet any number of merchant bankers and probably owners of stately homes and Scottish grouse moors, but rich gossip-column journalists were not likely to form part of his circle.

An hour later, her skin bright pink and slightly puckered and her expensively arranged hair rather fluffy from the steam, Willow emerged from the bathroom with no real idea of what to do next. She decided to try to put the whole matter of Algy's murder out of her mind until she had dealt with Richard.

It amused her to dress elaborately for him and to spend some time painting her face with the sort of cosmetics she would once have despised. By the time she had finished, her face (which was usually white and dull) still looked pale but really rather interesting. Her eyes looked larger and darker than in their unpainted state and consequently her nose was much less obvious, while the carefully chosen lipstick made her lips look fuller, more generous than those of DOAP's Miss King, even sensuous.

The dress she chose from her generous wardrobe was made of silk hand-printed with a flight of black butterflies against a sunset sky of subtle flame colours, and it clung to her figure, making her look slim rather than skinnily angular as she did in her DOAP suits. Looking at herself in a long glass, she was reasonably certain that even if she were to run into someone from the department they would never recognise daunting, plain Willow King in the sinuously glamorous romantic novelist she had become.

Richard's instinctive blink and wide smile when he arrived told her that he at least approved of the efforts she had made with her face and clothes. He kissed her, carefully avoiding her lipstick, and apologised for his lateness.

'I should be used to it by now,' said Willow, smiling at him in a way that would have astonished her DOAP colleagues. 'What was it? Tiresome clients or a new deal blowing up out of the blue?'

'Neither,' he answered shortly and then as he caught sight of her derisive glance, added: 'Well, yes, it was clients actually and their lawyers. . . . Nothing out of the ordinary, merely coming clean about some figures they'd fudged, which meant that all the listing particulars will have to be changed overnight. I think their lawyers must have been as horrified as we all were when they confessed.'

Willow wished that she were more interested in the goings-on of the City or less interested in the lengths to which Richard could go to avoid giving her any real information about his work. He clearly enjoyed talking to her about it, but was far too experienced a merchant banker to commit the slightest indiscretion, and she often felt how much more interesting his conversation would be if he could only include a few names or at least personalities in it. Just occasionally she tried to push or tease him into revealing them, forgetting how much she herself relied on his discretion. He was the only person in the world who knew that Willow King and Cressida Woodruffe were the same woman; and yet in all the years she had known him she had never been afraid that he would betray her.

They had met at a party of her publisher, soon after her

fourth book had been published and actually achieved the best-seller list in hardback. Richard had been invited only because his bank was handling the merger of her publisher and a larger house, and he was clearly bored by the chatter about royalties, affairs between editors and authors, redundancies and disastrous jacket flap copy. His lacklustre eyes brightened visibly when Willow's editor brought her up to be introduced and she found herself both flattered by his obvious interest in her and intrigued by him. As they talked she discovered not only that he had a dry sense of humour that appealed to her, but also that his brains matched or even exceeded her own. Although she usually hated parties and left after half an hour, on that evening she stayed talking in ever greater animation to Richard.

He took her out to dinner that first night and quite soon afterwards they went to bed together. Despite her total inexperience and their mutual dislike of admitting or discussing their feelings, it had been a wholly pleasurable interlude, which they were both happy to repeat. Gradually a routine grew up between them, and they dined together on most evenings between Thursday and Sunday, except when Richard was in New York, Paris or Tokyo on bank business.

Willow considered that their friendship was both civilised and eminently satisfactory. It gave each of them pleasure, an escort to the occasional party, theatre or cinema, and just as much overt emotion as each could handle comfortably. Willow knew quite well that 'Cressida Woodruffe's' readers would have found the arrangement unattractively cold, even selfish, but there was genuine affection between them. Neither made claims on the other (although just occasionally as the years passed Richard allowed himself the luxury of sentimental pleading, secure perhaps in the knowledge that Willow would never spoil things by yielding to his pleas) and both were considerate of the other's privacy. Willow had not consciously kept her secrets from him, but Richard had never asked any of the questions that might have elicited frankness from her. She told him the truth in the end only because it had come to seem impolite to withhold so much from a man with whom she made love once or twice a week.

Watching him on that Thursday evening in November admiring her new clothes, Willow remembered how he had burst out laughing as she told him of the life she led in Clapham, and she herself laughed at the memory.

'What's so funny?' he asked, rather defensive. 'Have I sat in something?' He twisted round to squint down at his own impeccable backview. Willow laughed again and shook her curly head.

'Nothing, Richard. I was just remembering how amused you were when I first told you who I really was. It was such a relief!'

He only smiled and picked up her fur coat for her. Willow shrugged herself into it and together they walked out into the icy street. Richard told her about the restaurant he had chosen, asked her what she had been reading since they last met and said nothing of any importance until they were sitting in immense comfort with their oysters and Chablis in front of them. Then he settled himself more luxuriously in the embracing red-velvet chair and said:

'And so how was the department this week? All of a flutter, I take it, over this ghastly business.'

Willow swallowed an oyster, enjoying the peculiar sensation of the soft, yielding saltiness sliding over her tongue and trying to ignore a sudden recognition of the highly similar sensations she felt as she recovered from a phlegmy cold.

'All of a flutter just about describes it,' she said. 'They're all inventing wilder and wilder solutions about whodunnit and causing untold umbrage to each other as they propound them.'

'And have you any theories?' Richard asked, wondering as so often before what she was like in her professional persona and whether it could really be true that none of her colleagues guessed who she was.

'Not yet,' she answered, not wanting to expose poor Mrs Gripper's sad secret (even if it were genuine). She picked up another oyster shell, 'But I shall pretty soon have to.'

'Oh, God, Willow, I've seen that look before,' he said, peering through the candlelight at her. 'What on earth have you done?'

She dropped the empty oyster shell on the plate, wiped her long fingers on her napkin, took a sip of wine and said coolly:

'Richard, you're as bad as the idiots at DOAP: you of all people can't really believe that I banged the Minister over the head with a cricket bat or something and killed him, can you? In any case, you and I spent the whole of that evening together with the Krug and fish fingers. You must remember.'

'I remember perfectly well, not least my perennial horror at what you do to a good wine by insisting on eating those disgusting, vulgar things,' he said. Then, sobering, he added: 'In any case, I know you far too well to imagine any such thing.'

'Thank you, Richard,' said Willow as soberly, and went on, as though disliking so much seriousness: 'And I don't see why I should scour a taste for fish fingers out of myself just because you despise them. They're almost the only thing I've retained from the Newcastle of my youth. Even after a childhood like mine, one should be allowed a tiny bit of nostalgia.'

'Were you so unhappy then?' asked Richard. It was the most intimate question he had ever asked her and for a moment she was tempted to laugh it off; but then she remembered his declaration of faith in her and thought that she had to answer properly.

'Not exactly unhappy, Richard, because I didn't know anything else. But I did feel as though I inhabited a world quite separate from anyone else. Don't look like that, my dear,' she said, stretching out a hand across the table. He held it for a moment, looking so sad that she felt that she had to try to explain.

'I don't blame my parents: they did their absolute best, but they knew nothing whatever about the emotional needs of children. They were both very busy at the university and confined their dealings with me to making sure that I was fit and healthy and would be able to cope with the world on my own. Since they were forty-two and fifty-five when I was conceived they were convinced that they'd die before I'd got a job with a secure salary and pension.'

'Hence the Civil Service,' said Richard. 'I wonder what they would think of Cressida Woodruffe.' At that Willow laughed and took a sip of Chablis.

'I rather think they would be appalled,' she said. 'For two professorial scientists to have produced a daughter with an academic record like mine was one thing – I think they were really quite proud of that – but to have a daughter who made a fortune out of romantic novels? No, Richard. They would have hated it – and despised half the things I've bought with the money. They seriously disapproved of luxury and in my place would have sent all the money to Third World aid projects, I suspect.'

Richard swallowed the last of his oysters and then looked speculatively across the table at her.

'Is that why you go on spending half the week at DOAP?' he asked. 'You obviously hated it and your Clapham life before you invented Cressida, so why do you go on? You're not a masochist by nature, as far as I know.'

Willow thought about it and wondered how much to tell him. In the end, she compromised.

'I suppose partly,' she said carefully. 'They worked so hard – as I did – to fit me for that life that something in me is tied to it. But more to the point is that if I'm to go on writing escapist fiction for other people, I need to go on living in a life from which *I* want to escape. Fantasy would wear very thin if it were worn every day.'

'Would it?' asked Richard, clearly not believing her. Willow shrugged, not wanting to delve into her own psyche, let alone expose it to Richard. It had occurred to her more than once that she might prefer to have two lives so that if anyone in either existence tried to get too close to her she could escape to the other. But it was not an idea on which she wished to dwell. To deflect Richard's attention, she said:

'But I may not have the option much longer. There is a risk that my DOAP life may come to a sticky – but I hope quite private – end.'

'Mixed metaphors, Willow! I'm shocked,' said Richard, drinking some more wine. When he had put the glass down again, he seemed to understand what she meant, for he said: 'What have you done? Oh no! It's to do with this murder, isn't it?'

'The police wanted alibis for last Monday evening and with the establishments officer sitting in on the interview, I could hardly tell them where I actually was, now could I?' said Willow.

Richard picked up his glass of white wine again, took a deep swallow as though to give himself courage and then spoke.

'Are you telling me that you have lied to the police in a murder enquiry? You must be stark staring bonkers! Yes, I'm not surprised you're looking a bit nervous.'

Willow, unaware that her expression had changed, shrugged.

'I had no option, Richard, unless I was going to throw all this away.' She gestured at their sumptuous surroundings, gobbled up the rest of her oysters and then looked across the table at him. 'Oh, come on Richard, smile! It's not that serious. Either I'm going to discover who did do it before they check out Aunt Agatha, or if they get there first, I can always confess – but privately. I really am not going to have Cressida Woodruffe trumpeted all through the lino-covered corridors of that hellish plague-ridden building for them all to point and giggle at.'

Richard, sighing as though he simply could not cope with her, signalled to a waiter to clear away their plates. He was half genuinely appalled by her lawlessness; but the other half of him was secretly excited by it. One of her greatest attractions for him had always been the hint of Cressida's irresponsible, self-indulgent wickedness, which was so easily kept in check by Willow King's unassailable probity: she had the tamed, almost contrived, wildness of an eighteenth-century 'wild' garden, and he had always felt free to enjoy it without fear of any real danger.

'Don't worry so, Richard,' she said, suddenly touched by the serious expression on his thin face. 'I can devote the whole time until next Tuesday morning to solving the mystery – the book's gone sticky on me anyway and a little mild detecting will probably clear my brain. I'm sure that I can discover. . .'

'Better than the police, forensic scientists and so on?' Richard demanded, with all the arrogance of which he was quite unaware. There were times when Willow found it so infuriating that she challenged him, but on that evening for some reason she found it merely amusing; perhaps her reaction was part and parcel of her dressing up to please him.

'I really do think you have gone mad,' he went on, and Willow began to feel a licking flame of anger somewhere in her mind. 'You think that your novelist's brain will invent the motive, don't you? And that you can present the guilty one to the police with a flourish next Tuesday morning? You need to rein in that imagination of yours. It could get you into serious trouble.'

'Don't sneer too much at my imagination, Richard,' said Willow with more than a hint of Civil Service crispness. 'It earns me even more than your banker's brain earns you.'

'*Touché*, b'gad,' he said with the rueful smile that always disarmed her. 'But you must be careful about pinning all your investigating on motive, mustn't you? I mean, do remember what Lord Peter said about motive to Harriet in *Busman's Honeymoon.*'

Before she could answer, the waiter brought their grouse and then made way for the sommelier with a bottle of Burgundy. When they had both gone and Willow had eaten at least half of the delicious bird, she took up the conversation where Richard had left it.

'But you know, Richard, it is really a question of motive. . . . Not the killer's,' she said quickly as he made as though to protest. 'But the minister's. I mean, what could he possibly have been doing bang in the middle of Clapham Common at the end of a working day in November? That's got to be sorted out before anyone – police included – can have any idea about who killed him, because there were no witnesses, there was no weapon left at the scene, no physical clues at all – according to the DOAP gossip anyway, and that's usually accurate.' She caught herself up at that, but did not bother to deny it aloud. After all Richard knew nothing of Algy's pursuit of her or the highly overheated speculation that that episode had generated.

'What about his driver? He must have had an official car, presumably,' said Richard.

'Albert – yes, but unfortunately he's in the clear. Apparently the minister told him to take the car to the top of Cedar's Road and wait there. Plenty of witnesses have been found to confirm the order and the fact that he sat there. After all a huge black car like that with a chauffeur is pretty conspicuous in Clapham,' answered Willow, who had already considered and rejected Albert as a possible suspect. She had always thought him a bit of a thug and without an alibi he would have seemed a likely murderer.

The word 'witnesses' seemed to jog Richard's memory.

'Are you certain that no one saw anything? As far as I can remember Clapham Common is remarkably open and fairly well lit. Hardly any trees. Could anyone have been killed without being seen? Of course, it is a very long time since I've been near the place.'

'I don't know,' said Willow, picking at the carcase of her grouse. 'There are lights along most of the paths, but when I was there last night, I discovered that it can get pitchy dark in the middle of the grass bits,' she went on, forgetting the previous day's fear in amusement at Richard's distancing himself from his days of struggle in a small Clapham flat.

Richard, not noticing her amusement, immediately demanded to know what she thought she had been doing wandering about in the dark in much the same terms that the inspector had used, and before she thought, Willow found herself explaining her actions and motives to him. He listened, expressionless, but when she had finished telling him about the joggers and her dramatic encounter with Inspector Worth, Richard put his head in his hands. Concerned for him, Willow reached across the table and laid one of her hands on his thick hair, mildly admiring the contrast of her raspberry-tipped nails against the darkness of his head. He looked up.

'Willow, I know I have no right to say this, but I do wish that you wouldn't do things like that. I. . . I. . .'

'What, Richard?' Willow asked.

'Oh God, you might think of me before you go and risk yourself like that. If anything happened to you. . . .'

Willow looked at him in surprise. Until that evening he had always been scrupulous in keeping his side of their unspoken bargain: Cressida Woodruffe was fair game, but he had no part in Willow's Clapham life.

'Oh I know, I'm sorry. What you do at DOAP is none of my business. But, Willow, it's just so damned dangerous – and if you go annoying whoever it was who killed Endelsham, then you're going to risk even worse. Willow, promise you won't do anything to get yourself hurt.'

'Richard, I. . .' she began, but then stopped herself from making him any dangerous promises of obedience.

'Let's get out of here,' he said far more roughly than she had ever heard him speak. He stood up and signalled impatiently for the bill. When it came, he added a hefty tip and signed it. Taking Willow by the arm he then whisked her out of the restaurant and into his Audi. Neither spoke on the short drive back to Chesham Place. When they were at last in Willow's bedroom, Richard tried to make up for his attempted infringement of her independence.

'I couldn't help it, Willow. I'm sorry.' He dropped on his knees in front of her, wrapped his arms around her waist and buried his face against her silken skirt. She laid both hands on his head and there was even a hint of tenderness in her smile as she said:

'Richard, my dear, don't worry so much. I shan't get hurt. Come on; get up and come to bed.'

He tipped back his head and she bent to kiss him.

4

WILLOW woke early the following morning to the depressing sound of heavy November rain beating against the windows of her bedroom. Hearing the soft snuffle of Richard's breathing, she twisted her head to the right to look at her illuminated clock. Six o'clock: there was an hour and a half to go before Mrs Rusham would arrive and make breakfast. Willow hated lying awake in bed with nothing to do, but she was loth to wake Richard by turning on the light to read. Instead, she slid carefully out of bed, wrapped herself in her thick velvet dressing gown and padded silently out to the kitchen to make herself a cup of tea and think.

The kitchen was a wonderful room, designed to fit all Willow's fantasies in the days before she had even envisaged having a housekeeper who would keep her out of it. In the centre of the long wall was a white four-door Aga, far too big for any single woman's flat, let alone one who was away for half of every week. But it was supremely cosy on a grey morning, and Willow loved feeling the warmth of it against her thighs as she leaned forward to lift the heavy lid of the fast ring.

While she waited for the kettle to boil, she took a pad of paper and a pencil to the cushioned rocking chair in the corner and sat down, tucking her feet up under her, to list the few things she knew about Algy Endelsham's life before DOAP. That done, she looked contentedly around the kitchen, noting the almost aseptic cleanliness of it all, and hoping that Mrs Rusham shared some of her delight in the soft redness of the quarry tiles and the silky gleam of the copper pans and bowls that hung on the wall opposite the Aga above the thick beech work tops. Whenever the housekeeper was in the flat she made it quite clear that she wanted her employer to stay out of the kitchen and she always greeted any sullying of its impeccable tidiness with a frigid politeness that was expressive of extreme disapproval. Willow put up with it not only because Mrs Rusham was an excellent cook and organiser, but also because she had never betrayed the slightest hint of curiosity about her employer's private life or unexplained absences. Willow prized that restraint even more than she prized her glorious kitchen.

The hiss of the kettle brought her approving reverie to an end; she made a pot of Earl Grey tea and poured some out into a fine bone-china mug, which she took back to the rocking chair. There she sat, nursing the warm mug and rocking herself gently as she turned over and over in her mind all the possible reasons why a man like Algy Endelsham might have been killed.

When she had first heard about the murder, she had assumed that it must have been his womanising that had angered someone so much that he or she (or even they) had killed him, and Gino's titillating hints had tended to reinforce the assumption. But there was still the frightful possibility that Algy had merely been the victim of mindless violence, or perhaps somebody's spite or even lunacy. What Willow had to decide was how to proceed with her investigation with so few facts.

She was nowhere near any kind of solution when, nearly an hour later, she heard the sounds of Richard getting out of bed.

'Tea, darling?' she called from the kitchen, and then smiled as he came in, his thick hair standing on end from a vigorous scratching and his long body clad in the heavy silk dressing gown she had bought for him. Navy blue with claret-coloured piping, it was, she considered, very suitable for a successful banker.

'Um,' he said, 'tea would be lovely, if it's not too much trouble.'

'I'll make a new pot – this is hours old. Go and run a bath and I'll bring you a cup there.'

Richard looked a little surprised, but obediently went away. Willow smiled as she acknowledged to herself that she rarely exhibited her slight domestic gifts when Richard was in the flat. She was less amused to realise that they had been stimulated by the faint sense of guilt she felt about what she was going to do.

She carried his tea into the bathroom and perched herself on the side of the bath. Richard put up a soapy hand to take the mug and looked at the position she had chosen.

'You're going to get your elegant dressing gown very wet if you sit just there,' he said.

'Never mind, my dear,' she answered. 'I wanted to ask you something.'

'Yes?' he said and his tone made it quite clear that he was prepared to block any question that might have a bearing on anything the bank was about to do. Willow was not surprised: she had often thought that Richard would find it difficult to tell anyone what the time was unless he had had it vetted by the bank's lawyers first.

'What do you know about Algy Endelsham, Richard?' she asked.

'Me? Nothing other than what I've read in the papers,' he answered sipping the hot tea. 'You make a nice cuppa, Willow.'

60

'Come on, Richard, wake up!' Willow said, leaning down to kiss his damp head. 'Bankers always know about politicians; there must be something.'

Richard lay obstinately back in the hot water. A wicked little smile teased the edges of Willow's lips and she sneaked her fingers behind his neck to stroke his top vertebrae in precisely the way he most enjoyed. 'Tell!' she commanded, still stroking. After about ninety seconds he could bear it no longer and sat up to grab a handful of her luscious hair with his free hand.

'I'd like to strangle you sometimes,' he said, laughing and twisting the hair into a rope.

'Like Porphyria's lover,' suggested Willow.

'You're irritatingly well read, you know,' he said, letting the hair go. 'For a mathematician, I mean. Yes, I do know a little about precious Algy, but it's not to his credit. Are you trustworthy?'

'It's Willow you're talking to,' she assured him, 'not Cressida Woodruffe.'

'Okay; well he was a swine at school.' He let his eyelids drop for a moment and then took another reviving gulp of tea.

Willow was surprised. It was well known that Algy Endelsham had had, among his innumerable other endowments, the benefit of an Eton education, while Richard had been taught at a rather humbler establishment. One of the things Willow had never learned to understand was the importance that people like Algy and Richard laid on the place where they went to school.

'You sound upset, Richard,' she said. 'What happened? And when were you at school with Algy – wasn't he at Eton?'

'We were at prep school together, and as I said, he was a swine. Bloody successful, of course, even then: captain of the first XI, head of school, leader of the choir. . . power crazy and a damned sadist.'

'My poor Richard,' she said, thinking for the first time

of what he must have been like as a child.

She had asked him very little about his family or upbringing, because it had quickly become obvious that he disliked talking about his more distant past. Since Willow shared his preference for the present, it had not been difficult to refrain from asking awkward questions. Now she realised that she had forced a confidence out of him and one that she might have to pursue if she were really to discover all the truth about Algernon Endelsham and his killer.

'Algy,' she said, the regret in her voice sounding to Richard like gentleness for him. He looked up at her unseeing eyes with a yearning smile.

'A sadist?' Willow went on. 'It's hard to believe. He was always so charming at DOAP.'

'To everyone?' Richard asked quietly and Willow looked down at him in ever-increasing concern.

'Come to think of it, no, not to everyone. He was fairly hard on the slow and the stupid and the obstructive members of the department. But, Richard, you couldn't have been any of those things at school - even prepschool: I think you're the most intelligent man I've ever met,' said Willow truthfully. It was, after all, Richard's formidable brains that had first attracted her.

He lay back against the curved end of the bath, smiling at her with such self-mockery in his eyes that she was reassured.

'Thank you for that testimonial, my dear,' he said, laughing. 'No, Endelsham always terrorised anyone who showed the slightest weakness – laughed at the homesick, derided the short-sighted who were bad at games; that sort of thing.'

'How unspeakably horrible!' Willow exclaimed. To herself she added silently: well there's that to be said for not understanding other people's motives and emotions – at least you think more kindly of them for not knowing too much about them. 'You must have been miserable.'

'Everyone's miserable at their prep school. It's a fact of life – and bloody good preparation for life at that.' He gave a short snorting laugh. 'Nothing, ever, is as bad again. And when you've learned how to cope with that at eight, you know you'll be all right for the rest of your life.'

'And people think that private schooling is so desirable,' said Willow, who had received an excellent and humane education at the grammar school to which she walked every day from her parents' house in Newcastle. In fact it had been the maths teacher there who had provided the only easy warmth in clever, isolated Wilhelmina King's life, and even shortened her ridiculous name.

'Oh it has its moments, Willow,' said Richard, yawning. 'But I must get on, darling. Shall I run you a bath?'

'Yes, please,' she said, leaning over to kiss his head again to make up for her reminding him of his childhood sorrows.

As soon as he had wandered into her bedroom to dress, she got into the bath, and they were both clean and dressing by the time Mrs Rusham arrived and started to make breakfast. Willow was horribly conscious of the dirty teapots and damp rings on the kitchen work surfaces. When she emerged from her bedroom for breakfast and greeted Mrs Rusham, the housekeeper made no mention of the mess, but a certain tightness about her lips and sharpness in her voice made it quite clear what she thought of her employer's invasion of the territory she considered her own.

Mrs Rusham had provided foaming cappuccino, canta-loupe melon, crisp bacon and wonderful fresh brioches, which she picked up from a baker on her way in to work every morning. The *Financial Times* was neatly folded by Richard's plate and *The Times* and the *Independent* by Willow's. She picked up *The Times* and turned to the letters page, but when Richard emerged, a little damp about the hairline but impeccably dressed, she refolded the newspaper and would not allow him even to glance at his. Instead she grilled him about Algy's days at prep school.

Richard, never at his best in the morning, tried to answer the questions tolerantly, but at last lost patience.

'For heaven's sake, Willow, you can't imagine that the roots of this murder lie as far back as that! The five beastly years we all spent between eight and thirteen can hardly hold the seeds of an enmity that surfaced more than a quarter of a century later.'

'Well no, of course not,' she answered, sipping her coffee. 'But it all helps to give me a picture of the man. . . and such a different picture from the one I got working in his department. It's extraordinary, but I had no idea he was like that. In fact if it were not you who had told me, I don't think I'd believe it yet.'

'Look: he probably wasn't,' said Richard, tucking into the bacon and looking at his watch between mouthfuls. 'The man doubtless changed as he grew up. Just because he was a bully as a child, doesn't mean that he could not have become the sweet charmer of the gossip columns or your girlish office dreams.'

'No,' said Willow, not even bothering to comment on his jibe. 'But it's intriguing. Look, Richard, have you got anything on paper about your school – lists, magazines, anything like that? It would be rivetting to find out what he was really like: not through the eyes of an unhappy contemporary, but with hindsight. Have you? I know you; you like to keep everything about your life somewhere about you.'

As she said that she began to wonder why he found it necessary to surround himself with all the evidence of his past; and it was not only that. He was also an inveterate collector of things. His house was filled with ramparts of paper, books, china, antiques. Perhaps, she thought, watching his good-looking, severe face, they really were ramparts; but against what? Willow

64

hardly even noticed that she was once more indulging in impertinent speculation as the fascination took hold of her mind.

'As it happens, yes,' said Richard, pushing away his bacon plate and finishing his coffee. 'I think there is a trunkful of stuff in the attic at home, and if it'll satisfy your curiosity you have my permission to search.'

'Bless you, Richard,' said Willow as he stood up and straightened his tie. 'Could you get someone to bring it round here today? This morning, perhaps.'

'I'd give a lot to see those Civil Servants of yours listening to you, wheedling like that,' said Richard, and he took a certain satisfaction from the frown that creased Willow's white forehead. 'But I'm afraid there's not a hope. I have to go to Paris this morning. I'll get you the stuff as soon as I can manage.' He looked at his slim, gold watch and gulped down the last of his coffee. 'I must be off. Thank you, Willow, for letting me stay.'

'Thank you,' she said. 'And don't forget the FT.'

He picked up the newspaper and folded it under his arm. Then he kissed her briefly.

'Thank you also for. . . giving me a lovely evening,' he said, 'and a delectable breakfast.'

'Despite the inquisition?'

'Yes. And, Willow, you made a promise not to take risks. You will keep it, won't you?' Richard's voice was heavy with the unaccustomed emotion of the previous evening, and Willow shuddered inwardly. But she nodded.

'All right. Have a good day. See you this evening.' He went out but put his head round the door again two minutes later to say:

'Did you know that the bandstand on Clapham Common is a gay meeting place? Perhaps that filthy rag has been right about Endelsham's preferences after all.'

'The *Daily Mercury*,' said Willow, looking astonished. 'Don't tell me that you read that, Richard.'

'Lord no, but the secretaries always have it and one

manages to see most of the juicy bits. 'Bye, Willow.'

When he had really gone, she accepted a second cup of coffee from Mrs Rusham and sat brooding on what Richard had told her about Algy Endelsham. The more she thought about it, the less she could believe that the Algernon Endelsham she had known had ever been a homosexual. Richard's account of the schoolboy bully seemed to fit in much better with some of Algy's behaviour at the department, and offered a more convincing reason for his murder. The man had obviously been less crude in his attempts at controlling his fellows than the boy had been; but the impulse that had made him torment the weak at school must have been the same as the one that drove him to make fools of his officials at every possible opportunity. Willow, disliking and despising so many of them herself, had found it quite amusing at the time, but looking back she was ashamed of herself.

In her uncharacteristically introspective mood, she found herself wondering for the first time whether the minister's embarrassingly public pursuit of herself might have been a product of the same impulse. After all, he had never been able to humiliate her over her work, because she had been able to keep up with him, and indeed overtake him. That would have left him with only the weapon of his sexuality and apparently unfailing record of seduction.

It was a new and rather disturbing thought, and it made her want more than ever to talk to Mrs Gripper. If she had really loved him, then she might be able to explain him to Willow. Without a clear idea of his real character, Willow did not think that it would be possible to unravel the mystery of his death.

When Mrs Rusham returned with a tray to remove the dirty breakfast crockery, she looked surprised to see her employer still at the breakfast table, scribbling down an address with one hand while she held open the telephone book in the other.

'Shall I clear now, Miss Woodruffe?' she asked in a tone that told Willow precisely what her housekeeper thought of women who idle around over breakfast at ten in the morning.

'Yes, do,' she said, smiling. 'I must tidy myself up, and then I have to go out. Don't bother about lunch; I'll have something out.'

'Very well, Miss Woodruffe,' said the housekeeper, carrying the heavy tray out of the breakfast room.

Willow made up her face quickly and then left the flat to walk through the high, white streets towards Graham Terrace. She had decided that the only way to speak to Mrs Gripper would be to ring the front-door bell and ask for her. Any other approach would take weeks and might well fail. If the worst came to the worst and Willow was rebuffed, she would not have lost anything, and there was a chance that she might succeed.

It took only ten minutes to walk from Willow's flat to the Grippers' front door, which was not quite long enough for her to prepare her opening speech. Looking up at the house as she passed, she walked on, thinking of the various possible introductions. At the end of the street, she turned back and approached the house again just as the front door opened.

Thinking that the fates were on her side, she hurried forward and reached the steps just as a burly man in a thick, dark-blue overcoat strode down them. He saw her and scowled. His already florid face seemed to redden even more and his bright blue eyes narrowed.

'Damn,' thought Willow, coming to a betraying halt. 'This must be Gripper himself.' But before she could either retreat or think of anything to say to him, he had walked right up to her and stood glaring at her. He had a fat, lighted cigar in one hand and a heavy-looking umbrella in the other. Standing squarely in front of her, with the umbrella slanted out to his left, he took up almost the entire width of the pavement. Without stepping into the gutter, walking backwards, or pushing him out of the way, Willow was stuck. There was no reason for her to be afraid of him; after all, he could have no idea who she was or why she should have been in the street where he lived; and yet she was frightened. It was an unpleasant sensation to one who had once thought that she feared nothing and nobody.

Not wanting to let him see her fear, she put back her head and looked him straight in the eye. She noticed that he was quite handsome, in his heavy, rich-looking way and that, although he displayed none of the romantic-novelists' gestures of hostility, there was more naked anger in his face than she had ever seen before. Trying to look both dignified and surprised to have been stopped by a stranger, she opened her mouth to ask him to move out of her path.

'Don't pretend it's not my home you were watching,' he said harshly in a voice that sent adrenalin pumping through her. 'I've watched you going up and down the street with your eyes on the house. Now, I don't know who you work for, but I can find out without any trouble at all. And I can tell you this: if I ever see you on this street again, if you ever try to speak to my wife, you will be sorry you were ever born.'

Willow stood absolutely still, unable to think of anything to say, but understanding at last why Mrs Gripper should have seemed terrified: Willow felt that she too would have been scared if she had had to share a house with such a man. Wishing that he was smaller or his voice less menacing, Willow tried to tell herself that she had no reason to be frightened of a middle-aged man in daylight in one of the most respectable parts of London, but she could not do it. His size, his arrogance and his threats made it almost impossible for her to think, let alone take any kind of action.

'Cat got your tongue?' he asked, and his voice seemed to grate in her brain. 'You're not even good at your job.

Beneath contempt in fact. But I won't have you worrying my wife even so. Now get off my patch.'

Gathering her reserves, Willow moved three steps back so that she no longer had to look up into his face, and found her voice.

'I do not know who you are,' she said, desperately hoping her voice carried conviction. 'And I think you must have mistaken me for someone else. I should be grateful if you would get out of my way, so that I can proceed.'

'You know bloody well who I am. And if I ever see you round here again, you'll discover that I don't make threats I can't carry out. If I read anything anywhere about my affairs, the libel writs will land on your editor's desk faster than you can telephone your lawyers. Got that?'

With her face relaxing slightly as she understood what he thought she was doing, Willow even managed to smile.

'You really are mistaken,' she said. 'I do not write for any publication and I have no interest in who you are or what your business is.'

Then with as much dignity as she could achieve (which was not very much) Willow brushed past him and walked back towards Eaton Square. She found that her hands were shaking, and she felt faint and rather sick. Despite the fact that he had not threatened any kind of physical violence, Willow knew that she had never been so afraid, not even the night when she had absurdly let off her pocket alarm on Clapham Common. She even found herself fantasising that Inspector Worth would materialise in front of her once again and restore her to herself, as he had on the common.

Knowing that if she returned to her flat she would have to make some excuse for her presence to Mrs Rusham, Willow decided to retreat to the anonymous safety of the coffee shop at the top of Peter Jones. There, at least, there would be no furious males to threaten the complete vulnerability that had just been revealed to her.

Ten minutes later, Willow was queueing for her coffee behind a row of smiling, chatty women with bags of shopping. One or two had babies in buggies and there were several blond toddlers rushing about in their blue-and-white-striped Osh-Kosh dungarees and red-leather shoes. The air of bright innocence and peaceful femininity began to restore Willow's damaged nerve. She took a large Danish pastry from the counter, vaguely thinking that the carbohydrate might help subdue her residual panic. Having paid for it and a cup of coffee, she carried her tray to a seat near the window overlooking the King's Road and sat down looking out and seeing nothing.

After a while the banging of her heart had slowed almost to normal and the sweat on her hands had dried enough for her to pick up her cup. The coffee was strong and still hot enough to help control the nausea she felt. She drank thirstily and when the cup was empty began to eat the sticky bun. When that, too, was finished she did feel better. Even so she could not help remembering what Richard had said the previous evening and wondering what she had let herself in for when she launched herself on the investigation.

In one way it was satisfactory to have had first-hand evidence of Eustace Gripper's temper and territorial instincts. The strength of his reaction to a possible snooper, and the precise words he had used, did suggest that Gino's tittle tattle might have some basis in fact. And a man who could so threaten a wholly unknown woman who just happened to pass by his house might well take violent exception to the seduction of his wife. But even so, would he go as far as murder?

Willow was just deciding that she would have to find some way of investigating both the Grippers and discovering whether they had alibis without ever coming face to face with him again when her gaze focussed on a bus which had just pulled up at a stop down in the street below. It was a number 19, which, she knew, went to Clapham Junction. Moving decisively at last, she got up from the small table and left the restaurant.

Having told Mrs Rusham that she would be out for lunch, she could hardly go straight back to the flat and had been wondering what on earth to do with herself. The bus had decided her; she would return to Clapham Junction station and try to inveigle the tramp to some place where she could question him without fear of being interrupted by helpful station staff.

As she was waiting for the lift, she caught sight of herself in a long mirror and realised that she would need something to disguise herself a little. The Burberry and black boots she had chosen when she hoped to talk to Mrs Gripper would not stand out too badly in Clapham, but her hair might well betray her. Ignoring the lift, she hurried down the stairs to the hat department and bought herself a large, not very becoming, black PVC rain hat, into which she could tuck all of the gleaming, dark-red curls. With the hat brim flopping irritatingly in front of her eyes, she was confident that no one would either recognise or remember her in the future.

Reassured of her anonymity, she went out into the street and joined the bus queue. It seemed strange to be heading south of the river on a 'Cressida Woodruffe' day, and Willow even felt a prick of conscience that she was not working at her novel; but her search for Algy's murderer had suddenly become serious. It was no longer just a matter of pitting her wits against those of the policeman who had interviewed her in order to avoid humiliating exposure. Now she had been threatened by a man who might have killed the minister. Gripper had not specified what he might do to her, except sue her for libel if she wrote about him, but she could forget neither the viciousness of his voice as he warned her off nor the aura of physical power that had surrounded him.

Her quest had taken on a personal quality. If Algernon Endelsham had been killed by Eustace Gripper, then

Willow wanted him behind bars. If he were innocent, then she needed to have proof in order to exorcise the terror he had induced in her. As it was, Willow knew that she would not be able to walk through that part of Belgravia again without fear.

A bus drew up at the stop and Willow shuffled on to it with the rest of the queuers. The drive to Clapham would have taken not much more than ten minutes in a car on a trafficless road, but on that Friday morning, with some commuters already leaving London for the weekend, shoppers milling into the road at every possible opportunity and the early lunchers clogging each crossing and junction of the road, the bus took well over an hour.

Willow left it in some relief and walked into the station in search of her tramp. She found him without trouble and was relieved to see that there was no sign of any station staff to interfere. The whole place appeared to be deserted. The tramp was sitting on a bench, a bottle of cider beside him and a filthy-looking, half-eaten sandwich clasped in one hand.

'You look cold,' she said cheerfully, sitting down at the opposite end of the bench. There was no reply. The man tilted his cider bottle – still wrapped in its paper bag – to his mouth. Willow tried again. 'I saw you here on Wednesday evening; you asked for the price of a cuppa. I should think you'd like something hot now, wouldn't you? It's a beastly day.'

She hated to hear herself sounding like Lady Bountiful, but the interrogation of an independent minded tramp was not something for which either her Civil Service training or her writing talents had prepared her. The man looked slowly round, as though the words she had used had taken time to penetrate his mind. There was no recognition in his eyes, and Willow waited without much hope. It suddenly seemed absurd to think that she would discover anything. Even if the tramp had seen anything unusual on the night of the minister's death, there was no guarantee that he would remember it or bother to pass it on even if he did remember.

'Wouldn't mind,' he said at last.

'A cup of tea?' said Willow brightly. Determined not merely to hand over some money, she went on, 'I'd like one too. I'll just nip across to the buffet and get them. What about something to eat, too? I expect there're hot pies or something.'

'Wouldn't mind,' he said again and rubbed the back of one filthy, mittened hand across his swollen lips.

Willow went quickly to the station buffet, hoping that she could buy the tea and get back to the bench before someone moved the tramp on or he decided to give her up as a bad source of nourishment. The whole episode seemed rather unreal, as though she were playing a detective in a rather poor play, but she was determined to go on with it and put up with whatever peculiar sensations of artificiality she felt.

Just as there seemed to be no passengers waiting for trains, there was no one queueing in the buffet and Willow was back on the tramp's side of the platform in barely five minutes, balancing a hot pie on top of two paper cups of tea.

'So what did you see last Monday?' she said, as she put her loot on the red metal bench.

'Nothing,' he answered, reaching for the pie. Willow handed it to him and asked her question again, adding:

'Was there nothing different, no one behaving strangely that night?'

The man shook his head and bits of pie flew off his beard with each movement. Willow tried to suppress her distaste, leaning back against the bench and sipping her tea. She could not think what to do next. None of the detective stories she had read – or wooden plays that she had seen during her student days – provided any model. Once again she felt a fool and most unlike herself.

'He was washing.' The tramp's voice jerked Willow's head round to face him again. 'Washing,' he repeated more loudly as though he had taken her blankly surprised expression to mean that she had not heard him the first time. An express rattled through the station just then, making any speech impossible to hear. When it had gone at last, Willow said:

'Who was washing?'

'Bloke in a mac. On Monday. Kept it buttoned all the time and the collar up. Washed his hands and face. Water all over the collar, but he kept it up.'

'How do you know it was Monday?' asked Willow, remembering her doubts about his intelligence and memory. She was disconcerted by the blaze of anger in the man's bright grey eyes, which seemed so incongruous in his dirty, pouchy face.

'I'm not daft, you know,' he said. 'Last Monday.'

'What did he look like?' Willow asked, unable to apologise to the man for underestimating him, but equally unable to leave before she had heard everything he had to tell. But it seemed that he felt he had done enough to repay her for the hot pie and tea, for he shook his head again.

'Just a bloke.'

'Old or young?' Willow prompted.

'Yes,' said the tramp irritatingly. 'It's too cold here.' Willow sighed and did not try to stop him as he heaved himself up from the bench and shambled off. She had got more information than she had expected, if considerably less than she had wanted.

It was little enough, though, and probably not even reliable. But if he really had seen a man washing on the Monday when Algy had died, perhaps. . . . No, there was nothing whatever to connect the washing man with the murder except her vague idea that the murderer might have left Clapham by a train from the Junction. She was no further on. Willow got up from her bench and carried the paper cup, still half-full of tea, to a large bin and dropped it in, wiping her hands fastidiously on a handkerchief, which she then threw in after it.

It dawned on her that as there was no longer a reason to hang about the undeniably depressing environs of the Junction, she might as well take a train back into the middle of London. There was no one around to tell her the time of the next train and it took her some minutes to find a timetable. Finding that there would be at least fifteen minutes to wait, she decided to take a quick look outside the station.

There was nothing much of interest to see and nothing to spark off any useful ideas in her mind. She passed dull shops and various pubs, including one called The Pig's Ear, which she vaguely remembered hearing discussed in the office. Annoyingly she could not remember the context. Thinking that it looked peculiarly depressing, she walked on, eventually buying a local paper in a tobacconist's shop.

She took the newspaper back to the station and read it while she waited for the train. There seemed to be almost nothing in it except crime; everything from an unsuccessful attempt to rob a building society to cases of child abuse and murder and rape. There was nothing about the minister in it, which surprised Willow until she remembered that it was a weekly paper.

As her train pulled slowly into the station, she threw the newspaper into the rubbish bin and then took her seat, strangely disturbed by what she had read.

Real violence had not touched anyone she knew until Algy's death and she had hardly thought about how much of it there was only just below the surface of everyday life. Suddenly it seemed as though there were a core of hot, molten violence rather like the lava at the centre of the earth that could erupt through any flaw in the protective crust. And if that were true, Willow thought, then it followed that almost anyone could have become angry or frightened enough to have killed the minister.

It might even, she thought, reducing the whole proposition to absurdity, have been Richard Crescent, wreaking revenge on the tormentor of his schooldays. At that thought Willow pulled herself up. Just as Richard was her alibi, so she was his. Besides, Richard was quite incapable of violence.

The train was held up outside Waterloo station, and as she sat in it, Willow asked herself how she could be certain that Richard could never resort to violence. With common sense slowly returning, she told herself that if he had shown no signs of it during the three years he had been her lover, he was unlikely to do so in the future.

But then presumably Algy had felt the same about whomever he had met on Clapham Common. Willow shivered and all of a sudden wished that she had not decided to unmask him. It was axiomatic that anyone who had killed once would not hesitate to kill again, if only in self-protection. Remembering that, Willow was disturbed to think that she had cut herself off from the protection of the police.

5

RETURNING to the haven of Chesham Place, Willow retreated at once to the small room in which she wrote her novels. She wanted to regain at least the illusion of safety that her writing had always given her.

Compared with the rest of the flat the writing room was plain and functional, but it contained one exceedingly comfortable armchair upholstered in deep heather-coloured corduroy as well as an ergonomically designed typing chair in front of the word processor. The only decorations on the plain silver-grey walls were two charming watercolours of one of the bleaker aspects of the North Yorkshire moors, but Willow had never felt that the room lacked sympathy for her endeavours, and at that moment it seemed like a sanctuary.

Willow pulled off her boots and left them sagging by the door; her mackintosh was draped over a tall bookcase; and she herself sat in the cushioned embrace of the deep armchair. Resting her aching head against a cushion, she allowed herself to come to the conclusion that it would be more sensible to avoid direct detection in future and proceed by analysis and deduction alone. Because she had never in her adult life let herself be deceived by wishful thinking, fantasy or exculpation, she admitted that her decision had more to do with her newly discovered fear of violence than with her well-known talent for analysis and rational thought. But she did admit in support of the decision that her amateurish attempts at physical detection had not taken her very far.

After all, she had learned only that Mr Gripper was an angry, apparently powerful man who resented the thought that a journalist on a rival newspaper might be watching him or his family with a view to writing about them with the snide salacity his own organ found so profitable, and that a man dressed in a mackintosh had washed his hands and face in the men's lavatory at Clapham Junction station one evening. She could not even be certain that the ablutions had taken place on the night of the murder, although it was possible that the tramp's memory was accurate.

Various useful inferences might be drawn from those two facts, but none that was irrefutable. Gripper's attitude might be said to give him a motive to do away with the man who had cuckolded him.

As though the word 'motive' had galvanised part of her brain, Willow stopped thinking over her frustrating morning and got out of her astonishingly comfortable chair to find a large, white notebook and a fibre-tipped pen. Returning to the chair, she listed on the first sheet of paper all the possible motives that might have led to Algy's murder: love; hate; revenge; money; fear. After a few moments' silent contemplation of the little list, she added 'other', and then tried to fill out each category.

Richard might be right that a case could never be solved by analysis of motive alone, but at least the isolation of a possible motive – or motives – would give Willow a useful starting point for more productive investigation. After all, she could not simply drift about London aimlessly asking questions and putting herself at risk of violence.

Love, or its less affectionate approximations, still seemed to Willow to have been the most likely cause of the killing. She grimaced as she remembered that most of her colleagues at the department seemed to have thought so too and that she had been their chosen murderess. Despite their views, it really did not seem likely to her that Algy's killer could have been a woman.

The least sexist of people, Willow had no sentimental feelings about her own sex and was quite certain that women could kill just as effectively or viciously as men; but it did not seem possible that any woman could have overpowered a healthy man, six foot four inches tall, broad of shoulder and muscular of build. Roger had definitely told her that the minister had been 'beaten up – his head smashed in'; to Willow that did not sound like a woman's killing.

It would follow, therefore, that if the motive had been love it would have had to be someone like Gripper, whose beloved had been seduced by the usually irresistible minister. Willow appended a note under the relevant heading to remind herself to find out who else had succumbed to Algy in the recent past, and another to find out more about Gripper, not least where he had been on the evening in question.

'Hate' would overlap with the previous possibilities, but ought to include more, she thought. She rather agreed with Richard, that it would be absurd to look for the roots of a man's murder in his brutalities at prep school and so she directed her mind to Algy's more recent victims. There were probably plenty at the department, from his private office staff all the way up to the permanent secretary, but Willow's mind boggled at the thought of any of them taking such desperate action to rid themselves of a bully who would in the natural course of political events be shuffled out of DOAP before too long.

Algy had had enemies in the House, too, and Willow had several times witnessed his cruelly brilliant destruction of opponents' speeches. But there again, it was hard to imagine a Member of Parliament being so deranged by professional humiliation that he lured his tormentor on to the dark South-London common and beat him until he was dead. Clearly the police thought that the answer to the mystery lay within the confines of the department, and Willow was inclined to agree with them; unless, of course, someone like Gripper had carried off an effective bluff. Might not the killing have been done elsewhere, and the body taken to the common by car and dumped?

'No,' said Willow aloud. 'That doesn't fit, either. Algy was last seen by someone in the department at a quarter to six. He spoke to his chauffeur on the telephone five minutes later to instruct him to wait on the far side of the common. He was not seen again until the chauffeur, alarmed by his long wait returned to the office and telephoned the police at nine o'clock.'

The door of Willow's writing room opened and Mrs Rusham's grey head appeared round it.

'Did you call, Miss Woodruffe?' Willow, remembering that she had been talking to herself again, nearly blushed.

'No, in fact I didn't, Mrs Rusham. But since you are here, do you think you could get me a cup of tea? And perhaps a sandwich? I didn't have time for lunch in the end.'

'Certainly, Miss Woodruffe,' she said and retreated.

If only the chauffeur had not been seen by innumerable homing commuters as he sat under the arc lights, Willow thought. Albert, tall and built like a boxer, was just the physical type to be able to batter a man like Algy to death. Disliking Albert's truculence and ill-temper as much as she did, Willow had little difficulty in persuading herself that he was capable of such a murder. Chiding herself for leaving the subject of motive and being trapped into speculation about personalities and timing, Willow thought that it was extraordinary how much she had lost of the discipline so carefully inculcated in her by her parents. In the old days, she would have been able to compel her mind to concentrate on the dullest subject. Now, it seemed to roam in any direction it pleased.

Doing her best to corral her imagination, Willow looked back to her list to find that money was the next topic. Algy had obviously had quite a lot; he had always been superlatively well dressed and in private life drove a thoroughly expensive BMW, besides having that indefinably confident swagger that comes from a hefty bank balance. Willow realised that she would have to find out who his heirs were and, unable to continue to sit still while there were so many questions to be asked, got up to rifle through an old address book she kept in one of her filing cabinets.

During her early years in London, her parents had often asked her to be kind to students who had left their care and arrived in the capital to start their careers. Such requests were almost the only contact Willow had had with her parents once she had left home. One of their protégés, Willow remembered, had deserted science for the law and ended up working at Somerset House. If she could only remember his name, she could ask him how to go about securing a copy of Algy's will.

She had given the young man supper in Abbeville Road not long before her father's death, and had even, she thought, helped him to find somewhere to live. He had quite liked her and even invited her out to restaurants once he had become settled. Willow had accepted the first time, but had disliked both the dinner and her host's amorous advances and had categorically refused all subsequent invitations. William Gaskarth! That was his name.

Willow walked across to the big mahogany desk that carried her word processor, reference books, stationery and telephone, looked up the number of Somerset House, dialled it and asked to speak to Mr Gaskarth. She was ludicrously insulted to be told that he no longer worked there and only slightly mollified to be asked whether anyone else could help.

'Well, I don't know; yes, perhaps,' she said with unusual indecision. 'I need to consult a will, and I understand that they are kept at Somerset House.'

The woman who had answered the telephone said that she would put Willow through to a suitable department and a moment later, she was talking to a younger, but still female, voice.

'Can you tell me,' said Willow, who had regained most of her self-possession, 'how I would go about consulting a will?'

'It is perfectly simple, madam: you simply present yourself at the desk here and bespeak a copy,' said the helpful voice.

'I see,' said Willow. 'And how long would it take for the copy to be produced?'

'It rather depends. When was probate of the will granted?'

'I don't think it has been,' said Willow. 'Does that matter?'

'Possibly not: when was probate applied for?' The voice had begun to irritate Willow and her own voice sounded positively snappish as she said:

'It hasn't. There hasn't been time yet.'

'In that case,' said the voice, 'we cannot help you. We do not hold wills that have not been the subject of a grant.'

'Oh. . . . So how can I find out the terms of a will? I thought they were public documents,' said Willow thoroughly annoyed.

'You could apply to the solicitors, but unless there is some very good reason for you to see the will, I cannot imagine that they would allow it.'

'I see,' said Willow, and then, belatedly remembering her manners, added: 'Thank you for your help. Good bye.' She replaced the receiver just as Mrs Rusham returned with a tray of tea and sandwiches. There was an enticing selection: some seemed to be crab and mayonnaise; some watercress; and the remainder cheese and cucumber.

Willow thanked her and then poured a cup of tea, trying unsuccessfully to remove from her mind a wholly unjustified resentment at the powers and freedom of Inspector Worth.

He, no doubt, had already seen a copy of Algy's will and if he found any obvious suspects among the beneficiaries he would simply go and interrogate them, whereas Willow was stuck with no help except her own brains and imagination. So incensed was she at the police's unfair advantages in her self-imposed competition with them that she decided to leave the investigation for the moment and go out and buy herself something.

Despite the riches that Cressida Woodruffe had brought her, Willow did not often allow herself the extreme delight of unnecessary, impulse spending, but when she did she generally found the exercise therapeutic. That particular day seemed a suitable one on which to seek solace and so she ate her sandwiches, drank the tea and took herself to Fortnum and Mason, where she spent a happy half hour browsing through various departments. Toying with the thought of buying a dinner service of charmingly decorated Italian porcelain, she decided instead to have a quick look upstairs at the clothes and completed her cure with the trying on of a deceptively simple, short black-velvet dress. Both the style and colour of the dress suited her, and she felt at ease in it, and so she told the sales assistant that she would take it. Murmuring mockingly to herself 'I spend therefore I am', she signed the credit card slip and took the parcel home to Chesham Place.

Hardly had she unpacked it than she heard the front-door bell buzz and then Mrs Rusham's voice, speaking in a far more friendly tone than any she used to her employer:

'Please come on up, Mr Lawrence-Crescent.'

Willow, glad that she had exorcised most of her various tensions, went out into the hall to greet him. One quick look at his face told her that he was still suffering from his own troubles. Before she could think of anything soothing to say, he said, in a voice raw with irritation:

'Don't say it, Willow. I've had an infuriating day in Paris and a bloody awful flight back.'

Willow shook her head.

'You look terrible, Richard. I wasn't going to say a word, except to invite you to come and have a bath.'

'What?' he demanded, looking at her as though she were a recalcitrant foreign client who had perpetrated some frightful banking solecism.

'Come on, dear Richard, and have a bath with me,' said Willow, infinitely relieved to find that the sickly emotion of the previous evening had been overtaken by one much easier for her to deal with and accept. A reluctant smile slightly relaxed his tight lips, but there was still a look in his hazel eyes that said, 'Don't think that you can take my bad temper away so easily; I want a bit longer to get the maximum enjoyment out of it.'

Willow knew the feeling herself too well to try to talk him out of it and instead went straight to the bathroom to run plenty of hot water into the huge white bath. There was ample room in it for two normal-sized adults, and she had forced the plumber to put the taps at the side so that both of them could lean comfortably against the smoothly curved enamel without the brass taps getting in the way. In deference to Richard's sensibilities she avoided the Chanel No.19 bath oil and instead added a splash of quite gentlemanly cologne-scented foam.

By the time Richard condescended to join her, she was already soaking in the aromatic, bubbling water, her hair tied up like a child's on top of her head out of the way. As though the sight of her, with whisps of red hair clinging damply around her face and drops of water sparkling on her shoulders, had galvanised him, he grinned a little self-consciously, undressed and joined her.

They proceeded to shed their tensions with some exceedingly childish romping, during which Richard's hair was quite soaked and Willow's painted toenails were reverently kissed one after the other in a parody of devotion. Richard had just reached the little toe of the second foot when he sat up with a rush, sending a tidal wave of scented water over the back of the bath on to the floor.

'Oh God, Willow,' he said through a mouthful of foaming bathwater, 'isn't tonight the night of Sarah Gnatche's engagement party?'

Willow, rubbing the stinging water out of her eyes and shaking it out of her ears, looked blearily at him.

'Friday! Oh, lord, yes you're right. You did tell me about it, but I'd completely forgotten. We needn't go, need we?' said Willow, who was often bored by cocktail parties, particularly when she knew none of the other guests.

'Well I must,' said Richard, 'and you did promise to come with me, Willow.' The slightly injured tone in his voice aroused considerable resistance within Willow.

'Didn't you say it was being held in the House of Lords? You know I never go to the Palace of Westminster as Cressida,' she said crossly.

'No one's going to recognise you. Who could be there on a Friday evening who might have had dealings with Willow King in the House of Commons? Do come, Willow. After all, we always do spend Friday evenings together and I thought we could look in there and then go on and have dinner somewhere,' said Richard, unfolding his long legs and getting out of the bath. 'Besides,' he went on, a slightly cunning look distorting his conventionally handsome features, 'the Gnatches live in Algy Endelsham's constituency.'

'So what?' asked Willow rudely, still lying back amid the bubbles.

'And they're old family friends of his. I'm sure you'd find someone there to give you some helpful hints about him. You never know, you might even find a suspect or two.'

Bearing in mind the vastness and difficulty of the task she had taken on and thinking that at least in such social contacts she might have some slight advantage over the police, Willow grudgingly agreed to accompany her lover to celebrate his ex-girlfriend's engagement.

Three-quarters of an hour later, late and a little damp but glamorous enough to be easily forgiven, they arrived at the party. The receiving line had long-since been broken up, rather to Willow's relief, but Sarah's much older brother was posted near the door to greet any late arrivals. Richard introduced him to Willow and with a stagily lecherous glance at her new black dress and long legs he sent Richard straight off to find drinks.

'Poor old Cress,' said Anthony Gnatche, 'just the same.'

'I've never heard him called that before,' said Willow coldly. She had disliked him from the moment of hearing his braying voice and decoding his tie and blazer buttons (which belonged to one of the smarter regiments), but she was determined to pump him for any information she could get out of him.

'We called him that at our prep school. The theory was that he was just like the kind of creeping green stuff that could be found growing on someone's slimy flannel on the window sill.' The rather handsome man's self-satisfied laugh put the finishing touches to Willow's dislike of him. She might occasionally find Richard irritatingly pompous, might even moan about his astonishing lack of ordinary practical skills, but she unreservedly admired his intelligence, and he was extremely kind to her. She certainly was not prepared to accept criticism from an upper-crust lout like this one, who obviously valued brawn miles above brain. With her face hardening into that of the assistant secretary (finance) of DOAP, she was planning to rout him with a brilliantly sarcastic comment when she realised that he had given her precisely the opening she needed.

'Oh, so you must have been at school with that poor murdered politician too. Do you remember him?' she said instead.

'Algy Endelsham? Yes, of course I remember him. We've been friends really ever since. Luckily I never got across him as people like poor old Cress used to. I suppose being pretty good at games helped, what? But d'you know, if old Algy were going to be bumped orf, I'd have thought it would have been his brother who'd have done it,' said Gnatche pressing his calves backwards and thrusting his manly chest towards Willow.

'I didn't know he had ever had a brother,' said Willow, mentally waking up. 'What happened to him?'

'God knows. Pathetic character, really,' answered Gnatche. 'Ah, Richard, great. Here, Miss Woodruffe, Cress has managed to find you some fizz. Buzz off there's a good chap; go and play.'

Richard laughed:

'You know, Anthony,' he said with an arrogance which Willow could only envy in the particular circumstances, 'it's lucky that you're never going to have to earn your own living. The real world is just that tiniest bit different from prep school life. All right if I leave you, Cressida?' he added, turning to Willow. With his back to Anthony Gnatche, he gave her such a broad wink that she could hardly refrain from laughing.

'Fine, Richard,' she said as drily as she could. 'Anthony is telling me all about the poor murdered minister during his schooldays, Richard,' she added brightly.

'Ah, thrilling for you,' he answered over his shoulder as he walked away.

'Now, where were we?' murmured Gnatche, drinking from the glass Richard had brought him. 'Algy's brother, yes. He'd have been all right, I suppose, if he'd been the younger. But there he was, Endelsham Ma., but lower down the school than Endelsham Mi., never in any of the teams, butter fingered, tone deaf and mocked for singing out of tune in chapel, dead loss really. Bogged his bags, too. Funny, I've never thought of him from that day to this.'

Conscious of a desire to whip out a tape recorder to collect the man's objectionable reminiscences so that she did not actually have to listen to them, Willow did not answer. Instead she took a sip of the 'Champagne' she had been given and had to exercise all her diplomacy and good manners not to screw up her face in disgust. It was, she thought, extraordinary that anyone should go to the trouble of having a party in such a place and then choose to serve sweet, cloying sparkling wine of the most blatant sort. He must have bought it himself, too, for the House of Lords catering people could never have chosen such stuff. A fat waitress passed just then with a heavy silver-plated tray of aspic-covered savouries. Willow, who usually detested such things, reached out for a couple and stuffed them into her mouth to take away the taste of the wine.

Anthony Gnatche, tall, dark, rich and county, had been accustomed from his late teens to finding any woman to whom he spoke so flattered by his attentions that she tried at once to elicit compliments and invitations from him. He was therefore extremely surprised that this woman did not even bother to answer what he had said and, worse, that her eyes were searching the crowd behind him.

'But that's all bloody dull, Cressida – if I may,' he said, expecting a better response and patting her shoulder. The pat if not the words drew her attention back to him.

'What?' she said vaguely. 'Oh, yes, do call me Cressida. I. . .'

'I wish I could take you out for some dinner later, but I'm stuck with my mother and sisters,' he said, trying harder than ever to evoke the usual reactions in the tall red-head in front of him. 'But perhaps some other night?'

'What?' she said again and then remembered where she was. 'Oh, it's sweet of you. Yes, perhaps. But I'd better wander off now; I mustn't monopolise you.'

Since that was an excuse Gnatche himself had often used to get away from the fat, the dull, the spotty, the poor, the provincial, the noisy and the too-obviously clever girls he had been landed with at parties, he was left in considerable discomfort. But it was not long before he had refurbished his self-esteem by realising that despite her glossy finish she must be a good thirty-five at least and, stuck with poor old Cress, obviously at her last gasp sexually speaking.

Willow, quite unaware that she had challenged his masculinity, dented his self-image or been anything other than perfectly polite was meanwhile congratulating herself on the fact that she no longer detested parties full of people she did not know. It would have been hard to pinpoint the moment at which such occasions had ceased to be ordeals and had become instead opportunities for a little discreet publicising of her books and for the collecting of useful copy, but it had undoubtedly coincided with her making real money.

Whenever the moment, it had given her ample confidence, and she used her newish social skills now to trawl the party for bits and pieces of gossip about the minister. She also collected innumerable compliments for herself. Some of them pleased her for the niceness with which they were delivered or the wit with which they were phrased (the witty ones were usually produced by men of at least sixty). But in the end they began to bore her, because they seemed as unreal as the person she was pretending to be. Determined not to drink any more of the disgusting wine and over-full of the damp and salty bits and pieces she had been offered to eat, she started to look for Richard to take her home at about half-past eight.

A gentle touch on her black velvet sleeve made her turn round and she found herself looking down into a sweet pink-and-white face surrounded with fine fair hair crowned with a velvet hairband. Amused that the uniform for 'nice young girls' did not seem to have changed in the last twenty years, Willow smiled encouragingly.

'I say,' said the blond child, who must have been about eighteen, 'aren't you Cressida Woodruffe? I absolutely adore your books and I recognised you from that smashing photograph on the jackets.'

'Yes, I am. How kind of you,' answered Willow, looking more carefully at her and noticing that the dark-green silk dress the child wore was much too old for her but added a certain style to her predictable prettiness. 'Who are you?'

'Oh I'm Emma. . . Gnatche,' came the answer and Willow thought immediately, yes, naturally you're Emma. A creature who looks like you could not be called anything else. Then she came to her senses just as the child went on: 'You know, Sarah's sister. Can I get someone to fetch a drink for you?'

'No, thank you,' said Willow, shaking her red hair. 'I was really looking for Richard Crescent, who's going to take me out to dinner.'

'Oh, I saw him a minute ago, kissing Sarah good bye.' The girl put a hand up over her mouth and her eyes, huge and blue, looked at Willow in terror. 'I am sorry. I mean, they weren't. . .'

'Don't worry, Emma. Richard and I are old friends,' said Willow.

'I am sorry,' said Emma again when she was sure that Willow was really not upset by her tactless revelation. 'It's only that I'm in such a state about poor Algy that. . . I mean, I'm not usually this ill-mannered or scatty.'

'Algy?' repeated Willow, delighted to have stumbled on yet another opening.

'Yes, Algernon Endelsham, you know the minister who's just been. . . killed.' The big eyes were glossy with unshed tears and Willow found even her stony heart a little wrung with pity.

'Why don't we go and sit on that sofa over there, and you can tell me all about it,' she said quite gently. They went, and out it all came. Emma had worked for Algy briefly during her last summer holidays from school, when she had been trying to decide whether she wanted to be a House of Commons secretary.

Hearing that, Willow spared a thought for the silent bitterness she would once have felt at the unfair, unearned and invaluable privileges given to girls like this one. Daughters of successful – or merely well-known – parents, they were able to swan into jobs in whatever field they chose: Members of Parliament would give them holiday jobs, publishers would take them on despite their total lack of experience – or often brains – auction houses would train them, interior decorators, art galleries and sundry other furnishers of the playgrounds of the rich would snap them up for the desirable effects of their voices on the telephone, irrespective of whether they could type, do accounts, or recognise a Leonardo da Vinci from a David Hockney, while daughters of the merely hardworking, like Willow herself, had to work and struggle for anything they achieved.

But the days of bitter jealousy – heavily suppressed though it had always been – were long over for Willow, and by then she was able to admit to herself that girls like Emma Gnatche could also be charming, well-mannered, sometimes clever, hard working and as thoroughly deserving of their good fortune as she considered herself to be.

Richard materialised in front of their sofa before Willow could ask any questions of the girl beside her and so instead she said:

'Here's Richard, so I'll have to go, but I'd love to have a proper talk with you. Are you in London this weekend?'

'Yes,' said Emma obviously finding herself very daring. 'We might have lunch or something. . . . I mean, if you wanted to.'

'Why not? answered Willow, smiling again. 'Look, what about the Café des Amis in Covent Garden. Do you know it?' Emma nodded her sleek blond head. 'All right then; twelve o'clock, so that we miss the worst of the crowds?'

'Gosh, super. Thanks. I'll be there,' said Emma, blushing and casting a distracted look at Richard before escaping.

'What on earth are you up to?' Richard asked, watching Willow watching Emma.

'What? Oh, she worked for Algy last summer. As you say, his goings-on at prep school aren't likely to cast much light on what happened to him this November, but last August is a different matter.'

'Be careful, Willow. I'm not sure I like the idea of your . . .'

'My what, Richard? If you're implying that I'll damage that child, you damn well ought to know me better.' He did not speak, and she tossed her red head at him as he ushered her out of the room.

'Where would you like to eat, Willow?' he asked a little later as they were sitting side by side in his luxurious car.

'Honestly, Richard, I'm not particularly hungry – especially after that dreary party. I ate such a lot of bits and pieces. I'd rather just go home. And I must do some work. I'm horribly behind. Could you just drop me off in Chesham Place?'

'Don't you want to hear about Algy's beastliness at school then?' asked Richard.

Willow turned her head and gave him a brilliant smile.

'I've decided that you're right that it can't be relevant, dear Richard,' she said. 'But I am a bit intrigued to know about his brother. That frightful Gnatche told me a little about him this evening. Did you know him too?'

'Not well; but I do remember that he suffered even more than the rest of us from Algy's dictator-complex.'

'Did they look alike?' Willow asked as the red lights in front of them forced Richard to brake. He looked at her and sighed. 'What's the matter?' she asked, bringing him back to his senses.

'Nothing really. I'd just hoped we could return to the bath and carry on where we left off. Never mind. Your work must come first.'

Detecting a certain sarcasm in that sententious comment, Willow did not deign to answer.

'As far as I can remember,' said Richard, apparently giving up hope of persuading her to change her mind, 'the brother was a nondescript little squirt – not as tall as Algy then, although he was older, but. . . Oh heavens, Willow, it's more than a quarter of a century since I left, I can't remember and it wouldn't do you any good even if I could – no man's going to look the same at forty as he did at thirteen.'

'There's no need to be so cross,' she said, genuinely surprised at his tone, 'I was merely curious. Ah, good, here we are. You're sweet to have brought me home, Richard. Good night. Sleep well.'

'I'll be lucky,' he murmured under his breath and then added more loudly, 'It was fun, Willow. May I see you tomorrow?'

'Depends a bit on the work. I'll ring you in the afternoon. Will you be in the office?' she asked, knowing that the quantity of paper generated by mergers and acquisitions meant that he usually had to work on it for at least one day each weekend.

'Probably,' he said gloomily thinking that if he couldn't be with her he might as well work.

Leaning over to kiss him briefly, Willow opened the passenger door and stepped out on to the pavement. The sudden cold bit through her thinly-stockinged legs and made her hurry into the comforting warmth of her empty flat without even waving at him. The last thing she heard as the front door banged was the engine of Richard's car revving furiously and the tires screeching as he pulled away from the kerb.

'What on earth is the matter with him?' she asked herself, peering out of the drawing room windows as his tail lights whisked round the corner into Lowndes Place. It did not occur to her that he might be suffering from intense sexual frustration.

Turning back to admire her drawing-room, she thought how pleasant it was to have the flat to herself. Much as she liked him his presence did sometimes become oppressive. She vaguely assumed that that was because she had lived alone for so long, and accepted it without fretting. Feeling hungry in the sudden release from his devotion, she went to the kitchen to see if there were any tasty morsels left in the fridge.

Not much to her surprise, Mrs Rusham had filled it with all kinds of provisions and Willow helped herself to a picnic of smoked duck breast, Italian fruits in mustard syrup and radishes, followed by some immensely dark chocolate ice cream, all washed down with half a bottle of mineral water. Then, comfortable, at ease with herself and not in the least tired, she settled down to work on her increasingly rounded picture of Algy Endelsham.

The only motive on her list that she had not yet examined was 'Fear', and she set about finding possible theories. There were a great many people in the department who were afraid of his impatience, his caustic tongue, his highly developed critical skills, but not – she was convinced – to the extent of killing him. The only type of person who could be both that frightened and that ruthless would be someone with a lot at stake, perhaps someone engaged in a particularly profitable bit of corruption.

If Algy had somehow stumbled on the corruption during his time at DOAP and perhaps threatened to expose it unless the perpetrators wound it up, then they might well want to get rid of him. For a moment she almost dismissed the idea, because any minister of the Crown would presumably report any such wrongdoing to the appropriate authority; and yet would Algy have taken so easy a course? Willow considered the proposition and, after a little exercise of her imagination, decided that perhaps he would not. A man so certain of himself – so powerful, so much enjoying the exercise of that power – might well try to tackle the matter himself.

Having got so far into her speculation, Willow found that her imagination had gone as sticky as her novel and she could get no further. She added the words 'possible corruption threatened with exposure' to her columns of motives and put pad and pencil away.

Willow found herself thinking of one of Shakespeare's sonnets as she undressed and got into bed three hours later, and during the night dreamed of Algy standing in all his glorious handsomeness surrounded by fields and fields of lilies turning brown and stinking in a morass of sludgy mud and stagnant pools.

6

ARRIVING at the Café des Amis the following day, Willow was suddenly assailed by an unwonted sensation of shame as she saw the shivering figure of Emma Gnatche standing outside the restaurant clad only in a pair of jeans, a fluffy yellow sweater and a sleeveless dark-blue and turquoise Puffa and her pearls. Willow felt that she ought to have known that the child would be too shy to go into the restaurant on her own, find a table and order herself a drink. Wishing that she had not been tempted by the cold to wear her darkest and glossiest fur coat, Willow hurried up to Emma and hustled her inside the restaurant, saying:

'You poor child, you must be solid ice by now. I'm sorry I'm so late. I was caught up by a telephone call just as I was leaving and then I couldn't get a taxi.'

'Don't you drive?' asked Emma, her teeth clattering like the shoes of a demented tap dancer.

'Not often in London. When I made some real money I bought myself an enormous Mercedes. It's wonderful and I love it, but it's far too big to park easily in London – and I'm too sentimental to sell it and buy a Metro or something,' answered Willow, trying to summon a waiter. As soon as one materialised, she said: 'Please fetch a whisky and ginger wine now, and then bring us some menus.'

He responded quickly and politely. Willow was not sure whether it was the obvious need in Emma's blue-tinged face, her own imperiousness or the thickness of her mink that had wrought the miracle, but in three minutes the revivifying drink was put in front of Emma.

'Go on, drink up,' said Willow. 'It'll warm you. And then I can put lots of hot food into you and stop myself feeling so guilty.'

Emma blushed, shook her head and said: 'It was my own idiotic fault I just never remember how cold it's going to be outside the car. This tastes frightfully strong, you know.'

'Never mind. It works. Let's choose what we're going to eat.'

When their order had been given to the waiter, Willow thought that she ought to try to set her guest at ease instead of wading in instantly with questions about Algy.

'That was a splendid party last night,' she said and watched Emma's face with interest. The first polite smile was chased by a look of doubt and then a slight hardening beneath the sweetness. 'Didn't you think so?'

Emma shrugged. 'Well, actually I thought it was pretty awful to have a party so soon after. . . after Algy died, although I do see that Sarah's engagement is much more important to her than an old family friend like Algy. . .'

'Yes,' said Willow as sympathetically as possible. 'He wasn't actually a relation, was he?' Emma shook her head.

'No, and of course Sarah didn't know him as well as I did. But still. . . And anyway, I can't stand her Charlie. He really is the pits. What Sarah thinks she sees in him, I can't imagine.' Emma stopped, as though relieved to see their waiter bringing a basket of bread and some butter. She took some and then looked sideways at Willow, who smiled encouragement.

'In fact he's awfully like Anthony – and you'd have thought even Sarah would know that it wasn't a very good idea. . .' Emma broke off in obvious confusion and Willow, highly amused and liking her more for her family loyalty, decided to prompt her.

'Your brother? He's much older than both you and Sarah, isn't he?'

Emma pushed her black velvet hair band right back with both hands and then brought it a little forward so that it raised a small halo of hair above her unlined forehead.

'Yes; he's a half brother, you see. And when Daddy died, four years ago, Anthony sort of took over.'

'And you don't like him much?' suggested Willow. Emma blushed again, but she was game and so despite her embarrassment she said:

'Not very much. I know it's an awful thing to say, but he's so different from Daddy, you see – and he's so horribly thick. He can't help that, but . . . well, it makes him lose his temper so often, which I hate. I'm terribly surprised that Sarah thinks she can live with someone so like him for the rest of her life. I always thought she ought to have married Richard.'

'I'm not sure I agree that stupidity is a concomitant of loss of temper,' said Willow drily, not wanting to go into the subject of Richard's old passion for Emma's elder sister.

'Oh, yes, it is,' said Emma earnestly. 'Algy explained it to me once. He told me that when people are as stupid and inarticulate as Anthony they find it very hard to talk rationally about anything that has upset them, and so they lose their temper and sometimes get violent.'

'You don't mean that your step-brother has ever hit you?' said Willow, horrified to think that anyone could have beaten the gentle girl at her side.

'No,' Emma assured her quickly, 'he's never been physically violent to either of us, but he does rage about a lot, which I've always found rather frightening. And that particular evening it was horribly embarrassing as well. He was so kind.'

'Anthony?' said Willow, thoroughly at sea. Emma's face looked quite shocked. She shook her head.

'Goodness no. Algy,' she said. 'He was always sweet to me, but that evening when Anthony had been so beastly, Algy really saved my life.' The unfortunate choice of words seemed to strike her, for her big blue eyes filled with tears again. Willow felt cruel to be reminding the child of her hero's death, but the opportunity of finding out about Algy and his enemies was too good to throw away.

'Tell me about Algy,' she said as gently as she could. 'That is unless you mind talking about him.'

'No. It would be rather a relief,' said Emma. 'I've been longing to talk to someone about him, but haven't been able to say anything about him at home since that ghastly evening when Anthony decided that. . . that I'd fallen in love with Algy. I mean; it was so embarrassing for us both.'

'What happened?' asked Willow, pouring them each a glass of wine.

'Well,' said Emma, looking speculatively at Willow. Whatever she saw in Willow's face seemed to reassure her, for in the end she told her story.

'You know I told you yesterday that I worked for Algy in the summer?' Willow nodded.

'Because we live in the constituency, he often used to drive me home on Friday nights, and he'd tell me things in the car, sometimes things that worried him. And I used to try to help.' Emma came to a halt there, drank a little wine and gazed across the table with an expression of such sadness on her face that Willow's conscience pricked again.

'I'm sure you did help him, Emma,' she said. The girl looked up and tried to smile.

'He used to say that I did,' she agreed. 'That was when it happened. We'd got back home by then and I'd thanked him for the lift and he just put his arm round my shoulders and told me that I'd been kind to him and helped a lot.

99

Then he kissed me – just in a friendly way. That was all. But Anthony happened to see and he went mad: he came storming down the steps, wrenched open Algy's door and started yelling at him.'

'What did Algy do?' Willow asked, suppressing a smile. The minister, she felt sure, would have been well accustomed to dealing with the angry menfolk of his string of inamoratas.

'He just told me not to worry about it and to go on into the house. Naturally I did as he said and I left them yelling at each other. At least Anthony was yelling, but Algy was quite quiet about it. I was so embarrassed that I thought I'd never be able to go back to the office. But I had to of course, and Algy was absolutely sweet. He told me that he'd known Anthony far too long to take him seriously and explained all about stupid people getting so angry.'

The waiter reappeared just then with their fish soup, and Willow was rather relieved to have a few moments in which to gather her rambling thoughts and decide which of the innumerable questions in her mind to put into words. The soup was delicious and kept them both quiet for a few minutes. At last Willow laid down her spoon and said carefully:

'I'm not sure you should blame your brother too much, Emma. He was probably trying to protect you; after all, Algy did have a rather dreadful reputation with women. It was pretty irresponsible of him.'

Emma's gentle face took on a much harder expression and Willow waited in considerable interest to hear her reaction.

'He only did that sort of thing because he was so unhappy. And anyway he was only being kind to me. He'd never have dreamt of trying to seduce me; I know he wouldn't,' she said, surprising Willow once again. She had a sudden vision of Algy leaving the irritations and burdens of office and shutting himself up in a car with this trustful child and reconstructing his picture of himself

100

through the reflection he saw in her eyes. No wonder he was kind to her, thought Willow, since she more than anyone else would have been able to feed his need for uncoerced admiration.

'You must have known him very well,' she said. 'I've never heard anyone else describe him as unhappy.' Emma managed to look both modest and rather pleased.

'He did tell me things,' she acknowledged and picked up her soup spoon again. Before she could drink any soup there was a shriek of 'Emms' from a girl who was threading her way through the restaurant to a table on the far side. Emma let her spoon drop back into the soup and waved.

'It's a friend of mine from school,' she said to Willow and then in a louder voice: 'Hello Grania! How *are* you?'

'Brill actually,' said the newcomer, sitting cheerfully down on the extra chair at their table. 'I've been to poor Simon's new exhibition. He's hardly sold any – but they're quite nice paintings and I told him I'd get Mummy to come in when she's next in London. Golly I'm hungry,' she said, reaching for a roll.

Willow sat up at the mention of paintings, because she was always on the lookout for new artists, and the movement attracted Emma's attention.

'Gosh, Cressida,' she said, conscience-stricken again. 'I'm so sorry. This is Grania Ballater. We were at school together. Grania, this is Cressida Woodruffe.'

'No!' said the girl. 'Fantastic. I say, I love your books.'

'Thank you,' said Willow. 'Who is Simon? Is the exhibition near here?'

'Yah, the other side of Covent Garden,' said Grania. 'He's the elder brother of one of our muckers.' Willow decoded the sentence with some difficulty and then asked for the address of the exhibition. Grania dictated it and then, perhaps remembering her impatient escort, said she really ought to go. She got up, scattering crumbs all over the table, and said good bye to Emma.

When she had gone, Willow looked at Emma, wondering what she thought of her 'friend'. Emma looked back and then nodded, a charming smile on her face.

'I know,' she said. 'But she really is nice under it all.'

'I'm sure she is,' said Willow, 'if noisy. But you were telling me about Algy and how he talked to you. What sort of things did you talk about?'

'Oh everything really. He used to talk about my career and what I ought to do. He didn't think that being a secretary in the House would be a good thing. He said that it didn't give one enough scope and that so many of the girls who did it got stuck and middle-aged and full of fantasies and bitter. He thought I ought to do something of my own, not be a bottle-washer for someone else.'

Well that was something positively useful for him to have done, thought Willow, wondering whether she had been trapped into misjudging him by Richard's reminiscences. She said nothing and Emma, clearly pining to talk about her hero, finished up her soup and went on.

'And sometimes he told me things that were worrying him.'

'Things about his constituency or the department?' At that question, Emma looked speculatively across the table.

'They were really pretty confidential,' she murmured, and Willow patted her hand in an auntly fashion.

'Don't you worry about it then. I just thought you wanted to talk. Have you decided what you are going to do? Why not university?' asked Willow, well aware that people with secrets long above all else to tell them to novelists; it was one of the odder phenomena she had discovered since the publication of her first book, but it cropped up again and again. Emma proved to be no exception.

'I suppose since he's. . . dead. . . .' Her voice broke and Willow wished that her informant could have been just a little older or more hard boiled. 'Since he isn't alive any more, it doesn't matter, and you won't pass any of it on, will you?' Willow shook her head.

'Well, personal things, usually. About his brother and things like that. But hardly anybody knew he had a brother, you see. I mean, even I didn't until that evening when he was so upset that he kissed me. You see he'd been telling me how worried he was about his brother.' She looked anxiously at Willow, but seeing nothing in her face except polite interest decided to get it all off her chest.

'His brother was a terribly pathetic sort of man, you see, a failure, Algy used to say, but so jealous of him that he was always thinking up schemes to embarrass Algy or the government or something. Algy knew that he couldn't – I mean, there wasn't anything Algy had done that would have embarrassed anybody. But Algy was afraid that if this brother of his tried, he'd make such a fool of himself that even he would realise how he'd sunk and then perhaps he'd commit suicide or something really frightful like that. It was so difficult for him to help his brother, you see, without making him feel useless.'

'Heavens!' said Willow, inadequately. The story was preposterous. She wondered whether Algy had been spinning stories for Emma's benefit or whether he had really succeded in deceiving himself. But there was a hint of a possible motive there. If the brother were really useless, he must be incapable of earning a living, in which case he must be in desperate need of money. For some reason, she remembered an amateur production of *Salad Days* she had seen at Newcastle University and suddenly thought of a reason why Algy might have been walking across Clapham Common.

If Algy's brother were a black sheep like the one in Julian Slade's musical, perhaps he would be destitute and sleeping rough. If Algy had been walking across the common towards Clapham Junction, might he perhaps have had an assignation there? No; that really would be too absurd, she thought and turned back to little Emma.

'Did you know if Algy was going to leave the brother something in his will?' Willow asked. Emma shook her head.

'He never talked about that sort of thing. I mean, why should he? He was only thirty-nine. And it's honestly not the kind of question one would ask someone one. . . oh, you know.' She turned away from Willow and blotted her eyes on the paper napkin before giving her nose a thorough blow. Willow had to smile, but the amusement was removed from her face when Emma turned back to say:

'You don't mean that you think that Algy's brother might have. . . might have killed him, do you? Do you think I ought to tell the police?'

'I imagine that they'll have thought of it already, and they've probably got a copy of his will, so they'll know far more than we. Don't you think so?' said Willow, carefully removing any hint of resentment out of her voice. She still could not forgive Inspector Worth for having so much easy access to vital information.

'Yes, of course,' said Emma, 'And they must be inundated by people thinking that they know who did it. What a relief!' She looked suddenly immensely relaxed, as though she had been released from some quite serious anxiety.

'What else did you think you ought to tell them?' asked Willow tentatively and was surprised to see Emma blush once again. She started to speak and was then saved by the waiter coming to clear away their soup plates and bring the steaks and salad. When he had gone, she whispered:

'It was just something that I'd promised Algy I'd never talk about – most frightfully secret. But it did occur to me that if it was so secret, then it might. . . that perhaps I ought. . . .'

Something about the unhappiness in Emma's face and her obvious loyalty to her late employer got through

Willow's defences and she found herself really minding that the child should be relieved of some of her distress.

'About Amanda Gripper, you mean?' said Willow and saw from Emma's expression of astonishment that she was right.

Willow, relieved to have Gino's gossip finally confirmed, was more interested in comforting Emma, and explained as kindly as possible that a secret as fascinating as that one was not likely to remain secret for very long and that it was likely to be shared by several people in Special Branch and probably in the various Civil Service vetting departments, as well as selected 'trusted' friends of each of the participants.

Emma digested that piece of worldly wisdom in silence. Then she looked up at Willow with a hopeful expression.

'So you mean that you think the police will know about it already?'

'I'm sure they will, Emma,' said Willow.

'Thank God,' said the child and turned back to her steak with far more interest than she had shown before. She finished it all, accepted Willow's suggestion of *tarte aux pommes* and then coffee.

Just before they parted, when Emma had thanked 'Cressida' profusely for the delicious lunch, Willow said:

'I think Algy was very lucky to have you, Emma. You must have helped him a lot.'

'Do you really think so?' asked the girl, looking so earnest that Willow understood why Anthony Gnatche would have been so furious when he witnessed Algy's attempted seduction.

'You loved him, didn't you?' said Willow gently and then was sorry when Emma burst into real, gulping, howling tears. Passers-by stopped and peered, but Emma seemed oblivious.

'I'm so sorry,' she said over and over again as Willow searched ineffectually for handkerchiefs. In the end she had to go back into the restaurant and beg some paper napkins from one of the waiters. When Emma had mopped her eyes and managed to stop crying, she apologised yet again. Willow broke all her unspoken rules and put an arm around the girl's shoulders.

'Don't apologise, Emma. It was cruel of me to have reminded you.' She took her arm away and said more briskly: 'Now, where did you leave your car?'

'Just down Maiden Lane. I'll be all right, Cressida. Thank you so much. I am sorry to have been a nuisance.'

Realising that anything she said would provoke only more apologies, Willow said good bye and turned decisively away.

Since she was in Covent Garden she decided to investigate the exhibition Grania had mentioned. It was some time since she had added to her small but choice collection of paintings. She had begun to have serious doubts by the time she had discovered that the so-called gallery was merely the basement of a shop that sold fantastically expensive knitted clothes. Regretting the probable embarrassment involved in walking out of so small a shop without making a purchase, she climbed gingerly down a precipitous helical staircase into a small whitewashed room hung with double rows of pictures and inhabited by a single person.

He was a pleasant, untidy, stammering young man, of about thirty-five who stood up to greet his only customer and blushed as she asked if she could look round. She was touched by his lack of arrogance and decided to buy something even if she hated it, knowing that she could always give it to Mrs Rusham if she really could not bear it, or even hang it in Abbeville Road.

Willow walked slowly round the small whitewashed basement, her spirits rising with each step she took. The pictures were oils, mainly landscapes, but what enchanted her was their gaiety. Each painting seemed full of light and an indefinable atmosphere of happiness, as though the painter had been smiling with every stroke of his brush. Willow knew enough about the business of creating something to know that that was most unlikely, but the results were a delight.

She turned back to the young man, an irresistible smile on her own face that woke an answering one from him.

'Did you paint them?' she asked. He nodded and blushed again.

'I like them very much,' she said. 'Have you a price list?' He handed her a typewritten list and she liked the fact that he had not thrust it at her when she first walked in. She circled the little gallery once again, consulting the list in her hand and then came back to the improvised desk and told him that she would like to buy numbers eleven, fifteen and twenty-two, which came to a total of £2,567.50.

'Oh, I say,' said the young painter breathlessly. 'You really don't have to, you know.' Willow laughed.

'No, I know I don't. But I like them very much indeed.' At last she managed to persuade him that she was not being charitable, agreed to leave her purchases with him until the end of his exhibition, signed a cheque and left him, thinking how well he would do as a friend for Emma Gnatche. They had a lot of the same gentleness, and a humility that was seriously appealing. Willow rather hoped that the ghastly Grania would introduce them.

Having nothing to carry, Willow decided to walk back to her flat so that she could think. She had discovered long ago that when one of her novels went dead on her and she could not think what to do with a tiresome character or difficult plot, the only thing to do was walk. Sitting worrying over the problem was never as effective as striding along the London pavements and just allowing a solution to come to her.

Setting off down Long Acre towards the West End, she hoped that the same process might help her sort out her apparently still-born investigation into the murder.

It was a pity, she thought, that she had allowed her

sympathy for Emma Gnatche's broken heart to stop her from asking more about the Grippers. Emma was unlikely to know much about them, of course, but it was dotty not even to have discovered what she did know.

The walk did help Willow's absurdly slow mind a little, because as she was passing the statue of Eros in the middle of Piccadilly, she realised that she had had a splendid opportunity of finding out about Gripper the previous day and had wasted it.

Her publisher's publicity manager would be sure to know about him, and might even be in a position to introduce him to her star author. After all, the publicity department must be dealing with journalists most of the time. Willow was irritated to think that she had had the whole of Friday to telephone her publisher. Now she would just have to wait until Monday.

The least she could do, she thought, was to buy a copy of the *Daily Mercury* and see what sort of thing Gripper wrote. It was not a newspaper that Willow King would have dreamt of touching in the ordinary way, full as it was of prurient gossip, simplistic tub-thumping, and photographs of naked teenage girls presumably designed to titillate the jaded palates of frustrated middle-aged men and pubescent boys. Willow bought her copy at a newsstand near Green Park tube station and stood transfixed in the middle of the street.

'Murdered Minister In Rent Boy Scandal?' screamed the headline.

Someone walked into Willow and produced an apology that was so loaded with accusation that she realised she would have to get out of the way. Dazed by the headline, she backtracked down Piccadilly to a café she sometimes used and ordered a cup of coffee.

Carrying it to a table at the far end of the restaurant, she sat down and perused the scandal sheet. When she got to the end of the article she realised that it was a masterpiece of innuendo and unjustified speculation. She went back to the beginning and re-read it slowly to see whether there were any facts in it at all.

'Close friends of glamorous minister, Algernon ('Algy') Endelsham deny categorically that he had ever been a homosexual. Nevertheless recent speculation about his private life might have led people outside his charmed circle to think otherwise.

'Did they include members of the South-London vigilante group whose recent gay-bashing activities include the smashing up of Junction pub The Pig's Ear last week?

'A youth involved in that punch-up is said to be "helping the police with their enquiries".

'The leader of the band said last month, "We hate rich pouffs taking advantage of homeless lads".

'Inspector Tom Worth, leading the Clapham-based enquiry into the minister's murder had no comment to make on the pub brawl.'

Willow drank her coffee and considered the newspaper. The pub fracas to which the article referred must have been the source of the talk about The Pig's Ear that she had overheard at DOAP, but as far as she could see, the paper had neither made nor even claimed any connection between it and Algy's death. They had merely interwoven speculation about the one with a brief report of the other. But at least one thing was clear to her: she now knew where the DOAP messengers had got the idea that the minister might have been a homosexual. The *Daily Mercury* had always been their preferred reading, and it did not take an intuitive genius, Willow thought, to work out why the paper might have wanted to suggest that the minister's sexual preferences might have been a little unorthodox. If the secret of Gripper's wife's affair with Algy were beginning to leak beyond what the paper called 'the charmed circle', then Gripper himself might well want to draw a red herring across the trail.

He must have been taking a bit of a risk that Algy would sue, Willow thought, although the articles that had appeared before his death had been much less explicit that the latest one; and yet would a man like Algy have bothered to take any kind of legal action? There must have been so many women who could have given him a testimonial of bedworthiness that he might have decided to brush off the whole campaign as part of the occupational hazard of public life; and presumably Gripper had never mentioned anything so crude as rent boys until his enemy was dead and outside the scope of the libel laws.

What a shit the man must be, said Willow to herself, draining her coffee. He couldn't keep his wife happy and so he had to resort to tactics like that to smear the character of the man she preferred. What else might Gripper do to assert his own superiority?

Remembering the heavy handsomeness of the florid man who had accosted her, Willow thought that if she had been Amanda Gripper, she would have chosen Algy over Gripper every time, even if she had discovered Algy's tendency to bully and mock the weak.

Willow read her way through the whole of the *Daily Mercury* and when she had finished even the sports pages at the back, she dropped the paper on to the table and retreated to the ladies' room to wash her hands. Seldom had she felt so grubby. The whole tenor of the paper was a kind of sanctimonious delight in all the pathetic squalor of human folly. As she rinsed the soap off her fingers, Willow wondered what kind of person made up its immense readership: they must be people of so little confidence or achievement that their only pleasure could be in *Schadenfreude*. What hope was there for a world where people felt like that? she wondered.

7

G OING TO BED that night, Willow promised herself that
she would work seriously on her novel for the whole
of Sunday. Important though it was for her to discover the
identity of Algy's murderer before she returned to DOAP
and the investigations of Inspector Worth the following
Tuesday, it was also important for her to fulfil her contract
and get the current novel finished by the end of December.
She had already been paid a third of the generous advance
and she had no intention of welching on the deal.

The Sunday newspapers thudding through her specially
wide letter box as she was drinking her coffee the next
morning heralded a tempting distraction, and Willow
had to struggle hard with herself not to succumb. But
she succeeded, finished the coffee and retreated to her
writing room without even picking up the papers from
the hall. Her work went reasonably well and, indeed, she
found that the short break had helped her to sort out a
particularly knotty problem with one of her characters.
By two-thirty, she realised that she was both hungry and
very tired, and decided that she deserved an interval for
lunch.

She found a mixture of delicacies in the fridge and picnicked on them happily in the kitchen with the newspapers spread out on the big table in front of her. Having done nearly six hours' real work, she felt that she could allow herself to return to the subject that had threatened to take over her mind whenever her concentration had flagged. Ignoring the magazines and book reviews (which she usually read first), she concentrated on any sections that might contain anything about Algy. There were plenty of relevant articles and she read every word conscientiously.

By the time she had finished her lunch she had confirmation of much of the DOAP chatter: that Algy had died between six and nine o'clock the previous Monday from blows to his head; that his body had been found soon after ten o'clock that night in the middle of Clapham Common; that there was no sign of a weapon by the body and so far no physical evidence of his attacker.

There was also an article in each of three papers about the incident in the Clapham Junction pub, but none of them suggested any connection between that and the murder. Each piece ended with the same words the *Daily Mercury* had used, that 'a man is helping the police with their enquiries', but the Sunday newspapers made no suggestion that the enquiries had to do with anything except the criminal damage to the pub and the various charges of assault against its patrons.

Even so, having read to the end of the last article, Willow retrieved her list of motives and added under the heading 'Other', vigilante killing. As she wrote, she wondered whether there were any law under which Gripper could be indicted if the gay-bashers did turn out to have murdered Algy. Without his decoy innuendo, no one in the world would have thought that Algy was a homosexual.

Willow also wondered whether she would dare to talk to Roger about the vigilantes. There was no doubt that he might be able to throw some very useful light on the murky subject, but Willow did not know whether she had the moral courage to ask for it. Having sedulously avoided any intimacies with her staff for years, she could hardly justify cross-examining Roger about his private life.

But still, she told herself, there was little point in worrying about that until she returned to DOAP on Tuesday. There were plenty of other things to occupy her mind; not the least of which was the fact that she was half-way through her allotted time away from DOAP and had discovered nothing of any consequence. She looked down again at the list of possible motives.

After a few moments' thought, she added to the 'Other' column, 'Political assassination?', and then crossed it out; it really did not seem possible. So far the only plausible motives she had accumulated were Gripper's rage at his wife's infidelity, the unknown brother's desire for any inheritance he might gain from Algy's death, and the vengeance of the vigilantes. Willow found that the least convincing, despite (or perhaps because of) Gripper's having seized on it.

Before she could work out precisely why she was not disposed to believe it, the telephone bell interrupted her. Assuming that it would be Richard demanding tender-loving-care, she almost left her machine to answer, but in the end did pick up her receiver and repeated her telephone number. A vaguely familiar male voice said:

'Might I speak to Miss Cressida Woodruffe?'

'This is she,' said Willow properly.

'Ah, good. Hello, Cressida; Anthony Gnatche here.'

'How nice to hear from you,' said Willow with more sincerity than she would have expected when she had last spoken to him. Since then her opinion of him had risen considerably. Stupid he might be, but he had diagnosed the state of his young step-sister's heart and been determined that it should not be exploited by the experienced charm of his old school friend.

'I was wondering whether I could tempt you out for some dinner, tomorrow evening,' he said. 'Emma told me how very kind you were to her yesterday.'

'It was a pleasure,' said Willow warmly. 'She's a sweet girl.'

'Well I think so, too,' said Gnatche. 'I must confess that my invitation has a slight ulterior motive.'

'Oh?' said Willow more coolly.

'Yes, I'm worried about Emma and I wanted to ask your advice. Are you free?'

'In fact I am,' she said. 'Shall we meet somewhere?'

'No, I'll come and pick you up, at – what? – about eight?'

'Could we make it seven-thirty? I like to get early to bed on Mondays,' said Willow, making it quite clear that she was accepting only the offer of dinner. Gnatche agreed and wrote down her address.

Willow put down the receiver, made herself a cup of black coffee and returned to the newspapers. The only other relevant article was a profile of Inspector Thomas Worth, which had been written by the paper's defence correspondent. Willow was slightly surprised by that: after all, an inspector was not particularly senior, and it seemed strange that he should have so much coverage. But when she had read the article, she understood.

Thomas Worth had, it seemed, been an officer in the SAS, and something of a hero. The profile did not go into any great detail about his army service or the decorations he had won, which did not surprise Willow. Journalists like the defence correspondent would need to keep their official sources sweet, and the SAS of all regiments would dislike any precise accounts of their officers and actions to be published. Where the detail came was in the accounts of his police career.

According to the article, Inspector Worth was greatly disliked by some of his colleagues and junior officers, not least for his insistence that the laws designed to protect the country's citizens applied as much to the villains in their charge as to the law-abiding public. They also disliked the fact that he had had a public-school education and 'talked posh'. When Willow read that, she thought that she understood why his voice had sounded so colourless: he must have tried desperately to remove its elitist accent and intonation without going so far as to pretend to regional vowel sounds and glottal stops.

By the time she had finished the profile, Willow had the strong impression that the journalist felt that Worth ought to have been promoted rather higher than inspector, and that he was given all the thoroughly unpopular cases. There was even a delicately masked suggestion that the Met. did not believe Algy's murderer would ever be found, because of the complete lack of physical clues and witnesses, and that Worth had been lumbered with the apparently impossible task to teach him a lesson.

With rather less antagonism in her mind than usual, Willow left the subject of the inspector and returned to work on her novel. When she eventually let herself decide that she had done enough for the day, she was so tired that she had no energy left for anybody's problems, least of all his. Forgetting them, her own, Emma Gnatche's and everyone else's, Willow had a deep, hot bath, dined in her dressing gown off scrambled eggs, mineral water and marrons glacés, and watched an old romantic film on the television.

Just before she went to sleep, she found enough energy to scribble a list of questions she wanted to ask various people the following day, in case she lost another op-portunity. She needed to ask Nan Hambalt, the publicity manager of her publisher, about the Grippers; she had to find out where Algy's brother lived and either talk to him or to people who knew him and discover at least whether he had had any expectations of an inheritance from Algy; and on Tuesday morning, she would have to pluck up enough courage to ask Roger whether the *Daily Mercury*'s hints about the minister's sexuality had any basis in fact, and whether he knew anything about the vigilantes.

Her list written, she laid down both pen and paper and switched off the lamp by her bedhead. Turning over, so that her face lay in the softness of the goose-down pillows, she remembered that there was still nothing substantial in the column headed 'Fear' on her list of possible motives. Before she could tease her weary mind even into speculation, she was engulfed in sleep.

The following morning, bathed, dressed and breakfasted, she rang up Nan Hambalt to put in train some enquiries about Mr and Mrs Gripper. The questions were disguised in a general request for information about gossip columns, explained by Willow's plans for a new book set in the fervid world of the tabloid press. An amused chuckle came down the telephone.

'Oh you could have such fun with that,' said the publicity manager. 'I have a couple of friends who might be useful. One works on the *Evening Standard* and the other on "Gripper's Gripes": would you like me to set up a meeting with them?'

'That would be terrific, Nan, if you don't mind? "Gripper's Gripes", what a superb name for his outpourings! I'd love to meet someone who knows all the ins and outs of that column.'

'Isn't it good? Jane once told me that that's what they call it on the paper. Look, I'll give her a ring and find out when she's free – is lunch or dinner better for you, Cressida?'

'Dinner, really, and any night between Thursday and Monday. If I'm not here when you ring back, leave a message on the machine or with Mrs Rusham. Okay?'

'Sure. How's the book?'

Willow answered politely but soon managed to extricate herself from the conversation and put down the receiver. Unable to think of any other way of finding out about the

Grippers that would not involve coming face to face with him once again, Willow realised a little bitterly that she would have to leave that part of the investigation until Nan produced her friend.

She turned instead to one of the other parts of her investigation: the possible existence of corruption in the department. At first sight the proposition seemed fairly unattractive, because it was hard to see how anyone could run any lucrative scam from so dreary an organisation. At that thought Willow told herself that she was thinking far too much as Cressida Woodruffe. The assistant secretary (finance) of the Department of Old Age Pensions ought not to be so naive. Billions of pounds were spent each year on pensions for the country's elderly: not enough, she believed, but nevertheless millions. There must be ways in which some of those millions could be diverted into the pockets of a clever swindler.

Unfortunately all the swindles that occurred to Willow were on a pathetically small scale, which might get their perpetrators sacked but would never result in criminal prosecution, and she could not imagine that anyone would kill to avoid being sacked. In any case, Algy himself would be quite uninterested in anything so paltry.

Willow's main difficulty in finding a possible source of major corruption was that if any pension were to be diverted from its intended recipient, that person would rightly set up such a squeal of protest that it would be found out at once.

'Unless,' she said aloud, wondering at her own absurd slowness of brain, 'the pensioner was no longer there to squeal.'

As she well knew from her early days at the department, when a pensioner died whoever was in charge of his or her affairs was bound to report the death and return the pension book to the department. Occasionally if the department had any reason to believe that the pensioner had died (if no one had drawn the money for some time, for example), a form would be sent to the pensioner's last known address asking for confirmation.

It might just be possible, Willow thought, to intercept a percentage of all notifications of death, collect the books, write as though from the address on the book to inform the department that the pensioners had moved from their original address and arrange to have the pensions paid by post to accommodation addresses or even collected from various post offices around the country.

Willow got up from her chair and prowled about the room, running her fingers madly through her red hair, trying to find first practical objections to the scheme and then possible perpetrators. If Algy were to have become interested, then the perpetrator must be relatively senior; he would have dealt quickly, ruthlessly perhaps, and openly with some peculating clerk.

What she found hardest at that stage to believe was that any of the dull but worthy men and women who staffed the department would have the imagination, the dishonesty or the human resources to carry off such an embezzlement successfully. Nevertheless she scribbled an account of her speculation on her list of motives and then turned back to her search for Algy's brother.

There was no one except Algy in the telephone book under the name Endelsham, and Willow began to wonder whether the brother could possibly be ex-directory, and if so why. Of course, if he were as hopeless as Emma's accounts had suggested, then he really might be destitute and 'of no fixed abode', in which case obviously he would not be listed in the telephone directory. Once again her mind was inexorably drawn to the tramp who lived in and around Clapham Junction station. But again she ignored him on the grounds that the coincidence would be simply too absurd. More realistic was the possibility that Algy's brother might live outside London; but Willow did not think so. It had definitely sounded from Emma's chatter as though the poor man lived in London.

There had been no references to a brother in any of the newspaper articles about the murder, and even the obituaries had ended merely, 'He never married.' The only certain information Willow had was that the brother had been at the Jeremiah House prep school in Hastings at least thirty years earlier. She dialled Directory Enquiries and got the number of the school.

Posing as a journalist, she then told the school secretary who answered that she was writing a mood piece about Algernon Endelsham's childhood for a women's magazine and was seeking any nice stories about his time at the school. Unfortunately, she was told, the school had changed hands three times since those days and was now a progressive co-educational establishment, specialising in speech and drama.

'I'm afraid that none of the teachers working here now would have the faintest idea of anything that went on here in the old days. It was a very repressive, out-of-date place, you know,' said the woman in an indefinably irritating voice.

'So I gathered,' said Willow, trying to make her own voice sound cosy. 'But is there really no one – even an old gardener or anything – who might have stories to tell about the old days?'

'Well,' came the slightly whining voice, weakening a little. 'There is old Mr Caldervale in the town. Frankly he's the most awful nuisance, turning up on Parents' Day and banging on about falling standards. God knows if he was here at the stage you want, but he certainly taught French here for years. I can give you his address if you like.'

'Thank you very much. That might help,' said Willow, and wrote down both address and telephone number. At first she thought of telephoning on the same pretext and in the same guise, but then the words 'banging on about falling standards' made her stop, just as her finger was landing on the first button of her telephone. An elderly man who minded so much about standards might well clam up at such an approach. Willow thought that she would have to go and see him – and not as a sexy, rich novelist either.

With her DOAP personality to hand, she thought that she probably would not have too much difficulty in gaining his confidence. Rejecting the idea of being a pensions investigator, she decided instead to be an emissary from a firm of solicitors in search of Algy's brother as beneficiary under a distant relative's will. She assumed that there was no reason to suppose that the casual-sounding school secretary would ever tell the 'tiresome old man' that she had given his name and address to a journalist.

Cursing, for the umpteenth time, her stupidity in having bought a vast cream-coloured Mercedes with leather upholstery instead of a small, inconspicuous car, Willow changed into the one suitable suit she had hanging in the back of Cressida's wardrobe, got out of the house before Mrs Rusham returned from her weekly shopping expedition, took a taxi to Charing Cross and a grubby, smelly train to Hastings, and at last found her way to a small house on the edge of the town. The sight of its sparklingly clean windows, lack of net curtains and general air of exposure to the sun and the wind gave Willow a moment's encouragement. A man who lived in such a house could not be the doddering old fool suggested by the secretary's contempt.

Willow, dressed in dark grey suit and white shirt, her hair put up and no cosmetics on her face, knocked briskly on the gleaming, dark-green front door. After a full minute's wait, she heard a halting tread and the soft thud and drag of a rubber-shod walking stick. Composing her face into an expression of unintrusive but friendly competence, she waited. The green door opened at last and she was confronted with a very tall, thin man, with bowed shoulders, who leaned on a stick. For a moment she was ashamed to have dragged a man obviously in pain from his warm chair and dropped her glance. She saw that

120

he wore brown brogues with so high a gloss polished on to them that they might have been made of enamelled glass. Allowing her gaze to travel slowly upwards, she noted the shabby grey flannel trousers, which had been carefully darned on one knee, the thick checked shirt, whose collar points were fraying, the plain tie and the well-worn tweed jacket. At last she allowed herself to look at his face and she thought that she was not going to be disappointed.

Never had she seen a man with such piercingly bright grey eyes. They dominated a face that must always have been thin but was now almost skeletal. Deep grey crescent-shaped shadows lay under the eyes, on either side of a harsh nose and drew all attention from the mouth, which she decided might look almost gentle if it were not so twisted.

'Yes?' the man said at last when she showed no signs of coming in or leaving him alone.

'Mr Caldervale?' she asked, coming to her senses. He nodded, leaning on his stick, and waited for her to explain herself. Willow, who had faced innumerable aggressive, obstructive and merely terrifying senior Civil Servants in her time, was not flustered.

'I am from Leonard, Friend and Winter, solicitors, Mr Caldervale, and we're looking for the beneficiary of one of our clients' wills. We believe that he was educated at your school until he was thirteen, but we have not been able to trace him since then. May I come in?'

'Certainly,' he said, moving stiffly away from the door to let her in. 'First door on your right.'

Willow followed his directions and found herself in an airy room, whose white walls were covered with bookshelves up to nearly shoulder height. Two modern wing chairs in sludge-green stretch covers provided the only seating, but there was a pleasant, shabby rug on the polished wooden floor. An exiguous gas fire popped and hissed in the blocked-in grate.

'Do sit down, Miss. . .?'

121

'King,' said Willow with the first honesty of the day. As she spoke she cast a backward look in her mind to her parents; no wonder they had been so insistent about her pension, she thought, if this kind of retirement was what they had envisaged for her. Telling herself that thanks to Cressida Woodruffe she need not fear it for herself, she smiled kindly at the old man.

'Now, what was this boy's name?' he asked briskly as he lowered himself carefully into the chair on the right of the fireplace. It had had an extra cushion in an unmatching cover added to heighten the seat, but even so he had difficulty getting down to it. He propped the stick carefully against one of the arms and seemed to give Willow his entire attention.

'Endelsham,' she said, still smiling. 'There were two of them, and it's perfectly clear who the younger was, but we're concerned with the elder, Jonathan. Do you remember him at all, Mr Caldervale?'

'A very great many boys passed through my French classes, Miss King; what makes you think that I might?' Mr Caldervale said. For a moment Willow was disappointed; but, catching a gleam in those extraordinary eyes, she took heart and spoke with what she hoped was engaging frankness.

'Well, given that his brother turned out so well – and became so famous – and has just been murdered, I thought your memory might, perhaps, have been jogged,' she said, speaking as one intelligent being to another.

'Hmmm,' he murmured, rubbing his strong, fleshless chin with one bent hand. 'I always liked honesty.' When he said no more, Willow wondered whether she had been mistaken in accepting that as a compliment. He glared at her and she had a moment's anxiety that he might disbelieve her cover story or perhaps demand a telephone number so that he could ring her supposed partners to check it. She tucked an imaginary wisp of hair back into the pins that kept it all off her face and waited.

'You're right,' he said at last. 'I do remember them both, poor little things.' Willow was so surprised that she repeated the last three words. The old man nodded.

'Yes, Jonathan was the obvious victim, but I often felt sorry for his brother, too; something was always driving him on to prove that he was so much cleverer, more popular, tougher and so on than anyone else. I've occasionally wished that I made more effort to find out what it was, but they were not in my house and it mightn't have gone down well.'

Willow was surprised to see that he appeared to be genuinely troubled, which seemed extraordinary. Surely his acquaintance with the two boys had been far too long ago to make him anxious still.

'Did you like them, then?' she asked. Caldervale looked at her, but she had the impression that he saw something quite different for his clear eyes were not focussed on her.

'Like them? I can't remember.' He put one knobbly, arthritic hand over his eyes for a moment and then said: 'I loathed most of the little beggars I had to teach for all those years, and when they snivelled with homesickness or terror of my temper, I loathed them all the more. Poor little beggars.'

'Were they good at French?' Willow asked, in order to change the subject. She was appalled by the sadness in his face, and by the loneliness that made him confide such sadness to a stranger.

'Not very, but I can't imagine what that's got to do with your enquiry,' said Mr Caldervale with such cold surprise that Willow was both reassured about his state of mind and rather glad that she had never had to recite French irregular verbs to him in her own youth.

'Nothing at all, Mr Caldervale; sheer vulgar curiosity, I'm afraid. No, all I need to ask you is whether you have any idea what happened to the elder brother? I – we, that is – can't find any trace of him through the normal channels; might he perhaps have emigrated or something?'

'It's possible. They loathed each other you know. . . you might find that Jonathan left of his own accord – or even that his brother forced him out. I don't know,' said Caldervale, hauling himself up out of his chair. He reached for the stick and walked painfully towards her. Willow wondered what on earth he wanted and shifted uncomfortably in her chair. He walked straight past her and opened the window behind her head. A blast of icy wind blew down the back of her neck.

'I hope you don't mind the air,' he said, and she thought there was a certain note of malice in his voice. 'But I always have the windows open when I have a pipe – couldn't bear the kind of stinking fug most old men live in.'

Willow watched him walk slowly back to the mantel-piece, take a pipe out of his pocket and fill it from a stone jar that stood there. Then he eased himself back into his chair and set about lighting the tobacco. He sucked gently on the end of his pipe and Willow was suddenly transported back to her parents' ugly house in Newcastle: the tobacco he smoked must have been the same as her father's. There had been no alcohol drunk in Dr William King's home, and his pipe was his only extravagance. In some ways, he had been rather like the old man in front of her: clever, acerbic and reserved. She had not thought of him or his pipe for years, but the sweet, pungent smoke caught at her throat and she had to blink away the sudden memories.

Mr Caldervale shook his bald head suddenly and the spare flesh under his chin swung gently with the move-ment. To her own surprise Willow forgot her mission and was once again filled with pity for the old man; he seemed to her to be managing his old age with great dignity, and yet there he was living alone, obviously in pain and with not quite enough money. The school to which he had devoted his working life found him a terrible old nuisance, and he was filled with regret at his strictness with the 'poor little beggars' he had taught.

'I am afraid I've not been much help, Miss King,' he said, sucking comfortably on the pipe, the bowl lightly clasped in one arthritic hand. 'What you need to find out is where Jonathan went after they left Hastings. I don't know which school it was, but it must have been somewhere less imposing than Eton certainly. If you could find that out, they'd probably know much more than I. I am sorry, Miss King, but at seventy-four one's mind does begin to slacken its hold on detail.'

Looking at his clear eyes, Willow found that hard to believe.

'Why do I think that you know more than you are telling me?' she asked him. She was answered first by a short bark of derisive laughter.

'Probably because you have an over-vivid imagination. Girls generally have, I've always been told,' he said.

What with the icy air biting at the back of her neck and Mr Caldervale's sexism arousing her rage, Willow realised that she was not going to shake his determined silence and bully or charm out of him any information he did not want to give up.

'I'm most grateful, Mr Caldervale, nevertheless,' she said with some truth. 'Thank you. Oh, no, please don't bother to get up again. I can see myself out.'

But he would not allow that and heaved himself out of the chair once more. Willow felt that uncomfortable pricking of her conscience again. Life had been very much easier, she thought, when she had not involved herself with other people, even if it had been a trifle lonely. With that word in her mind, she turned on the doorstep and offered her hand to the old man.

'Thank you again, Mr Caldervale. Good bye.' Looking a little surprised, he shifted his stick to his other hand and took hers. His palm was warm and dry and he shook her hand firmly.

'I wish you luck, Miss King,' he said, his eyes flashing fiercely, 'with whatever it is you are really doing.'

Willow blushed, but was too experienced to say more or try to persuade him of her bona fides. As she walked away from his aggressively clean cottage she felt as though his sharp old eyes were fixed on her retreating figure and even tightened and relaxed her shoulder blades once or twice. At last she could bear it no longer and turned to look back, but his front door was well and truly shut. Mocking herself for the over-active imagination he had diagnosed in her, she walked down to the sea and watched the grey waves crash down on the beach and suck backwards at the gravel in a violent undertow.

There were a few sad-looking children playing on the edge of the sea and two or three old men trudging along in wellingtons, but that was all. The whole scene was grey and forlorn. Willow thought of what the place must have looked like in its heyday as a holiday resort, with the pier gleaming, the beach full of people and the now-tatty shops and eating houses doing a brisk and comfortable trade. As it was, on that cold November day she thought she had never seen a more depressing place and pitied the miserable victims of Algernon Endelsham even more than she had before. It must have been bad enough to be sent away from warm, well-mothered homes at the pathetic age of eight, but to have to live for three-quarters of the year in a place so gloomy must have been horrible, let alone being tormented and mocked for their tears by a ferocious bully. Even the Newcastle of her own arid childhood had been more enticing.

Shivering suddenly and wrapping the jacket of her suit more firmly round herself, she turned away from the sea, and walked up into the town. There she found herself in slightly less tawdry and depressing surroundings, with one or two antique shops that made her want to stop and browse. She yielded to temptation after a while and toyed for a few minutes with the idea of buying a supposed Regency breakfast table, in lovely glowing kingwood, but in the end decided that the price was outrageous and the provenance doubtful. The proprietor's resigned acceptance of her polite excuses suggested either that she was right or that he had wasted too much time with impoverished tourists using his shop as a free wet-weather amusement. Despite her disenchantment with the breakfast table, she went on into each shop that looked as though it were more than a junkyard and in the end found herself in a print shop, leafing through piles of engravings, aquatints, etchings and lithographs.

There were several that caught her fancy and she bought a series of four hand-coloured etchings of exotic birds, which had obviously been cut from some Victorian natural-history book, for her Abbeville Road flat and a very much more expensive woodcut for Richard. Her conscience had been agitating her for her inaccessibility at the weekend – and at her irrepressible amusement at his prepschool nickname – and she thought that the spending of really quite a lot of money might help. She chose him a print of an ancient monastery herb garden, which seemed to her very charming with its distorted perspective and beautifully lettered instructions for the planting and cultivation of various medicinal and culinary herbs. Cress did not feature in the woodcut, which made her smile once again.

Willow paid cash for the Abbeville Road prints and put Richard's woodcut on one of her credit cards and waited until the pictures had been wrapped between sheets of stiff card. Then, still cold and dissatisfied with herself, she went into a teashop and ordered a pot of very strong coffee to drink before she could catch a train back to London.

Sitting on the train, it suddenly dawned on her that Algy's elder brother might well have tried to escape the bullying attentions of his tormentor not by emigration but simply by changing his name. If he did that and kept out of Algy's way, then he might have been able to get on with his life, perhaps even become qualified in some way and found himself a viable job. He could be anywhere.

Turning the new idea over and over in her mind, Willow then tried to remember anything she had ever known about the rules of Deed Poll. If there were a register of people's original names, Willow could search it for 'Endelsham' and then interview anyone who had once been called Jonathan Endelsham whatever his new name. Unfortunately she could not remember whether there was any such register and was amazed to find yet another topic of which she knew nothing. It was years since she had been faced with such inadequacy in herself and she did not like it at all.

8

WILLOW timed her return to Chesham Place to avoid Mrs Rusham, who might have been dangerously surprised to see her fastidious employer dressed in a manifestly ready-made suit that disguised all her good features and made her look ten years older and about fifty times poorer than she was. But evidence of the housekeeper's industry could be found all over the flat, and Willow relaxed into its gentle comfort with a sigh of relief. There was no message from Richard on either the machine or Mrs Rusham's pad and that too was a relief, even if, as Willow rather suspected, it meant that he was sulking. But there were various other messages, including one from Emma Gnatche thanking 'Cressida' for giving her lunch.

Emma's little speech was so charmingly phrased that Willow thought she would have to pursue her acquaintance with Emma even when her information was no longer needed for the investigation. The sound of her voice also reminded Willow that she had agreed to go out to dinner with Emma's brother. A quick look at her watch told Willow that he would be arriving in less than twenty minutes' time to collect her.

Ignoring the rest of the messages, Willow ran for the bathroom, unbuttoning and unzipping clothes as she went. She turned on both taps at full blast and flung some Channel No. 19 essence into the water. While the bath filled, she retreated to her bedroom to choose some clothes. Not at all certain where Anthony might take her, she was in a slight quandary as to what to wear. Emma's appearance and manner suggested that the family were perfectly well off, but the quality of the wine offered at Sarah's engagement party had led Willow to think otherwise. It would never do to embarrass her host – or indeed herself – by wearing a couture dress to a tiny, informal restaurant, but on the other hand it would do Cressida Woodruffe's publicity no good at all to be seen at a richly fashionable restaurant wearing jeans.

In the end she compromised and wore a plain black wool dress, whose cut would carry it almost anywhere. She pinned an antique emerald brooch just below the neck, hoping that if they did go to some bistro full of scrubbed tables and candle ends stuck in old chianti bottles, the jewel would be taken as fake.

With her tall, slim figure and her red hair, snaking down her back, she knew that she looked reasonably attractive, and was pleased three minutes later to see that Anthony Gnatche thought so too. Three minutes after that, though, she had remembered all the reasons why she had disliked him at Sarah's party. His braying laugh irritated her whenever he produced it; his crass compliments made her want to hit him; and the tedium of his mind and conversation suggested that an evening being grilled by Inspector Worth would be preferable to eating even the best dinner in the company of Anthony Gnatche.

Willow's sympathies for Emma grew as they arrived at the restaurant Anthony had chosen (happily one where the emerald pin could safely be taken as genuine) and he started to flex his importance in front of the waiters. First he decided that their table was in a draught and then as soon as they had been settled at a different table, started impatiently drumming his fingers on the table because the drinks he had ordered did not appear instantly. Willow wanted to tell him how bored such antics made her, but instead smiled as sweetly as her remaining honesty would allow.

'You wanted to ask some advice about Emma,' she said, hoping to turn his conversation from its tedious mixture of compliment and self-advertisement. Gnatche looked surprised for a moment and Willow could have kicked herself for believing that he had wanted her advice, but eventually he coughed and began to tell her that he was at his wits' end about what to do with his younger step-sister.

'She got very hung up on old Algy, you see,' he said at one moment. 'I expect she told you that. She said you were terribly sympathetic.'

'Did she?' said Willow, not wanting to betray little Emma's confidences and remembering how the child had said she was sometimes afraid of her brother.

'Oh, yes. And he was such a swine with girls; I just want to be sure. . . well, you know,' he said, giving her a look which she could not interpret at all.

'Not really,' said Willow. 'Have you thought of suggesting that she goes to university? It seemed to me that she was far too intelligent to waste her time on cookery classes and nice-young-girls' jobs. She ought to have some real work to do. And if she really was – what did you call it? – hung up on Mr Endelsham, that might distract her.'

Anthony's reaction to that suggestion left Willow in no doubt at all as to his views on women and their proper function in men's lives and her pity for his sisters grew. She tried to distract him by asking him about his work and he expatiated at great length about his farming methods and excellent man management. Willow listened, reminding herself both that it was all good copy and that the evening would end in due course.

Eventually Gnatche tired of talking about himself and returned to the subject of Emma. To Willow's highly critical ear, he seemed to be trying to pump her about what Emma might have said about her late employer, and she decided to say nothing. As she listened to him, Willow found her resentment and her boredom growing at such speed that she could hardly taste any of the delectable food that the now-morose waiter put in front of her.

It was just as she was biting into a perfect hot Cointreau soufflé as though it were tinned rice pudding that she decided to do something to make the best of the evening instead of letting it drive her into a frenzy of boredom and rage. She put down her spoon and waited for Gnatche to finish his sentence.

'I'm sure Emma'll be all right,' she said. 'She seemed far too sensible to let whatever she felt for Endelsham spoil her life. By the way, you knew him well: do you know who his heir is?'

'Why on earth do you want to know that?' demanded Gnatche. Willow, surprised by his abrupt – almost rude – tone, produced the first excuse that came into her head, and it was not a particularly good one.

'Oh, it's just that I was talking to my editor this morning, and she asked me whether I had any idea. My publisher is apparently thinking of commissioning a biography of Algy, and they'll need access to his papers.'

'Bit vulture-like, don't you think?'

'Perhaps,' said Willow, as though she were really considering the proposition. 'But, I suppose that is why they're so anxious to get the approval of his heirs. Do you know who they might be? Had he any family?'

'Just the brother as far as I know. They must have had parents, but Algy hadn't said a word about them in all the time I've known him,' said Gnatche, shaking his head. 'Presumably his brother gets something, however much

132

Algy loathed him when they were boys. Perhaps Algy left the rest to one or other of his mistresses. . . perhaps the party. Who knows?'

'What about Emma?' suggested Willow, not entirely seriously but in order to keep the conversation going. She was surprised to see her host's face change. His voice was cold and clipped as he said:

'I cannot imagine why you should think Algernon Endelsham should leave my sister anything. She has never been his mistress; and she would not dream of accepting a legacy from him even if she had been.'

'Please don't misunderstand me,' said Willow quickly. 'I never meant to suggest anything derogatory to Emma. She seemed wholly delightful and it was clear from her accounts of her work with Endelsham that he valued her highly. That made me wonder.' After a little more soothing, Gnatche allowed himself to accept Willow's excuses and even went so far as to answer her question.

'I think it's most unlikely that Emma stands to inherit anything,' he said at last. 'After all, no sane man alters his will to include a temporary typist, however sweet and helpful she may be, particularly as he can have had no suspicion that he would die.'

'I suppose not,' said Willow, unfairly irritated that Gnatche had not been able to help. She was left with his assumption, which she shared, that in the absence of other relations Algy's brother might be in line for a fairly substantial inheritance. It did just occur to her that Gnatche himself might have had some expectations, which could have explained why he had reacted so angrily to her suggestion about Emma. He might well be in some kind of financial trouble, despite his boasts about his wonderful farming techniques and man management. After all, the Common Agricultural Policy had resulted in serious trouble for many farmers and the value of agricultural land had fallen catastrophically. Perhaps he was fighting hard to keep up appearances while struggling to pay off crippling mortgages. That might well explain the disgusting wine served at Sarah's engagement party. And yet Willow could think of no reason why Endelsham should have bequeathed anything to Anthony Gnatche: it was true that they had been friends of a sort since prep school, but she simply could not imagine a man as sophisticated and intelligent as Algy being so fond of the tedious Gnatche that he wanted to enrich him.

Determined to get her hands on a copy of the will if she possibly could, Willow sat back and waited in some impatience for her host to finish his dinner. At last the grisly entertainment began to draw to a close. Willow watched while Anthony Gnatche paid the bill and then got up from the table in relief. She felt the weight of her fur coat sink on to her shoulders and thought that the sensation of returning freedom almost compensated for her headache and the rigid tension in her neck and shoulders.

'Thank you for a lovely dinner,' she called from the steps of the Chesham Place house when he had driven her home. 'Let me know when you're next going to be in London.'

'Will do,' he said, putting the car into gear again. She did not wait for anything else, but let herself into the flat and shut the door behind her with a deep sigh. But her home did not give her the usual feeling of sanctuary. She felt slightly uneasy and much less safe than usual. Perhaps something in Gnatche's attitude to life and his fellow mortals had upset her more than she had realised.

Poor Emma, she thought to herself as she went to hang up her coat. What a man to have in one's life! She wandered into the kitchen to make herself some soothing cocoa (which she remembered from childhood as having a good effect on her spirits) and then carried the cup into the drawing room to listen to the rest of her messages. One was from Eve Greville, her literary agent, asking her to ring to discuss some amendments to a Japanese contract for one of 'Cressida's' books.

134

Willow checked her watch to make sure that it was not too late to ring Eve, and then thankfully punched in the number. Ever since she had sent her first, unpublishable, novel to Eve Greville and received her amused but highly critical assessment of it, Willow had liked the clever, astringent woman, and she felt that a few minutes of discussion with Eve might help to remove both the memory of an excruciatingly boring evening and the uneasiness from her mind.

Eve answered the telephone promptly and brushed aside Willow's apologies for ringing so late. They thrashed out the problems on the contract and then Eve asked her usual question:

'How's the writing going, Cressida?'

'Not all that well, actually, Eve. I've got stuck and have been diverting myself with thoughts of the next one,' said Willow, not wanting to talk about the murder.

'So I hear,' came the ironic and amused voice of her agent. 'I was having lunch with Nan Hambalt today and she told me you were thinking of setting the next one in a newspaper gossip-column office. Nice idea, if you can get it right.'

'Do you think so?' said Willow, deliberately forgetting that her approach to Nan had been part of her investigation. 'I'll have to be careful, of course, because I've heard that the gossip chiefs are even more litigious than their victims.' Eve laughed and Willow heard the effect of years of smoking sixty a day rasping down the telephone.

'Yes and some of them are vile, too. Have you ever come across a man called Gripper?' Willow sighed inaudibly. Clearly she was not going to be able to ignore the hornets' nest she had stirred up in her own mind.

'Yes,' she said. 'But don't tell me you've had dealings with him?'

'Once, ages ago,' said Eve. 'He wanted me to represent him, and sent me a full synopsis and about five chapters of a novel he was writing. It was absolutely terrifying.'

Willow, remembering the fear that Gripper had induced in her, asked why. Eve said:

'He thought it was a literary novel as though "literariness" could excuse that kind of cruelty. It was about a woman married to a man she hated and the revenge she took on him for the things she had imagined he had done to her. Told from her point of view. . . . But all it told me was that Gripper knew nothing whatever about women. Made me feel sick, and very sorry indeed for his wife.'

Willow was silent for so long that Eve said:

'Are you still there, Cressida?'

'Yes. Sorry. I was just thinking of what a vile man he must be. Never mind. I haven't asked yet: how are you?'

'Fine, as always,' answered Eve. 'Pretty excited at the moment. I've just taken on a new client. She's young – very young; just out of university – but she has written a really rather remarkable novel. I even think it's quite a strong Booker possibility.'

'Why, is she foreign? Or is it one of those brilliantly written, excruciatingly boring, posey, storyless numbers?' said Willow with more than a hint of snappishness. 'Sorry, Eve. I didn't mean that. Cheap sneers are all too easy and lots of Booker winners are bloody good. I know that perfectly well. It's only jealousy.'

'You're probably tired, Cressida,' said Eve, sounding as nearly soothing as she ever did. 'And I've been boring on for far too long. Go and get a good night's sleep, and don't worry too much about the novel. They generally do get a bit sticky in the middle. You'll be all right.'

'Thanks, Eve. You're very good to put up with all my moans,' said Willow with rare insincerity. After all, she reasoned, she was paying Eve ten per cent of everything she earned. As that miserly thought entered her mind, she nearly laughed, remembering a story she had heard at a publishing party of an agent who always referred to his authors as 'those bastards who take ninety per cent of my income'. The amusement warmed her voice as she said goodbye to Eve and thanked her properly.

It was as she was replacing the receiver that Willow felt an inexplicable sense of panic. She looked down at the letters that Mrs Rusham had left beside the telephone answering machine and saw that they were not piled into the usual neat arrangement; but that could not account for her sudden terror. When she looked around her drawing room, trying to work out what could have caused it, she saw that there were other signs too. Mrs Rusham would never have left the sofa cushions overlapping as they were, and the fringe of the heavy silk rug was turned under at the corners as though someone had lifted the rug and then let it drop back carelessly.

Even more alarming was a very faint but quite revolting smell, which must have been what had first warned her subconscious mind of possible danger. Normally the flat smelled of fresh flowers, beeswax-and-turpentine furniture polish, Chanel No. 19, and just a little of whatever Mrs Rusham had been cooking. That evening there was something else as well: something slightly stale, acrid, and with overtones of some artificial sweetness. There was old tobacco smoke in it somewhere, Willow decided, male sweat and a faint hint of some kind of scent, possibly aftershave.

Dropping the envelope she had picked off the pile, she nerved herself to search the flat. Not surprisingly, there was no one there, but in each of the rooms except for the kitchen there was the same faint horrible smell as well as innumerable little signs to show that someone had opened, lifted and pushed aside her possessions as though looking for something.

As she went from room to room, Willow could not pretend that she had imagined either the smell or the small betraying untidinesses. Someone had been searching right through her flat. But the more she checked the more puzzled she became. Her floor safe was intact and when she opened it, she found all her jewellery there. In her writing room all her papers had obviously been rifled through, but they were still there and all in the order in which she had left them.

Willow grew more and more uncomfortable. Straightforward robbery would have been less upsetting, she thought, as she walked back into her bedroom for the second time. Even the bedcovers were slightly disarranged. She quickly stripped the bed and remade it with sheets from Mrs Rusham's linen cupboard, determined that she would not sleep in sheets touched by whoever had been there. She flung open the bedroom windows, too, to try to get rid of the smell, which was beginning to make her feel sick as well as afraid. That done, she went to check that all the other locks in the flat were intact and even pushed home the two big bolts on the front door as well as double locking the Chubbs.

At last, knowing that there was nothing else she could do to secure her flat, she went back to the drawing room to deal with her post, hoping that concentrating on something else would help her to get rid of the sense of outrage – and almost horror – that afflicted her whenever she thought of who might have invaded her home and fingered all her clothes and books and possessions.

None of the letters looked particularly interesting, but there was a large, brown-paper parcel under the table with one of her publisher's labels stuck on the top. The package seemed to promise more useful distraction from her fears, and so Willow pulled it out from under the table.

She broke an expensively varnished nail trying to get into the parcel and swore as she marched into the kitchen to get a knife. Wielding it as Madame Defarge might have done, she slit the tape and pulled apart the cardboard flaps that sprang free. The box proved to contain a large selection of glossy magazines with gossip columns and a heap of back numbers of the *Daily Mercury*. There was also a note.

Dear Cressida,

Goodness knows if these will be any help, but I thought it might amuse you to browse through them to get your background for the gossip-column book. I've taken the liberty of mentioning it at the editorial meeting and everyone else is just as excited as I am by the prospect. I've rung June, but she's out of London on some investigation. She's very reliable and I've asked her to ring me back as soon as poss. Happy hunting.

Love Nan.

Smiling at the characteristic style, which she had long ago learned disguised an extreme efficiency, Willow picked a pile of magazines off the heap and took it to one of the soft, grey-green sofas. Half an hour of frivolous magazines might help put her in the mood for sleep. Sipping at her cool cocoa, Willow flipped through the fashion pages of the magazine and browsed through the reviews for books and films and plays that had appeared nearly two years earlier. They quite amused her and when she had finished them she reached down for another magazine. But the lure of the diary section at the back of the first one proved too much for her determination to ignore the subject that seemed to loom all around her, and she looked through all eight pages of small square black-and-white photographs searching for Algy Endelsham's face.

There was no sign of him on the first of the diary pages, but she did come across a photograph of both Mr and Mrs Gripper, standing side by side. Eustace Gripper had his arm casually around the shoulders of his wife, who looked as though she had just tossed back her fine, fair hair and was looking sideways at him as though she really liked him. A consummate actress, perhaps? Willow wondered whether it might really be possible for someone to love two people so different from each other at the same time.

Then, almost to distract herself from that thought (which made her feel extraordinarily uncomfortable), she examined the background to the photograph. The occasion was some smart race meeting and the Grippers had been photographed just in front of their car. Both carried binoculars with clusters of cardboard shields attached to the straps to show that they were habitués of the racing scene. What intrigued Willow, however, was neither the pose nor the accessories they sported but the big burly figure of their chauffeur. The man was not in focus – because who, reading a society magazine, would want to identify a chauffeur? – but to Willow his outline and stance seemed familiar. She did not for one moment really believe that he was Albert, the minister's driver, but the similarities were surprising.

Shrugging, Willow turned the pages, looking for Algy's face. It cropped up often enough, at weddings, race meetings and even at one debutante dance. Willow was surprised enough by that to look more closely at the other photographs taken at the same dance.

'Dance held by the Lady Gnatche for the Hon. Sarah Gnatche,' read Willow, looking down at the young, bland faces on the glossy page. Sarah herself was there, posed against a large fan-shaped arrangement of roses and lilac between her mother and her half-brother. Willow found herself feeling a little sorry for the girl who stood there, looking rather plump and a little bit spotty but horribly expectant in her best frock. But in the end she found herself concentrating on the large and handsome figure of Algernon Endelsham, as though she could wrench out of the photograph some of the information she so badly needed.

Of course it told her nothing that she did not already know and she fell to imagining ways in which she could get hold of a copy of his will. That at least would tell her who or what Algy really cared for, quite apart from giving her the identity of the people who stood to gain from his death.

The woman to whom Willow had spoken at Somerset House had said that her only hope would be to ask the solicitors for a copy. Willow did not imagine that they would be likely to hand the will over to a complete stranger who had no official business with it, but she ought at least to try. Somehow she would have to find out who Algy's solicitors were and invent some reasonably plausible excuse to request a copy of the will. Apart from a straightforward request, which was likely to be denied, the only plans she could think of all involved crime, and Willow King was simply not equipped to burgle a solicitor's office, blackmail a partner or bribe a clerk.

Looking at her watch, she realised how late it was and told herself to go to bed, knowing that there was nothing she could usefully do that night. But she dreaded the thought of lying alone in the dark thinking of the people who had searched her flat – and why and for what. After five minutes' useless rationalisation, she obeyed her own instruction, but allowed herself to take two of the little yellow sleeping bombs her doctor had once prescribed for her.

9

THERE WERE many Tuesday mornings when Willow locked the door of the Chesham Place flat with a certain satisfaction. Although Tuesdays meant leaving behind the down-soft luxury of her writing life, they also meant leaving Richard's sometimes irritating behaviour, Mrs Rusham's overbearing efficiency, the requests of publisher and agent – and, of course, The Book. Whichever book it was, there were always moments during its writing when it seemed to be an enemy, dull but insatiably demanding of her time and effort. Sometimes the page or screen would mock Willow, telling her that she would never be able to write another word that anyone would want to read, that all her success had been no more than a fantasy. Such moments usually occurred as she reached the end of the first draft, when she was frequently tempted to tell Eve Greville that the whole thing would have to be thrown out because the plot was dreary, the characters absurd and the jokes the unfunniest she had ever read. Luckily, Eve was adept at nursing her over such obstacles and generally persuaded her to fill out, de-absurdify and tickle up the relevant parts of the book.

On that Tuesday, 29 November, it was not relief from a fugitive muse that she sought, but answers to four questions, the most important being: who had searched her flat and why? Less upsetting but probably more useful to her investigation into the minister's murder was the likelihood or otherwise of her half-formed suspicion that Algy might have uncovered some corruption at DOAP. The last was the irritating question of how to find out about the conditions of Algernon Endelsham's will.

Willow was quite clear that there was nothing 'Cressida Woodruffe' could do, short of persuading someone like Emma Gnatche to ring Algy's solicitors for her, and Willow knew too well that Emma would never do any such thing. There was nothing obvious she could do as Willow King, of course, but at least she would be within reach of Inspector Worth, who must already have the crucial information in his pocket.

She walked through Belgravia towards the bus stop, seeing nothing of the grand cream-coloured façades of the embassies and offices which she passed, but trying to think of ways in which she could get it from him without exposing her amateur investigation (which no doubt would merely make him laugh at her) or her real identity.

It seemed infinitely longer than four days since she had last been at DOAP, and she had almost forgotten that she had been arrogant enough to believe that she would have tracked down the murderer in that time, just as she had forgotten some of her first hostility to Inspector Worth. She was annoyed to discover that she badly wanted to see him, to tell him what little she had found out, to learn any useful facts he had accumulated, and to share with him all her wildest speculations.

Reminding herself, as she waited at the stop for a bus to take her across the river into Clapham, that she was Willow King who had brought the art of self-sufficiency to a pitch of perfection seldom achieved, she still found it hard to shake off the bundle of visceral emotions that were making her so uncharacteristically introspective and dependent. It was not until the tinny red bus was actually jerking and jolting its passengers across Vauxhall Bridge that she remembered how dangerous it would be to confide anything at all to Inspector Worth. Determined to regain her self-control, she reminded herself that she was in competition with him, and that it was still perfectly possible for her to find out who had done the murder without his help.

The proposition was a little hard for so rational a woman to believe, but by the time the bus had wandered all over the place and at last deposited her on the south side of Clapham Common, Willow thought that she had absorbed it and was once more recognisably the cool, unemotional star of the finance committee and terror of the fumbling and the foolish officers of DOAP.

She walked up Abbeville Road and let herself into her flat, dumping on the floor the small parachute bag she always took from one life to the other as camouflage in case she should meet any early-starting colleague before she was actually ready to face them.

An hour and a half later, changed into a suit and with a cup of instant coffee and a bowl of muesli and skimmed milk inside her, Willow walked out of the lift on the eighth floor of the DOAP tower. She was stopped at the door of her outer office by a uniformed constable, standing with his helmet in his hand.

'Would it be Miss King?' he asked in a soft South-London accent.

'It would,' she answered, smiling at his gentleness and extreme youth. 'What can I do for you, Officer?'

'The inspector would like a word, if you've a moment to spare, Miss King.'

'Certainly,' she answered, hoping that her voice had not given the sudden lurch that her insides had suffered. 'When?'

'Well, now Miss, actually,' said the constable, looking and sounding rather less gentle.

'Good heavens!' Willow said with entirely assumed cheerfulness. 'The inspector starts work early.' For some reason he must have decided to test her alibi and discovered that Aunt Agatha had no existence outside Willow's imagination. She felt cold all over. Then she saw a sudden shaft of light. 'I don't suppose poor Mr Englewood has been dragged this early from his home?'

'Oh yes, Miss,' said the constable, opening the lift door for Willow and putting out the light in her mind. 'He'll be there to see you're not pushed into saying anything you don't want or shouldn't say.'

With that exasperating reassurance echoing all round her, Willow found it hard to smile properly at Mr Englewood when he stood up to greet her. But she made herself do it, and began to feel as though she were looking at him for the first time. She wondered at the lines in the skin around his eyes and nose. Had it always been like that or was the strain of listening for any hidden brutalities in the inspector's interrogations beginning to exhaust him? Willow realised that her mind and feelings really were more disordered than she had believed when she found herself thinking that Englewood looked startlingly familiar to her and yet almost as though he were a complete stranger. The flesh that veiled his cheekbones seemed slacker than usual, and his grey eyes were dragged at the corners as though with anxiety.

'Good morning, Miss King. I'm sorry to drag you away from all the urgent matters on your desk when you've only just got back to it.' The sound of the deep, noncommittal voice of the policeman brought Willow's contemplation of the establishments officer to an abrupt halt. She swung round and nodded with modified politeness to the inspector. The vitality of his expression and the extraordinarily healthy-looking whites of his eyes made the contrast between him and the establishments officer complete, and

Willow rediscovered all the hostility she thought she had lost. She bitterly resented the policeman's power, of course, but there was more to her hostility than that, although she would have sacrificed a year's royalties before she would have admitted it. She did, however, admit to herself that it would have been comforting to have been able to tell him about the searching of her Belgravia flat. But she could not do that while Englewood was listening to her every word.

Inspector Worth smiled at her. He was standing at his desk, taller than Willow but dwarfed by his magnificent sergeant, and dressed in a plain suit of such conservative cut that its quality was hardly noticeable; but it did much to disguise the width of his shoulders and splendid bearing.

Pretending that she would have to make an inventory of his clothes as a way of controlling her feelings about him, Willow made a mental list of the grey worsted suit, plain white shirt, dull navy tie with some small unintelligible emblem woven into it. She could not see his shoes and socks, because of the desk, but as he gestured for her to sit down, his cuff rode up a little way and she saw his watch. For some reason it seemed incongruously personal. Willow would have expected some big, masculine-looking watch on a metal bracelet, but in fact it was an exceedingly old-fashioned rectangular gold watch on a worn, brown-leather strap. With her spectacles on she could see that the face of the watch was worn too, and its small black roman numerals badly rubbed.

'Miss King?' he said and for once there was a hint of individuality in his voice; it had warmed up a fraction. Instinctively she looked at him and discovered that his mouth looked friendly and his dark eyes smiled. Only the broken nose and firm, rounded chin still looked formidable. She smiled back despite her antagonism.

'That's quite all right,' she said, at last answering his first question. 'It's obviously something urgent. What can I tell you?' she went on, sounding to her own ears at least quite calm.

146

'Please sit down, Miss King. We've fixed up a coffee machine now: would you like a cup?'

Willow nodded, not trusting herself to speak any more than necessary as she took in the new courtesy and apparent concern for herself. The young constable poured coffee into a thick, ugly mug, offered milk and sugar and then handed it to her. Willow thanked him, glad to hear that her voice still did not shake. Gripping the mug and grateful for the warmth that was slowly reaching her hands through the thick earthenware, she faced the inspector.

'Now, Miss King, you do understand that in a murder enquiry we have to fossick about in the private affairs of a great many people, ninety-nine per cent of which turn out to be entirely irrelevant to the enquiry, don't you?'

Now it's coming, said Willow to herself. Is there anything I can say to Englewood, anything I can offer him, to make him keep it to himself? And what of the constable? What if his mother or – worse – his girlfriend were soon to be seen reading the latest Cressida Woodruffe: would he ever be able to resist boasting of his discovery that the glamorous rich author is really the plain, feared spinster of this dullest of all government departments?

'Yes, I quite understand that,' she said in a small, cold voice and waited.

'Good. That being so, I have to ask you some questions about your relations with the deceased.' He paused, as though he expected her to protest. Willow, hardly understanding that she had been reprieved for the moment at least, said:

'Naturally I shall answer any questions you feel that you have to ask, but might I perhaps speak to you alone? Presumably anything that I can tell you will remain confidential unless you find that you need it in some eventual prosecution.'

Inspector Worth looked across her navy-blue shoulder at the establishments officer, who got out of his chair and came to stand in front of her. She concentrated on

147

the details of his suit, which was made of hairy lovat
tweed quite inappropriate for a London office, although
it did go with his brown country brogues and the cravat
he wore again at the neck of his thick checked shirt.

'Miss King,' he said with unfamiliar formality, 'surely
you do not think that I would pass on anything that is
said during interviews such as this?' His tone was of such
personally injured honour that Willow smiled rather sickly
and assured him that she had had no such doubts.

'I can promise you that anything you say will remain
confidential as far as I am concerned,' he said as he
retreated to his chair. 'I am here only for your protection.'

'Thank you,' said Willow and looked back at the inspector, squaring her shoulders.

'Very well,' he said. 'I have heard from various sources
that you were the object of the deceased's attentions – if I
may call them that – and I wondered whether you could tell
me the story from your own point of view.'

'It is a very simple story, Inspector,' Willow said, her
voice quite steady. 'Mr Endelsham did indeed – what was
your phrase? Ah yes, make me the object of his attentions.
It started about two years ago, perhaps a little more, and
I think that by the following May he had understood that
I genuinely did not wish to be such an object and was
not merely being coy and trying to inflame him. Having
grasped that, he eventually ceased to single me out.'

'Ah,' murmured the inspector, fiddling with the pencil
in his hand. 'May I ask why you did not want his
"attentions"?'

'Well really, Inspector!' snapped Willow, banging her
thick mug down on the desk in front of her and spraying
coffee over some papers that were lying there. 'I fail to
see what that has to do with your investigation. But perhaps
you are at one with the entire population of this office
in thinking that if a man as goodlooking, famous and
well-off as Algernon Endelsham should start to pursue a
middle-aged unattached woman like me, she should be

148

so dumbfounded with gratitude that she would lie on the floor like a spaniel with all four legs in the air.'

Willow was yet more enraged when she looked furiously into his face and saw that he was laughing at her. He shook his head as he caught her eye.

'No, Miss King, I do not think any such thing. I merely wanted to know what it was about him that did not attract you so that I can get some insight into the man he was. I did not know him and in order to find my way through this investigation I need to find out what he was like. All right?'

At that appeal to reason, Willow's flaming anger cooled a little. After all, the inspector was doing no more than she herself had tried to do in the five days since her last encounter with him. It was an unsettling realisation to make.

'I beg your pardon. The reaction of my colleagues has caused me to be a little jumpy on the subject and would itself have constituted a perfectly good reason to avoid any close relationship with the minister.'

'I can understand that,' said Inspector Worth seriously. 'But the way you have said it suggests that you had other reasons as well.' Willow laughed a little and was glad to see him smile back at her.

'I had indeed. There was the unsuitability of the whole idea. I cannot imagine anything more prejudicial to the smooth running of the department than any kind of romance between a minister and a relatively senior official. Had I wished to encourage the minister, I should have had to resign, I imagine, and quite frankly my career is a great deal more important to me than a few months of doubtful felicity as the mistress of such a man.'

'Such a man,' repeated the Inspector. 'What kind of man?' Forgetting that there were any other people in the room, Willow spoke to the inspector as to an equal, quite forgetting that she had had gentler thoughts about Algy and perhaps even mixing him up in her disordered mind with the character she had invented for Eustace Gripper.

'The kind of man who knows who he is and where he is in the pecking order only by constantly reassuring himself of his sexual power over the women he meets,' she said. 'Most of the women the minister encountered were only too obviously drawn to his looks, money and success and he therefore had no need to impress them. Unlike many of my sex I do not find such things aphrodisiac. On the other hand, I greatly enjoyed the minister's company and found his attitude to the work of the department and his incisive intelligence highly invigorating. I can only suppose that the combination of my sincere admiration for his mind and complete lack of interest in his perhaps more obvious attractions made him wish to see whether he could break down my resistance.' Willow knew that she had fallen into the style of some of the more pompous of her colleagues and almost expected the inspector to ask her to have her statement typed and signed in triplicate.

'I see,' was all he said, drinking some of his own coffee, which must have been quite cold by then. 'I have come across men like that, and it is interesting that the deceased was of their fraternity. Do you know whether there were any other women in the department who had a similar experience?'

'I am afraid I do not,' said Willow, relaxing a little now that he seemed to have left the subject of Algy's attempted seduction. 'But I do not partake of the gossip of this place and since I work only part time I might easily miss something that the rest of my colleagues know intimately.' There she was sounding idiotically pompous again. But with luck, she thought, the very dullness and arrogance of her phrasing might bore the policeman so much that he would decide that she was a nonentity.

'He seems to have had the knack of arousing deep emotions in almost everyone he came up against: devotion from some, considerable antipathy from others,' suggested Inspector Worth.

Almost unbearably tempted to tell the inspector all the things she had learned about the dead man since they had last met, Willow knew that there was little she would have enjoyed more than a real talk with him. She could have told him about Gripper and described her other suspicions and asked him everything she needed to fill in the gaps in her knowledge. Opening her mouth to ask him whether he had even considered Eustace Gripper as a possible suspect, she suddenly remembered who and where she was. She hastily shut her mouth again, shocked by her reactions to the policeman's rational kindness.

'Were you angry with the minister?' he asked suddenly. At that short question Willow stiffened again and forgot her wish to have a really good talk with him.

'I was extremely irritated that so intelligent a man should be so damned silly, since you ask. But personally angry? No,' she said, sipping her coffee.

'Not even that – as I think you said earlier – your colleagues were all discussing the affair amongst themselves?' suggested Inspector Worth carefully. Willow smiled.

'I was exceedingly angry with them,' she said. 'But that was for their unwarranted if understandable assumption that I had succumbed to the red roses and flattering attention, been, as it were, enjoyed and then discarded. Their gloating so-called sympathy was what angered me, not the cause of it.'

'I see. Well, thank you very much,' said Inspector Worth getting out of his chair. Willow looked a little startled, but since it was clear that he was dismissing her she too rose.

'Not at all,' she said automatically. She knew that there was going to be no easy way to ask him about Algy's will and so all she said was, 'Please let me know if there is anything else that I can tell you.'

'I shall indeed. Thank you again,' he said. As she walked

past Mr Englewood towards the door, he too stood up.

'Well done, Willow,' he said. She saw that there was a most curious expression in his tired, grey eyes and she had the strange feeling that he was commending not her performance in front of the police but her determined chastity in the face of the minister's pursuit. For some peculiar reason that seemed to be almost more insulting than everyone else's view that she had been used and discarded. The intensity in Michael Englewood's eyes and voice bothered her and, since there seemed to be no suitable answer to his compliment, she merely smiled coldly and left the interrogation room.

Safely in the lift once the doors had closed, she leaned back against the stainless steel wall, let her head fall back and breathed deeply. Her idiocy in making herself compete with Inspector Worth seemed worse than ever before. As Richard had annoyingly warned her at the beginning, the police had endless resources and back-up teams, from accurate information to forensic scientists, with which to find the murderer. She had nothing except the information she could disentangle from the DOAP gossip and her own powers of analysis and imagination. Self-pity (the cardinal sin in Dr William King's household in Newcastle) threatened to engulf her.

Recognising the danger, Willow straightened her head, rubbed her eyes and said out loud: 'Well at least Aunt Agatha's safe for a little longer, thank God.'

The steel doors parted with their usual soft swishing noise on the eighth floor and she straightened her shoulders and walked into the outer office to confront her staff. Roger's pale eyes were alight as she walked towards his desk.

'Well, how did it go, Miss King?' he asked, clearly as avid for sensation as ever. 'Did that terrifying ex-SAS man give you the third degree?'

'SAS, Roger? What are you talking about?' Willow said over her shoulder as she put out a hand for the papers

Barbara was offering her. She had quite forgotten the profile she had read in the Sunday newspaper. 'I'm glad to see you're better,' she added noticing that the scars on his face had almost disappeared.

'Thank you, Miss King. My colds never last that long, though they're beastly while they are there. But the SAS, Miss King: the inspector downstairs used to be in it; rather a hero in Ireland, they say. But, you know, officers aren't allowed to stay very long in the SAS and he didn't fancy ordinary regimental soldiering again after all the high-jinks and so he left and joined the police.'

'Goodness!' Willow found that her uncharacteristic tensions were dissipating slightly under the ordinary conditions of her office. 'How did you discover all that?'

'Roger doesn't ever need to discover anything,' said Scottish Barbara in her usual caustic tone. 'Little pockets of information open themselves out in front of him and tiny drops of gossip just drop into his flower-like ears. Don't they, Roger? And then he just can't resist passing them on.'

'Do they, Roger?' said Willow in a tone of exaggerated interest. 'Then you can probably answer something that was exercising Barbara and me last week.' Roger looked happily expectant, and Willow drove all thoughts of embarrassment out of her mind in the interests of her enquiry.

'The messengers seem to have been reading about the minister's private life in the *Daily Mercury* and to have formed the impression that the minister's sexual orientation was not of the most obvious kind.' As Willow spoke, she could have kicked herself for both the pomposity and the ambiguity of the words she had chosen. But when she saw Roger's face quiver and become suffused with a deep-tomato-coloured blush, she wished that she had never embarked on the subject.

'Never mind,' she said at once. 'I'm sure you know no more than we, and no doubt that dreadful rag had it all wrong.' Roger seemed to make a tremendous effort to pull himself together. Turning away from Willow to face Scottish Barbara, he said:

'There's more than one secret I've never passed on, Barbara.'

'Really, Roger?' she said, her voice at its most Morningside, 'and what might they be?'

'Well, honestly! If I told you that, they'd not be secret any longer,' said Roger, shrugging. Then he saw that she was laughing at him, and added: 'Besides, I've never noticed that you're bored with the things I tell you, Barbara. Have you, Miss King?' He did look at Willow then, and she thought that there was a pleading expression in his eyes. She was not sure whether he wanted protection from the Scottish girl, whose sarcasm could sometimes get a little vicious, or whether he was begging her not to talk any more about the minister's possible preferences.

'No indeed,' said Willow, wondering whether she had been wrong about Gripper and all the rest of her suspicions. Could Roger really have had anything to do with the death? Could those horribly deep scratches have been driven into his face by Algy's scrabbling hands? Telling herself that the proposition was ludicrous, she went on: 'But we all have more than enough work to do to listen to any more of them now. I'll deal with these, Barbara. Thank you. Roger, bring in that report as soon as you've finished it, will you?'

'Yes, Miss King,' he said, settling to his keyboard once more.

Willow shut the door of her inner office, ready to be grateful for the familiarity of it all, the heaps of crested paper on her desk bearing their no doubt irritating minutes from the PUS or the junior minister and their impossible drafts of answers to parliamentary questions from her staff. But as soon as she leaned back against the door she had just shut, she was jerked out of her growing relaxation.

154

'That damned smell,' she whispered as she caught the faint cigarette-and-sweat-and-aftershave stench that had so frightened her in Chesham Place. All thoughts of Roger's scratches were pushed out of her mind.

Trying to tell herself that the smell was some unreal product of her mood – some symptom of paranoia, perhaps – Willow carefully examined her office. After even the most cursory search it would have been horribly clear that she should no longer doubt the reality of the smell. Drawers that were usually firmly closed were slightly open, papers that had been neatly stacked in trays were slightly askew, and there were scratches around the keyholes of the only two locks in the room. The safe in which she kept most of her confidential papers was impregnable, but the bottom left-hand drawer of her desk had been broken into and left unlocked and unlockable.

Despite her horror of the idea of people searching her rooms – and her terror of someone apparently having connected Willow King and Cressida Woodruffe – she allowed herself a small smile at the thought of her bottom drawer: all she kept there was her London Atlas, a box of sulphur-free dried apricots in case of desperate hunger, and her emergency supply of tampons.

10

WILLOW sat in the ruined sanctuary of her inner office, thinking that the stresses of Algy's death and her investigation of it must be turning her brain. It simply was not possible that the person who had searched her Chesham Place flat could also have found his way into her office at DOAP. There was no one (except of course Richard, who did not count) who could have connected the formidable spinster of DOAP with the absurdly rich Cressida Woodruffe, she told herself, and then remembered with a sickeningly deep intake of breath her feeling that someone had been watching her at Sloane Square tube station on the night of her last weekly transformation. Had someone actually followed her from DOAP that night?

Willow dropped her head in her hands. Rationally she knew perfectly well that it did not really matter if she were to be unmasked – however awkward or embarrassing that would be – but the idea of someone creeping behind her, cheating his way in to her flat, going through all her most personal possessions and lying in wait to expose her was horrible.

Quite apart from the fact that such an invasion of her much-cherished privacy must have a bearing on the case, Willow knew that she could not ignore it. Trying to keep calm, she thought about the people who might have wanted to follow her and expose her, but her analytical talents seemed to have deserted her. With the faint, but nauseatingly familiar smell of her adversary in her nostrils, all she could think of was the sinister intensity in Michael Englewood's eyes and voice as he had commended her so little time earlier, of her unprecedented meeting with him on the steps of DOAP the previous week and his extraordinary concern for her.

Without stopping to think any more, Willow flung open the door to her outer office, saying sharply, 'Barbara!'

'Yes, Willow?' said the young Scottish woman, sounding a little surprised at the unusual urgency of her chief's voice. But Willow ignored her, having seen Roger staring at her, his mouth open in surprise. At his side stood the bulky, threatening figure of Albert, the minister's driver.

'And what on earth are you doing here, Albert?' she demanded, wishing that she could get away from the smell of the man who had searched her home and her office.

'He. . . er. . . he just brought up a message, Miss King,' said Roger, patently terrified.

'Oh yes,' said Willow, heavily sarcastic. She held out her right hand for the message and, to her considerable chagrin, the driver handed her a standard DOAP brown envelope.

'I beg your pardon, Albert,' she said formally. 'I'm so busy at the moment I don't know whether I'm coming or going. Thank you for bringing it,' she added, far more ashamed of her fear than of the sarcasm in which she had indulged herself.

'It's my job to do what I'm told, Miss,' he said, with slightly less than his usual rudeness. 'And while the police need to keep me hanging around like this, I've been turned into a bleeding messenger. I'll be off then – unless there's an answer.'

Willow shook her head and retreated to her own room. The message proved to be a complete anti-climax, being no more than one of the establishments officer's standard memos about getting submissions for the annual promotion boards to him in good time.

There was a faint echo of the vile, stale smell hanging about her desk, which made her screw up the envelope and hurl it into the wastepaper basket. The uncharacteristically savage gesture did nothing about the smell, but it served to relieve some of her feelings of powerlessness.

Just as Willow was putting Mr Englewood's note in her filing basket, the door of her office opened and Barbara put her dark head into the room.

'Did you want me, Willow?' she asked.

'What?' said Willow, raising her head. 'Oh, yes, come in please.'

Barbara sat down opposite Willow's desk and looked interested. Willow suppressed a smile.

'I just wanted to ask you who had been up here while I was away?' she said, considerably calmer then than she had been when she had erupted into Barbara's office.

'Let me think,' said the girl irritatingly. 'The usual batch of messengers, the establishments officer. . .'

'Why?' said Willow sharply. Barbara shrugged.

'He quite often looks in when you're away – keeps Roger up to the mark anyway; that man has an awful tendency to skip off when there's no one to check up on him – and unfortunately he's not at all afraid of me,' she said.

'But Mr Englewood was not in this actual room, surely?' said Willow.

'Oh no. I didn't realise you meant in here. I've been in – obviously – and Roger. . . oh, yes; yesterday I was just

158

coming back from lunch when I found Albert emerging through your door. He'd been sent with a message, he said, and didn't like to leave it in the outer office where anyone might find it. The message was real – it was that confidential one from the PUS, which I didn't open. I didn't cross-examine Albert, I'm afraid. I was just relieved that he'd been while Roger was out,' Barbara said, puzzling Willow.

'But why?'

'Oh, he seems to terrify Roger. . . he's always even less able to work after Albert's been in,' she said, apparently not finding anything odd in the statement.

'I see,' said Willow. 'Thank you, Barbara.'

The administration trainee left and Willow found it quite hard to believe that it had been Albert of all people who had searched her office, let alone followed her or got into Chesham Place. He certainly disliked her, and she could well imagine him capable of breaking and entering; but he just did not seem intelligent enough to find out who she really was – or to have got into the flat without actually breaking in.

Having reached that conclusion, it was not hard for Willow to imagine circumstances in which Albert might be used by someone much cleverer. Remembering her speculations about a possible pensions fraud being run from the department, she thought that Albert might well have been retained for his muscle and aggression by someone more sophisticated or intelligent who had organised such a scheme.

Tapping her blotter with a piercingly sharp lead pencil, Willow was afraid that she could easily put a name to someone who might have done so: Michael Englewood.

His determination to sit in on all the police interviews with the staff had always struck her as a little excessive (as well as being highly inconvenient for her). Could it have been because he had been afraid someone might say something that would betray his fraud?

Ideas began to fall into place like pieces in a jigsaw puzzle: there was Michael Englewood's apparent satisfaction with his cul-de-sac of a job; his quick turnover of secretaries, which Willow had blamed on his self-confessed temper and inability to tolerate gossip and giggles, but which might have been designed to get rid of anyone bright enough to work out what he was up to; his determined solitariness; the feeling she was increasingly coming to trust that he had a great deal of anger tucked away somewhere behind his mild public persona. Did they all add up to the picture of an intelligent man who had somehow gone wrong and chosen to take his power and money from the perpetration of a widespread fraud instead of through ordinary career success? Or was she simply letting Cressida's imagination run away with her?

Could a man like that have decided that she herself was a threat to him, followed her, discovered the secret of her double-identity and ransacked her papers and possessions to find something he could use to stop her betraying him? Somehow the necessity of finding out who had murdered Algernon Endelsham was beginning to take second place in Willow's mind to her determination to find out who was trying to expose her, although they were likely to be the same person.

Knowing that there was little she could achieve by speculation while her imagination was running riot, Willow deliberately tried to sedate her teeming brain with work and turned to her in-tray. By the time she had dealt with her incoming letters, read the minutes that had accumulated on her desk since her departure the previous Thursday, corrected the drafts of answers to various parliamentary questions that concerned finance, and absorbed the agenda and papers for the weekly meeting of the finance committee, she had regained enough calm to get on with her double investigation. Summoning Roger, she first dictated the day's letters and minutes and then asked him whether he had yet been interviewed by the inspector.

'Why yes, Miss King,' he said looking at her as though she were mad. After all, he had already told her about his interrogation in exhausting detail the previous week.

'Oh yes, I'd forgotten,' she said carelessly. 'And was someone from estabs sitting in on your interview as well?'

'Yes indeed, the under secretary himself. To protect us all, I suppose, from Inspector Worth and his merry men. You'd never have thought he cared so much for us all, would you now?'

'Mr Englewood? Why on earth not? I've always thought he was particularly concerned with the well-being of members of the department – or at least as far as it affected the performance of their duties,' said Willow, remembering Barbara's comments on the under secretary's visits to their office.

Roger wriggled a little and then admitted that Mr Englewood was indeed concerned about the health of his staff and their ability to work.

'But,' he went on, his voice changing from that of misunderstood subordinate to privileged gossip, 'I'd have thought he'd run a mile rather than get really involved with any one of us. He's a very solitary sort of man, wouldn't you say?'

'I've never given it a thought,' answered Willow, trying not to show her amusement at Roger's frank relish for tittle-tattle.

'Well he is – ever since his wife ran off with that man to America.' Roger looked expectantly across the desk, clearly hoping for some questions about the wife and her mysterious American, but Willow was too experienced to allow herself to be sidetracked and so Roger had to go on without encouragement. 'So now he lives alone. And he's only interested in chess and crime novels – oh and fishing on his holidays.'

'He can't be that solitary if he plays chess,' Willow protested.

'Oh yes, poor man, he plays it on a pocket computer, you see. Takes it everywhere with him, so that he can play on the train and places and never have to talk to anyone else.'

'Oh. . . . Poor man indeed. But he must have some friends whom even the department doesn't know about.'

'Quite likely, Miss King. After all, he's not nearly as old as he looks. I've often wondered why he wanted to dress and present himself as though he were in his late fifties. But in fact he's even younger than me.'

'Really,' said Willow, genuinely startled. 'How old is he?'

'Forty-two,' said Roger shortly and Willow could not think why he should be irritable until she realised that he liked to think no one knew his own age.

'Good heavens! Well he's very self-contained, so I suppose even if he is lonely he can deal with it,' she said, hoping for some more of Roger's inexhaustible supply of gossip.

'He's quite a good hater,' said Roger slyly looking at her as though wondering how far he could go. 'He hated the poor minister at any rate.'

'You are a proper fountain of information, aren't you, Roger. How on earth did you discover that?' said Willow, finding the possible confirmation of her wild theories seriously disturbing. 'I thought it was only the PUS who really loathed him.' Roger wriggled in self-conscious pleasure and leaned a little closer to the desk.

'I've never told anyone else this, Miss King. But I know I'm right. The establishments officer hated him even more than the permanent secretary; I could swear to that in a court of law.'

'You might have to,' said Willow drily and then cursed herself silently as she thought she might have frightened him off. But Roger's interest in other people was far too intense to be daunted by a little thing like that. 'Go on, tell me. I dare you. How did you discover the dark secrets of his soul, poor man? And why, come to think of it, have you kept that very juicy secret from everyone else?'

Roger's entire face and scalp suddenly blushed vividly again under his thinning grey-blond hair. He shifted in his chair, picked up his shorthand notebook, fiddled with the pages and then put it down again.

'Well,' he began in a slightly weedling tone. 'Do you remember that evening when I had to retype that fantastically wordy finance report – the one that was seventy-five pages long, full of figures and statistics and had to be done in two days flat along with all the ordinary work of the office? With all that tabulating?'

'Yes,' answered Willow, pretending not to notice the still-warm resentment in his voice. 'About a month ago, wasn't it? I remember.'

'Well obviously I had to stay late to get it done.' He paused, but yet again she let go the opportunity of sympathising with him for the way she had been overworking him. 'And, well. . . You see. . .'

'Come on Roger, out with it. What happened?' Willow asked, really curious by then.

'Well I didn't have enough of the right paper. I ran out on about page ten.' He blushed again and Willow, understanding his embarrassment, refrained from reminding him of how often she had begged him to check his stationery cupboard regularly and restock it in good time. The number of productive hours wasted in his hunts for last-minute supplies of paper, ink, carbons, ribbons and so on had often driven her to say things that made him waste even more time in self-justification, recrimination and moaning about his status.

'And I knew that I'd never get any from normal channels at that time – I mean, it was after six. . . well after. So, I'd been down in the establishments office earlier in the day and I'd seen a whole stack of boxes of just the right kind of paper next to Valerie's desk.' He broke off, still blushing, and Willow decided to help him out.

'And so you thought you'd go and borrow some. Very sensible.' The flush died and he smiled brilliantly at her.

'Just so. It was the only sensible thing to do.'

The next part of his narrative – or confession – became sticky and Willow had to squeeze it out of him like the last bits of toothpaste from the very bottom of the tube, but in the end he told her that just as he was purloining a box of paper from the top of the stack, he heard angry voices from the under secretary's office. Being Roger, of course, he simply could not leave without discovering what was going on.

'Yes, Roger, I can quite understand that,' said Willow, desperately trying to keep all irony and even amusement out of her voice. She knew that she had failed as she watched Roger's face close up. Saying nothing, she waited for his need to talk to assert itself. In the end, amid many conscious looks and evasions, he told her that the two men were having the most vicious-sounding argument about betrayal.

'Betrayal?' repeated Willow, wondering whether she really had stumbled on proof of some scandal of corruption and blackmail. 'What was being betrayed? No, wait. Who were they?'

'Why the minister and Mr Englewood, of course,' he answered, wide eyed.

'There's no "of course" about it, Roger. I'm not a mind-reader. All right, so now tell me: who and what were being betrayed?'

'I'm not totally sure,' confessed Roger. 'Sometimes one of them must have turned away from the door or something because they kept becoming hard to hear.'

Willow suppressed the comment that rose to her mind and merely smiled, she hoped sympathetically. 'But you must have heard some of it,' she said at last.

'Well yes. One of them kind of hissed, with the most appalling savagery, "If you think that I'm going to throw away everything I've ever worked for just to allow you the comfort of security in your fraudulent character, you've another thing coming." I was that frightened, Miss King, I call tell you.'

'Golly,' said Willow, taking refuge in the kind of school-girl slang in which she had never indulged at school.

'Exactly,' said Roger with heavy emphasis on the second syllable. 'Wasn't it frightful?'

'But which of them was it who said it?'

'The tricky thing is, Miss King, that I don't know,' said Roger putting his notebook down on her desk as he leaned confidingly towards her. Willow had to suppress her own impulse to lean forward too.

'Come on, Roger, you're holding out on me. You must have known which of them was talking,' she said, regaining a little of her traditional crispness.

'Honestly I don't. I suppose it was because whoever he was, he was half-whispering – and in that very vicious tone of voice which we've none of us actually heard from either of them. At least I had never heard it.'

'No, I suppose not.' Willow glanced down at her watch just then and was horrified to see the time. 'We really can't sit here all morning like this, Roger. I've a mass of things to do and you've the report for the PUS, which I don't suppose is finished.' Her voice lifted at the end of the sentence, turning her statement into a question, and Roger gave the persecuted little sigh he always delivered when she chased him for work.

'Actually no, Miss King, not quite. But it won't take long now. Would you like a cup of tea?'

'That would be excellent,' she said and turned in her chair to pick up a file lying at the edge of her desk. Roger accepted his dismissal and went off to make a pot of tea.

Willow was left to face the fact that she had enough support for her suspicions to justify some real investigation into Michael Englewood. Reminding herself that she already had more than enough to do and that it was far more important to discover who had murdered the minister than whether the establishments officer was making money from some fraud, she seized the opportunity of Roger's absence to do the one thing she still wanted to do for the original investigation. It was important, she still considered, to establish the identity of Endelsham's heirs.

She reached for her telephone and dialled the number of Emma Gnatche's flat.

'Hello?' came a voice, which might have belonged to anyone of Emma's background and education.

'Is that you, Emma?' she asked brightly and then blessed the powers that be for her soundproofed office as she announced herself. 'It's Cressida here.'

'How are you?' said Emma, and Willow wondered whether there was really some constraint in Emma's voice or whether she had imagined it.

'Fine. Look, Emma, your brother kindly took me out to dinner last night and I ought to drop him a post-card to thank him, but absurdly I never asked for his address. Could you give it to me?'

'Oh, of course,' said Emma, sounding relieved. She dictated it, and then said curiously: 'Did you enjoy the dinner, Cressida?'

'Well,' said Willow, drawing out the vowel sound. 'The food was delicious.' Emma laughed, and Willow was emboldened to embark on the question she had really rung up to ask. She had spent some time trying to invent an excuse but in the end had decided that Emma would probably not ask her for one.

'Emma, I've been wondering: do you know who poor Algy's solicitors were?' she said rather tersely, hoping to jolt Emma into answering.

'But why. . .?' said the nice child, before breaking off. After a moment's silence, she went on: 'Yes, actually; I sometimes had to write to them for him. They're Feathers, Fox and Co.'

'Marvellous, Emma. Thank you,' said Willow, preparing to ask which partner of the firm dealt with Algy's affairs when she heard the sounds of Roger's return.

'Cressida? Are you still there?'

'What? Oh, yes, sorry, Emma. There's someone at the door. I'll have to go. See you soon. 'Bye.'

She put the telephone down just as Roger reappeared in the doorway. He gently laid the thick white office cup and saucer on her desk, murmuring:

'It's Earl Grey, Miss King: I thought you ought to have a proper cup of tea. Is that all right?'

'Very kind of you, Roger,' she answered, apparently immersed in a file that lay on her desk beside the telephone. He tried again to put off the dreadful moment when he would have to get back behind his keyboard.

'The poor minister always used to say that I made a better cup of Earl Grey than anyone else he'd ever met.' The hint of real sadness in his voice reached Willow's concentrating brain even before the sense of what he had said. Leaving the file open, she pulled down her spectacles and looked across the desk at him.

'Of course,' she said. 'I'd forgotten how often he happened to be passing this office at tea time when he first came here. You must have got to know him quite well.'

'He always had time to pass a friendly word; not like some I could mention, who seem to think one's no more than a piece of furniture just because one's only a clerical officer.'

'There, there,' said Willow lightly, knowing full well that Roger enjoyed a moan about his status almost as much as the opportunity to pass on gossip. She pushed the spectacles back up her big nose with one unpainted fingernail. 'I hope my differences with him didn't mean that you were too badly deprived of his company.'

Willow was repaid for her moment of sarcasm when Roger gave her a pitying little smile.

'Oh,' he said happily but with a self-conscious shrug of his plump shoulders, 'I still managed to get my fair share of him. Didn't you know? He occasionally used to drop in for a cup of my tea on the days when you were with your poor aunt. He'd send Barbara off for something and we'd settle down to a cuppa and a little chat as often as not.'

'Goodness,' was all Willow could think of to say, remembering Roger's earlier blushes – and the scratches on his face.

'In fact, he was here the afternoon before it happened. That's why the terrifying inspector said he'd probably have to send for me again. But,' he added with a sure instinct for a good exit line, 'I've far too much typing to do and you're far too busy to listen to chit-chat, so I'd better leave you to it.' He walked to the door and Willow smothered a smile of appreciation at his tactics.

'Oh by the way, the T. A. stands for Thomas Angus, always known as Tom. Tom Worth – the inspector, you know. . . worth a lot I'd say, wouldn't you, Miss King?' Roger threw artistically over his shoulder as he reached the door.

'Be off with you,' said Willow laughing out loud at last. It dawned on her that perhaps it was Roger's facility for amusing her that had made her like him and put up with his maddening dilatoriness and sloppiness for so long. That and his basic kindness, she added more charitably to herself. Perhaps it had been the same things that had drawn Algy to him, she thought. The minister had clearly valued the kindness in Emma Gnatche. Unfortunately, Willow could not entirely suppress the far less charitable – and perhaps more realistic – thought that Algy might have enjoyed basking in the uncritical admiration of people so far subordinate to him that they would never to able to constitute a threat to him.

As soon as Roger had shut the door behind him, she stopped pretending to read her file and swung her swivel chair round so that she could look out of her window across the common. It looked an innocent place in all the clarity of the winter sun, full of children and nannies, bicyclists, solitary but perfectly respectable-looking men; young blond women (all looking rather like Emma Gnatche and Mrs Gripper) dressed in wellingtons and waxed cotton jackets pretending they were in the country as they walked their black labradors, and a few mysteriously hurrying figures.

Where could they be going? Willow asked herself. She got out of her chair to have a better look down at them all. Perhaps a few of them were walking from offices on the southside of the common to restaurants in Lavender Hill or Battersea Rise, but surely such business lunchers were more likely to drive? It would be a longish walk to cross the common. Yet again she asked herself what on earth the immaculately dressed minister could have been doing picking his way across the muddy grass in the pitch dark coldness of that November evening. The bland, innocent-looking grass and trees and paths and ponds could tell her nothing and after a few minutes' staring, she sat down again and reached for the large-scale London map she always kept in the bottom drawer of her desk.

The paths that criss-crossed the common were clearly marked and, she remembered, as clearly lit at night. If Algy had been seized with a sudden desire for air after the stuffiness of the office tower, he could perfectly well have stuck to the paths and been reasonably safe. Or, safer still, he could have walked along the pavements that circled the common. As she stared at the black-and-white patchwork of roads, open spaces and railway lines, her eye was caught by the black mass of Clapham Junction railway station on the left of the double-page spread and she remembered what the tramp had told her about the washing man.

Could anyone who had just battered a man to death walk through the lit and crowded streets to a bustling railway station undetected? Willow wished that she had been able to ask the inspector about the body. Would there have been much blood? Would the assailant have been badly marked? Could a man of Algy's height and bulk have succumbed to such a battering without at least bruising his attacker? Surely not. For a sickening moment she thought again of Roger's scarred face, the scars freshly pink on the day after the murder; but then she consoled herself with the conviction that Roger would never knowingly hurt a fly – and in any case must have weighed at least three stones less than the magnificent Algy. Surely, if Roger had launched some maniacal and frenzied attack on the minister, Algy would have been able to deflect it like a schoolboy swatting a fly, she thought.

No, decided Willow turning back to the real investigation, Roger could have nothing to do with the solution, but she would definitely have to go back and talk to the tramp again and somehow force him to tell her more about the man he had seen. She might even be able to discover the tramp's name and finally put to rest her utterly absurd idea that he could have been the minister's unsatisfactory brother.

Suddenly she sat up straighter and pulled her internal telephone forwards. Discovering what the tramp was called might be no help at all if she had been right in her suspicion that the minister's brother had actually changed his name.

Having dialled the number of one of the department's lawyers, she said as soon as the telephone was answered:

'Robert? Good. Willow King here. I need a bit of background information.'

'Yes?'

'Tell me, if someone changes his or her name by deed poll, is there any way that one could find out what the original name was?'

There was a short pause at the other end of the line and Willow hastily assured Robert that she knew this was not the sort of question he was employed to answer. He laughed.

'Thinking of changing yours, Willow?' he asked. 'Well, I think if it really was done by deed poll, your best bet would be to go through back numbers of the *London Gazette*: all deed poll changes have to be advertised in that, if I remember my Josling on *Name Changes* correctly.'

Willow digested that piece of information, thinking that it would take a week of constant work to look through the possible years' issues of the newspaper.

'But you just said, that "if it really was done by deed poll": is there some other way?' she asked.

'Oh, yes. It's much cheaper and easier to do it by stat. dec.,' said Robert cheerfully.

'Tell me more.'

'You make a statutory declaration – which involves reciting an oath to a solicitor and paying £3.50; instead of fifty quid or so for a deed poll. And there wouldn't be any record of a stat. dec. name change except possibly in the solicitor's files. . . if there,' said Robert, blighting Willow's hopes of confirming her suspicions.

'I see. Thanks very much, Robert. If I ever want to change my name I'll come to you for a nice, cheap stat. dec.,' said Willow. He laughed again and said good bye.

'Before you go, Robert,' said Willow hastily.

'Yes?' came the cautious reply.

'Do you know any of the partners at Feathers, Fox & Co.? They've been recommended to me.'

'I don't think so. They're reputed to be excessively expensive. Anything I can help with, Willow?' he asked with more generosity than she would have expected.

'Thank you, Robert. But it's nothing to bother you with. How would I go about finding out who the partners are?'

'You could always try ringing up their switchboard and asking, but I think there're probably at least eighty, so it might take some time. The alternative is to look them up in the Waterlow diary,' said the lawyer.

'Thanks, Robert. You've been very helpful.'

'A pleasure, Willow,' came the answer. 'Though you are being a bit mysterious. Aren't Feathers, Fox the minister's solicitors? Don't tell me you have expectations. . . .' There was a note of teasing in his voice, but Willow was too annoyed with herself to hear it. To think that she had bothered to ring up Emma Gnatche when she could have got the same information from someone in her own office! Then she realised what he had said and her irritation was subsumed in embarrassment. That anyone in DOAP should have thought she wanted any of Algy's money was bad enough; that she should have given someone a hint that she expected it was worse. Somehow she managed to laugh and assure the lawyer that she had no such expectations. As she put down the telephone, she realised that she had probably just given substance to the department's assumption that she herself had killed the minister.

'Ah well,' she said aloud, 'so long as he doesn't go and confide in the inspector that ought not to matter.' There had been as yet no suggestion that anyone had even tried to check up on her alibi, let alone discovered that Aunt Agatha did not exist.

It was then, just as she was shutting up the map she had been studying, that she began to wonder about the other alibis she had heard, particularly Albert's. She opened the map again and checked what she already knew: that the top of Cedar's Road, where he had been told to wait with the car, was very little distance from the place where Algy's body had been discovered. It would have been so easy for him to leave the car, kill the minister and be back within less than half an hour. The only trouble was that the police had witnesses, all of whom had identified Albert, to prove that he had never left the car until he had gone to raise the alarm.

Having reminded herself of that depressing fact, Willow thought again and remembered that she had mistaken the chauffeur in the diary photograph of Mr and Mrs Gripper for Albert. If that had been so, then why should total strangers hurrying home in the dark not have mistaken some stand-in for him as well? It would have been easy for Albert to have persuaded a colleague – or even a friend or relation dressed in his uniform – to sit in the car under the street lamp while he enticed the minister on to the common and murdered him.

Willow allowed her imagination to roam for a moment or two over the possible reasons for the enticement. The only one she could think of that seemed even remotely possible was that Albert knew someone who had a piece of information the minister wanted. Suppose Albert had been employed by Michael Englewood (or indeed anyone else) to provide bodyguard services and assist in a bit of profitable corruption and had known that the minister was getting too close to the conspirators. Might Albert not have been able to say, 'Look here, Minister, my friend X can give you all the information you need about Y if you will just step this way and talk to him where no one can see him'? Algy might well have gone with him to the common and met not the informant but his own death.

11

TOWARDS the end of the afternoon, during which Willow worked like a demon to make up for the time she had spent idling in detection, the delights of assessing the financial implications of a proposed restructuring of the way pensions were calculated and paid began to pall. Roger had brought in another cup of tea and a bundle of letters for signature soon after four o'clock. Willow read through them all and then called him back.

'Roger, are you all right?' she asked, looking carefully at him. 'Or is your cold coming back?'

'Yes, I'm fine, Miss King – apart from having a cruel amount of work to get through,' he answered. 'Why?'

'I'm concerned about you. You haven't made so many typing mistakes for a very long time. Correct them, will you? And then bring the letters back. I've marked the mistakes in pencil. Thank you.'

Roger picked up the two piles of letters and left the office with a gesture that was almost a flounce. Willow shook her head at his departing back and then stretched her cramped neck and shoulder muscles before picking up her tea cup.

It was true, she thought after taking a sip, that Roger did make exceptionally good tea. Even so, it was hard to imagine the highly sophisticated, arrogant minister consoling himself with a cup of it at the price of Roger's chat and a wasted fifteen minutes.

That thought led inexorably back to what Algy might have been doing on the common or who could have lured him there and with what excuse. Willow wished that she could have interviewed Albert, the driver. She knew that she was being both snobbish and unkind, but given that she hardly knew the man, and disliked what she did know, she would have much preferred him to be the murderer than any other suspect except Gripper, whom she knew even less and had a more positive reason to dislike. But as she had no excuse to approach Albert and could only draw attention to herself by doing so, she decided that she could no longer put off talking to Michael Englewood. Taking a deep breath, she picked up the telephone and instead of the car pool dialled the number of his room.

'Ah, Valerie,' she said when the telephone was answered. 'Willow King here. Is the under secretary in his office?'

'Yes, Miss King; he's just got back from sitting in on Inspector Worth's question sessions. Hold on a moment.'

Willow could hear a muffled conversation and then Valerie's comforting, almost motherly voice saying: 'I'll put you through.'

'Willow,' said Mr Englewood. 'What can I do for you?'

'I'm sorry to disturb you,' she answered, much against her principles, which precluded apology for anything except a real and planned misdemeanour on her part. 'But I simply wanted to thank you for your support this morning. It made an otherwise daunting experience into something quite bearable.'

'I'm glad,' he said, his voice much warmer. 'I hope that you have not been too much troubled over this unhappy business.'

'Well obviously it has been very upsetting. I imagine that we must have all been rather upset – I mean all those of us who had any real contact with the minister. Look, I wonder. . . . I know this is short notice, but if you are not busy this evening I wonder if I might buy you a glass of wine or something? It would be such a relief to talk to someone who can be trusted not to indulge in prurient speculation or coy *double entendre*.'

'I could safely promise you that,' came the reply, 'and I should be delighted to have a drink with you. Six o'clock, perhaps?'

'Yes. Splendid. I'll meet you by the front desk. Thank you.' Willow put down her receiver and promised herself that she would get back to Clapham Junction to interview the tramp again on the following day. She turned back to work for the last hour and a half of the day, but she was interrupted by first one and then another of her junior staff with problems that had to be solved. It was almost half-past five before she had a chance to look at her own work. There seemed little point in starting anything new and so instead she sat, a scribbling pad in front of her, trying to see her way through the maze of suspicions, counter-suspicions and wild speculation that would lead eventually to Algy's murderer. But before she reached any conclusions it was time to lock away her confidential papers and proceed to the surreptitious interrogation of the under secretary (estabs).

The lift she was in seemed to her to be impregnated with the smell she now associated with the searching of her rooms. Was it, she wondered in sudden hope, merely one of the normal smells of the department, which she had never particularly noticed before she allowed herself to become so wrapped up in the investigation? If so, then she could have transferred it to Chesham Place herself.

Smiling a little in relief at that comforting hypothesis, Willow ignored the usual jerky inefficiency of the lift until it eventually stopped at the ground floor. As she stepped out, she looked across the cold lobby to the conference room where Inspector Worth had his temporary office. Instead of the tall, frighteningly attractive figure of the policeman, she saw Albert walking across the hall, his uniform cap dangling casually from his left hand and a crumpled newspaper jammed under his right arm. Thinking that she really ought to ask him what he had been doing in her office while her staff were absent, she was about to call out to him when she saw the door of the room that the police had commandeered open. She stood still by the lift doors, waiting and watching.

Inspector Tom Worth stood in the doorway and it was he who accosted the driver. Albert walked over and stood to attention in front of him. The inspector said something and Albert answered, but they were just too far away for Willow to catch anything either of them said.

'Ah, Willow,' said the establishments officer loudly from the other side of the hall. 'Have I kept you waiting long? I am sorry.'

Willow looked towards him and smiled, but before moving from her vantage point by the lifts she looked back at Albert and the inspector. She was only a little surprised to find herself under his scrutiny. With what Cressida would have described as a gracious inclination of her head, she moved off to join Mr Englewood and together they left the building.

'Where would you like to go?' he asked as they both shivered in the bitter cold.

'What about Selina's in Abbeville Road,' suggested Willow. 'They do mulled wine there and on a night like tonight, I'd have thought that was our best bet.'

'Selina's it shall be. But you'll have to show me the way,' he said. 'I'm not a great one for after-office socialising and I've never been there.'

'No, of course not,' said Willow suddenly remembering the piece of information that had eluded her earlier in the day. Didn't you tell me that you've taken the six-fifteen from Waterloo every night for years?' Then in case he read any kind of sneer – or suspicion – into that, she added: 'I really admire such self-discipline. One can waste such an astonishing amount of time fiddling around in the office after hours and never get enough done to justify the incursion into one's own time.'

'I've always admired the amount of work you manage to get through yourself, Willow,' he said, making no reference to his own habits. 'Ah, this must be your place.' He held open the door for her and together they sat down at a small table in front of the gas log fire.

Willow ordered a large jug of mulled wine without even thinking about it; after all, it had been she who had invited Mr Englewood to have a drink with her. But as the waitress took her order, she was aware of a coldness and quickly tracked it to its source.

'How silly of me,' she said, smiling frankly at him. 'I get so used to organising things in the office that I forget the old courtesies of social intercourse.'

'Please,' he protested. 'Pay no attention to me. It's a great many years since I had the opportunity of entertaining a woman, and I know that customs have changed immeasurably in the interim. Since my wife left – I'm certain that the office will have regaled you with every detail – I don't think I have been alone with a woman outside the DOAP tower. You must forgive my pre-women's-liberation gaucherie.'

Willow laughed, quite kindly, finding it increasingly difficult to believe in her own suspicions of this man. As she laughed, she realised that she was at last free of the disturbing smell. Michael Englewood smelled of tweed, the department's soap and ink.

'You're the first man I've met who would apologise – or phrase an apology so charmingly,' she said, so relieved that her voice was light and friendly. 'Yes, the office has regaled me with a little of your history, but don't let's talk about it, unless you particularly want to.'

'God forbid!' said Englewood with much greater emphasis than she had ever heard him use before. 'I think we have both suffered from the effects of office tittle-tattle. One small comfort of living alone as I have had to is that at least the office can't be exciting itself with details of my existence. Although,' he added consideringly, 'knowing some of the worst gossip-merchants, they have probably invented some appailingly lurid stories about me.'

Willow shook her head.

'Even I should probably have heard if they had done. But all I've been told is that you live alone; that your chief interest is chess. Oh yes, I've heard that you play it on a computer you take everywhere with you. I'd love to see it,' said Willow, trying to put him at his ease. But something she had said obviously had the reverse effect and he twitched visibly and began to flush. She decided to cover her unfortunate request.

'They also say that you like detective stories and that you spend your holidays fishing. There's nothing there to make you sweat and blush in the night,' she said to him kindly.

'Was that what happened to you when they were all chattering about the minister's glaringly public attempted seduction?' Englewood asked in a tone of such bitterness that Willow could not help staring at him.

'Sometimes, I must admit. It has recently dawned on me that I absolutely hated being humiliated in public like that,' she said, hoping to elicit some confidences. 'Although at the time I just thought I was irritated.'

'Yes, humiliation was always one of his specialities,' said Englewood. 'Ah, here's the wine. Might I pour it out? Just to bolster my failing masculinity?' There was more than a hint of charm in that smiling request. Willow merely smiled and nodded, leaving her probing for a minute or two. She sipped the hot, fragrant drink and sighed in satisfaction.

'There is one thing to be said for mulled wine apart from its warmth on a night like this,' she said. 'Despite the horrible quality of some "house" wines, once it's been hotted up and sugared and spiced it really is quite drinkable.'

'It's very good,' he said, 'but it does taste rather strong. Would you mind if I ordered something to eat with it? Some *pâté* or something? Will you join me?'

'That's very kind,' she said, mentally cursing him for his caution. 'In fact they do a wonderful if eccentric hot *pâté en croûte*. We might have that.' But as soon as he had given the waitress his order, Willow returned to the attack.

'You sound as though you knew the minister rather well.'

'Not particularly,' answered Englewood, sounding tired. 'But what I did know I disliked. He seemed to take such pleasure in making other people look foolish.'

'For example?'

'Well apart from you, there was the PUS – I can't be breaking any confidences because you must have seen it happening in meetings: how Algy would lead him on by apparently guileless questions until the poor man had made more and more of an ass of himself; and nearly everyone else who came within Endelsham's orbit had a taste of it.'

'It sounds rather as though he did it to you, too,' said Willow and then added hastily as she saw his face beginning to redden, 'not that I ever witnessed it, but you sound so angry that I can't help feeling that there is something more personal in your dislike than what he did to the PUS.'

'You're right, of course. Ah, here's the *pâté*. You know,' he said turning to face her for a moment, 'this really is rather a treat. At home I live on the dullest food – usually something cold on a piece of bread. It is a long, long time since I did something like this. You could say it was my fault – and you'd be right – but it is hard to pick yourself up again after. . .' He broke off, took a deep swig of the warm wine and then said: 'But I don't know why I'm boring you with my maunderings: I get the impression that you are just as lonely as I, except for your old aunt, and she can't be much of a friend for someone like you.'

'I get by well enough,' said Willow shortly, very much disliking the idea that Mr Englewood thought himself at all similar to her. 'But never mind. Tell me something: what will happen to Albert now? Will he be assigned to the next minister or will he have to go back to the pool?'

'Albert? What makes you ask about him?' The question came out as a kind of bark. Willow could not decide whether she thought Englewood was trying to protect a fellow conspirator or was simply surprised at her curiosity.

'Curiosity, I suppose,' answered Willow with a deceptively frank smile. 'I saw him in the hall while I was waiting for you and I wondered what makes a man choose to drive for a government department and whether it's thought to be better to drive a minister exclusively or be at the beck and call of all the pool-users.'

'I see. Albert used to be a private chauffeur and so it was thought that he might perhaps have more polish than some of the men who've spent their entire careers at DOAP. . . .'

'Polish!' repeated Willow with a squawk in her voice. 'I'd have said that he was the most gauche, most unhelpful employee in the entire department. Sorry, Michael. I shouldn't have interrupted. Do carry on.'

'Well yes,' he said. 'He didn't turn out to be quite what we'd expected, but the minister was always quite amused by him and he was a more than competent driver, so we kept him on. I expect he'll be assigned to the minister's successor.'

Englewood took a deep swallow of the wine and Willow began to hope that despite the *pâté* he might drink enough to loosen his tongue. To keep him unsuspicious of her motives, she asked another question about the driver as she refilled Englewood's glass.

'What would make a private chauffeur switch to the public sector? Presumably the pay is much worse,' she said.

'I imagine so. As far as I can remember, Albert told his interview panel that he was sick of hanging about for hours on end for a man he disliked and despised and would rather work regular hours even if it meant sacrificing a few pounds a week. We were rather relieved that he so obviously disliked his previous employer.'

'Really?' said Willow. 'Why on earth? As a justification for his wanting to come to a dreary place like DOAP?'

At that Englewood gave her another rueful smile as though to say that he too found the place deadly dull.

'Not entirely. I can't see why you shouldn't know if you really want to – there's no particular secret about it. Albert used to drive for one of the worst gossip-columnists in Fleet Street – we had been a little worried that he might be a plant. But good drivers are hard to find.'

'A plant? In DOAP?' Willow protested, genuinely astonished and wondering whether the coincidence that was suggesting itself to her so powerfully could really be true. 'I really can't imagine a gossip column being remotely interested in our doings.'

'With a man like Algernon Endelsham at the helm, so to speak?'

'No, you're right, of course. I can think of lots of journalists who'd have been pleased to know about his goings on. But go on, do tell me who it was.'

Englewood shook his head and so Willow, putting on one of Cressida's smiles, said:

'You're not going to tell me it was that frightful man Gripper are you?' The establishments officer, used though he was to keeping secrets, was not at all used to keeping them in the face of determined enquiry. No one had ever been interested enough in anything he knew to try to winkle it out of him before, and his face gave Willow all the answer she needed and set her thinking furiously. Not the least of the ideas skimming through her brain was that her investigation had thrown up more peculiar coincidences than she would have believed possible.

'Never mind,' she said at last. 'It was only shameless curiosity. But it's odd; Albert has always looked more like a boxer than a smooth private chauffeur.'

'Well he was, originally. That was another reason why we liked the look of him. Security and all that,' said Englewood, obviously happy to talk about something that was not classified.

'I wonder what he made of the minister. If he hated his previous employer, I mean,' said Willow, trying to wrench the conversation back to the real subject of her enquiry.

'I don't imagine he thought much either way. Even Endelsham wouldn't have wasted his time proving his superiority to a chauffeur; he was nearly always polite to what he called servants.'

'Unlike the rest of us,' said Willow, 'who were all treated to one or other of his techniques.' Englewood said nothing, but took another gulp of wine. Willow refilled his glass and signalled the waitress for a second jug. After nearly five minutes' silence, he said morosely:

'He even thought – or pretended to think – that I had a passion for that miserable emotional cripple who works in your office.'

'Roger, you mean,' said Willow carefully, wondering what on earth she was going to hear next.

'Yes. You know how work shy he is unless there's a drama on or someone's breathing down his neck?' Englewood paused for so long that Willow eventually nodded encouragingly. 'Well, I've always liked you, Willow, and you work a damn sight harder than some of the full-time assistant secretaries and so I was determined that when you weren't around to check up on him I'd try to keep him up to the mark for you.'

'That was good of you,' said Willow, touching his arm gently. 'I often wondered why he managed to work so much better when I wasn't around. Thank you.'

Englewood acknowledged her gratitude with a funny, formal bow and carried on with his story.

'I used to drop in really whenever I was up on the eighth floor, just to keep him on his toes, and for two or three days in a row I happened to be going in or coming out just as the minister was passing the door. Seeing me there so often, he invented this ludicrous fantasy and started working on the deluded Roger, exercising his famous fatal charm. The poor man can't have had so many compliments paid to him since his mother died. He pretty soon became completely enslaved, and to keep him in that condition, Algy used to drop in for a cup of tea almost every day when you were out of the office. All simply to torment me, you see.'

'Only this time,' said Willow with considerable vicarious satisfaction, 'you weren't tormented.'

'No,' he agreed, but there was in his voice a sound so expressive of pain that Willow nearly gasped. 'Oh God,' he went on, taking another mouthful of wine, 'I can't think why I'm confessing this to you, but I'll go mad if I don't tell anyone.'

Willow gripped her hands together beneath the ugly wrought-iron table, terrified that Englewood was about to admit to the murder. She suddenly felt desperately guilty for making him tight, pushing him and pushing him until he dropped his defences. Her detecting had long-since ceased to be the lighthearted game she had planned, but now it seemed despicable and she felt an unwonted hatred of herself and her irresponsibility. Forcing herself to look at her companion, she was relieved to see that he was slowly pulling himself together. He picked up his knife and fork again and ate the last corner of his *pâté en croûte*.

'I'm ashamed to say that I did nothing to disabuse Algy of his ludicrous fantasy. It seemed that if he thought he was successfully tormenting me about Roger, then he might have laid off all the other things that could really have hurt. Absurd, isn't it, Willow, that a grown man should behave so like a terrified schoolboy?'

'But understandable,' said Willow gently, remembering the tales of the schoolboys the minister had actually terrorised. Englewood suddenly gripped her wrist and she was surprised at the steel-like strength of his fingers, surprised and a little frightened. In her fear she wondered whether her certainty of his inability to kill was an error.

'Yes, but don't you see what terrifies me?' he said urgently. 'Mightn't Roger, inflamed by Algy's foul charade, have thought it was real and propositioned him or in some way approached him? Then Algy, with his inimitable cruelty, might have explained to the poor man precisely what was what. And then, Roger. . .'

'Might have killed him, you mean? Oh surely not. Really, I don't think you need worry about that. Roger is the least violent of men; don't you remember that time a year or so ago when he was set on by a gang of "gay-bashing" youths on the tube and he told us all he thought they'd hurt him less if he just sat there and didn't even try to hit back?' Willow said, remembering the scars once again, but also asking herself whether Englewood's 'confession' put him in the clear or whether it might merely be a bluff. If she could prove it to have been a bluff then she would have a little more evidence to back up her wild ideas about conspiracy.

'Have you told any of this to Inspector Worth?' she asked.

'Oh God,' was all the answer Englewood made, and he dropped his face in his hands. 'No, of course not. You're probably right that it's impossible and so I couldn't tell anyone official, but whoever did the murder must have been driven to it by that bloody man's cruelty – and if so he deserved it.' He raised his head again so quickly that Willow had no time to wipe the expression off her face. 'Does that shock you?'

'Yes,' she said honestly, 'but I can understand it; if he was as horrible to you as . . . as he obviously was.'

'You sound doubtful,' he said quite quietly, apparently calm again. 'Quite apart from humiliating me almost daily in the office, it was he who seduced my wife. After that I knew that I should never have married – that it would never be safe for me to let anyone know that I cared for anyone else, or he'd do it again. But I mustn't maunder on about all that now. I'm sorry to have bored you.' Willow, her mind suddenly blank with the shock of what she had heard, could think of nothing to say that might comfort him and simply sat with her mouth open, looking at him.

When she had recovered from the shock, she said:

'But that means you must have known him before he ever came to the department.' He nodded.

'Yes. She was a television researcher and she met him when he appeared on one of her programmes. He wasn't nearly so famous in those days and must have thought that even she could be useful to him. When she invited him to our home he came.' Englewood broke off.

Willow looked at him curiously and saw that his face had taken on the angry tension she had first seen that morning during her interview with the inspector.

'I had to watch it, you see,' he said, regaining a little calm: 'the whole process of seduction. It didn't take very long and then she went off with him. As soon as he'd got her, he dropped her of course. And then she went to America. She told me that she couldn't bear the thought of living with me who had witnessed every stage of her humiliation. And I couldn't persuade her that I loved her enough to make humiliation in either of us an irrelevance.'

'I am so sorry,' said Willow inadequately. Englewood shook his prematurely greying head.

'It's long over now,' he said. 'But you see, that was why I was so afraid for you when he started on you.'

As he said that, he grasped Willow's wrist again. The sweatiness of his hand disgusted her, but she could not

186

pull away. At last he released her and she resisted the temptation to wipe her arm with a napkin.

'All Endelsham's moves were the same,' he said. 'It was as if he was so full of contempt that he didn't even bother to change his technique – at first. I was certain that if you did let go to him, he would drop you too and then you would suffer terribly.'

'But I didn't succumb,' said Willow brightly, trying hard to reduce the emotional charge of their horrible conversation.

'No, I know. And I have never respected anyone more than I did you when I realised that,' he said. Highly embarrassed, Willow waited in silence.

'I'd have done anything for you then,' he said very quietly. 'Chasing your pathetic clerk to make sure he worked decently when you weren't there was all I could think of.'

He turned his face away from her as though he had embarrassed himself as much as he had her. At last he stood up, swaying slightly against the black iron table.

'I'll see to the bill and then leave you in peace. Will you be all right getting home, Willow?' he asked, still not looking at her.

'Lord yes,' said Willow, really concerned for him. 'I only live about two minutes from here, but what about you?'

'I'll be fine. Take a taxi to the station. Catch the train. No problem.' He signalled for the bill and when it came put down a bundle of five pound notes. Before Willow could thank him, he said: 'Thank you for listening. I can't tell you how good it is to talk to a woman like you. I'd never have said it while Algy was alive. But I can now. Thank you.'

Her heart squeezed with pity and her mind recoiling almost in disgust, Willow could only smile and watch him blunder up the steps out of the wine bar. When she was certain he had gone, she collected her coat and bag and followed him out, trying not to think of any of the implications of his various bombshells.

But it did seem quite obvious to her at last that whatever else he had done – and for whatever reason – Michael Englewood had not been running any conspiracy to defraud the department. The raw unhappiness he had revealed to her made her rather ashamed to have invented such an idea and also produced an innocent explanation for all the suspicious facts she had collected to bolster it.

The cold outside bit into her cheeks and she put her head down against the wind-born sleet so that she had reached the front door of her flat before she saw the man standing there in the shadows like a figure in a Thirties' black-and-white film. For a sickening moment, her heart seemed to stop altogether and then to resume beating, but hard and noisily in her chest.

12

'*I* HAVEN'T a warrant, Miss King, but I want to talk to you,' said a familiar, classless voice, and Willow's heart went on banging against her ribs. It was unfortunately not only the shock of his unexpected presence that disturbed her so much. She took a full minute to control the shaking in her knees and voice, but by telling herself savagely to brace up, she managed. Her toes and the top joint of each finger still tingled with the receding adrenalin fear had driven through her.

'But of course, Inspector. Have you been waiting long? You must be very cold,' she said breathlessly as she unlocked the door and held it open for him. 'Come on up. Search the flat. Search my life. I have nothing to hide.'

In the ugly yellow light of the streetlamps she saw a derisive smile flash across his craggy face and wondered how many of her innumerable secrets he had managed to discover. As they climbed the gritty stairs, she thought how refreshing it would be to talk to someone as strong and secure in his own esteem as the inspector after the revelation of Michael Englewood's bitter unhappiness and almost unhinged devotion to herself.

'May I make you some coffee?' she said, wondering whether the policeman seriously suspected her of murdering the minister. 'It might warm you up.'

'Yes indeed,' he answered cheerfully. 'As you correctly divined, I am frozen stiff. A cup of coffee would go down a treat.'

'Good,' she answered, letting him into the flat and going straight to the kitchen. As she put on the kettle she thought to herself that if he truly believed that she was a killer, he would never accept hospitality from her. Then, laughing at herself, she decided that she was allowing Cressida's romanticism to infect her proper cynicism. There was nothing in the world to stop a tough man like the inspector from eating and drinking his fill with a suspect. It was not, after all, as though Algy's killer had been a poisoner.

On that thought, she poured boiling water on to the instant coffee granules and carried the two mugs back into her living room.

'There's sugar on the table, if you like it,' she said, handing one to the policeman. Taking off her spectacles to wipe away the steam, she looked at him from under her pale eyelashes.

'Yes,' he said smiling at her with something like bitterness in his eyes, 'you're quite right. I do not suspect you of murdering Algernon Endelsham. But I do want to know what the hell you're up to.'

Willow shrugged, sat down on the lumpy dark-blue and pink sofa, and drank some coffee, burning the roof of her mouth. The tiny pain and sensation of a loosened tassel of skin hanging from her palate removed all her remaining resistance.

'All right,' she said, shrugging her thin shoulders. 'If I'd been allowed to see you alone in the beginning, I'd have told you all about it then, but I couldn't just blow my cover at DOAP after all these years.' She looked up, surprising a most peculiar expression on his face. 'Oh blast!' she cried. 'Don't tell me that you didn't know about Cressida after

190

all.' He shook his head.

'I haven't a clue what you're talking about, but you'll have to tell me now. Come on: who is Cressida? Another of the deceased's bits of crumpet?'

It did not occur to Willow that he was trying to make her angry in order to get her to tell him everything; she was just surprised that so intelligent a man should use such an offensive expression.

'Certainly not,' she answered, with such a bite in her voice that she surprised even herself. She was torn between saying nothing more without a solicitor present, telephoning Richard Crescent for help, and pouring out the whole story to the inspector. Reminding herself that she had originally planned to tell him the truth if she could only get to see him alone, she said: 'Off the record?'

'Don't be silly,' he said without heat. 'You're quite intelligent enough to know that I could never agree to that.'

Willow, who had been accustomed for many years to people virtually fainting at her intimidating brilliance, found his lack of awe of her brains almost as attractive as his intriguing face and broken nose. She took a breath so deep that her voice came out wobbly as she made her confession.

'She is what you might call my alter ego. The days I am thought to spend with my Aunt Agatha are in fact spent writing novels under the name of Cressida Woodruffe.'

'Here?'

'No. Since I made money as Cressida, I've also had a flat in Chesham Place,' said Willow not quite able to disguise her pride. 'I was there the night the minister was killed.'

'Alone?' The sharp monosyllabic interrogations unsettled her and she peered towards him as though she could bring sympathy into his cold dark eyes.

'I thought you didn't suspect me,' she said sharply.

'Stop wasting any more of my time, Miss Cressida Woodruffe, and tell me the whole lot now,' he said, but with the increase in words, his voice became marginally warmer, which helped her over the brink.

'No, I was not alone. There was a friend with me called Richard Lawrence-Crescent, but he's dropped the "Lawrence" bit. I'd rather you did not interview him if you can help it, because he would simply hate it. He thought I was mad enough anyway.' She drank some more coffee, realised that she had ingested quite enough liquid already, and put the mug down on the low painted table in front of her.

'Mad in what way? I don't think that's quite the adjective I'd have used,' said Inspector Worth, glaring at her over the rim of his own steaming mug.

'I thought that if I could find out who had murdered the minister by the time you discovered that my alibi was false, we could do a deal. Richard was certain that I'd find out nothing and merely cause maximum embarrassment all round.'

'Women!' said the inspector. 'Can you imagine how much easier my life would be without you? No never mind. That wasn't a question,' he added, seeing her open her mouth, 'nor was it meant as an insult. So tell me, what have you discovered so far?'

'Are you quite sure you want to know the thoughts of a member of my despised sex?' The anger in Willow's voice was quite obvious, but the inspector only laughed.

'Don't be so prickly,' he said. 'I've enough respect for your brains to want to know what you think you've discovered about this case.'

'Discovered would be putting it too high,' she said slowly. 'There are various possible motives and various opportunities, but I can't really get any further, because I have no access to your information.'

'Such as?'

'Oh, the state of the body; precisely what was done; whether the murderer would have been, for instance, covered in blood; who stood to gain financially from

192

Algy's death. That sort of thing,' said Willow casually.

'Considering that the deceased was by all accounts madly in love with you, you're taking a commendably cool look at it all,' said the inspector, betraying nothing more than mild interest.

'My gossiping colleagues have always been rather unsophisticated in their judgments,' she said carefully. 'I don't in fact think that Algy Endelsham was in love with me at all.'

'No?' said the inspector. There was very little colour in his voice, but something in the way he produced that interrogatory word made Willow blush.

'No,' she said firmly. 'I think what he was in fact trying to do was to make me fall in love with him so that he could have me at a disadvantage. I've realised since he died that he hated having to deal with people who were not somehow in his power, and there was no other way he could control me. Besides, I find it easier to control my disgust and horror at what Algy must have suffered in those last minutes if I exercise my brains rather than my emotions.'

As she spoke, Willow realised that she had just told the truth. Despite what she had heard of Algy's seduction of Mrs Englewood, Willow was still disgusted and horrified at what had happened to him. Nothing, no humiliation, no pain could justify murder, she thought.

'In some ways, Willow King, you're a girl after my own heart,' said the inspector, half-smiling at last.

'That is almost as insulting as your previous statement about my sex,' said Willow, trying fruitlessly not to like him.

'I'll do a deal with you,' he said. 'I'll tell you about the body and so forth, if you tell me about the motives and so on.'

'All right,' she said, deciding to amuse him so much with her stories about her encounter with Gripper, her hairdresser's gossip, the tramp, and even poor Roger that he would take no notice of the fact that she had been interrogating Englewood and forget to ask her about him.

'There are several people with motives,' she said lightly. 'Starting with the least likely, there is Roger Coverly in my office. I gather you've had several goes at him. The gossip is that he was infatuated with the minister, made some kind of approach, was crudely or cruelly repulsed and – as you might say – like a woman scorned lured the minister to the darkest part of the common and killed him.'

'So likely,' was the only comment made to that by Tom Worth, and Willow played her next card.

'Next is Eustace Gripper.'

'Who?' demanded the inspector, apparently startled. 'Not the gossip man – journalist?'

'Yes. Surely you've ferreted out the fact that his wife was Algy's mistress?' She waited, but got no reaction. Not being at all sure whether he was merely leading her on or whether he had really not considered Gripper, Willow plunged on. 'He's said to be a bully, prurient about other people's sex lives, possibly because of the barrenness of his own, viciously protective of his own dignity – and the previous employer (I think) of Albert the chauffeur.'

'Albert's got an alibi,' said Worth coolly. 'That is if you're thinking that this Gripper might have paid the bloke to kill Endelsham.'

'Well,' said Willow, 'I don't know enough about either Fleet Street or the world of contract killers, but wouldn't it be easy enough for Albert to get a brother or even just a mate to dress up in his uniform to sit under the street light at the top of Cedar's Road while Albert, perhaps alone or perhaps just in charge of hired desperados, did the deed?'

'Easy enough,' said Inspector Worth. 'But why would a man like Endelsham agree to go for a ramble across Clapham Common with his chauffeur?'

'Was that why you were grilling Albert this evening?' Willow asked, distracted for the moment from her own speculation on the subject of the minister's enticement.

194

'I can't really imagine that you hadn't thought of all this before.'

Inspector Worth smiled but did not answer. Instead he put another question.

'What were you doing with Mr Englewood this evening?' There was enough seriousness in his tone to make Willow realise that she would have to answer and could forget all ideas of entertaining him with stories of the tramp.

'How do you know I was doing any such thing?' she asked.

'When I saw you leave the building with him, I got one of my constables to follow you,' he said impatiently. 'Well?'

'We were simply having a drink,' said Willow crossly. 'The poor man has been under tremendous strain the last few days, you know.'

'And you were being the dear little woman comforting him? I find that hard to square with the Willow King who terrorises the department. Now, please stop playing games. I want to know.'

'Is that why you lay in wait for me in the cold?' He nodded. 'I simply wanted to find out whether he might have had a motive. He clearly had the opportunity – but then about a million people had that,' said Willow, hoping that she was not going to have to betray the bitter misery that Englewood had let her see.

'You know perfectly well that he had a motive,' said Worth, getting out of his chair and coming to stand in front of Willow. She felt him looming over her and was suddenly aware of his size and obvious strength, and of his power. Seldom had she felt so female or so fragile. Never had she expected to enjoy such a sensation. Unfortunately she did. Despising herself, she looked up into his face and made her admission.

'Yes, I know he had a motive of a sort. And yes, I do think it is possible – just possible – that he might have killed his wife's seducer at the time. But I find it impossible to believe that he would have waited ten years and then done it. Even if the awful coincidence of Algy's having been put at the head of the ministry had unhinged poor Englewood, he would surely have acted as soon as Algy got there – not waited three years. Englewood's basically such a gentle man, even if he has repressed a lot of hatred and anger; even if he is lonely as sin and seems to have been paranoid about the minister.'

'And what part have you been playing in all this?' The inspector sat down beside Willow on the uncomfortable sofa. 'You clearly know him extremely well; no one else in the department has tumbled to the fact that his wife levanted with the minister. Did you plot the whole thing together? Your enchantment and public refusal of Endelsham, and then when that didn't shut him up, the murder?'

'What, as revenge for Algy's seduction of poor Michael Englewood's wife? Good God, you can't believe that,' said Willow, her mouth snapping shut on the last syllable. 'You cannot. He never even told me about his wife until tonight. Besides,' she added, her sense of humour returning, 'you cannot seriously believe that a man who has someone as rich and beautiful as Amanda Gripper as his mistress would fall into a trap set by a plain, middle-aged, ill-dressed woman like me?'

To her extreme surprise, the inspector did not laugh – or even smile at that. Instead he put out a hand and pulled Willow's chin round so that she was facing him. She kept her eyes firmly staring at him, refusing to let him frighten or shame her. After a bit he let her go, saying:

'You don't really believe that, do you?' he said. 'However much you dress the part, you know perfectly well it is a part, don't you?'

Not liking his tone or the fact that he seemed to have seen what no one in DOAP had ever seen, Willow tried to distract him. Playing the scene for all it was worth, as though that might make it all seem less real, she massaged her chin.

'Physical bullying of suspects now! You might like to know that I bruise extremely easily and could no doubt have you put off the case if I displayed my chin to the complaints bureau,' she said, her voice quivering with rage, or perhaps the other, damnably inconvenient emotions that were churning around inside her.

'I could strangle you, Willow King,' he said bitterly.

'But why?' she demanded; then her voice changed infinitesimally. 'Funny, someone else said that only a week ago. I wonder why?'

He lunged forward and grabbed her shoulders with one arm. With his other hand he gripped her chin again, forcing it upwards so that he could kiss her. All her cynicism, all her highly developed critical faculties and her determination to ignore her instinctive liking for him, were overtaken by physical sensations, of which the uppermost was the feeling of his exceptional strength. Richard's considerate embraces had not prepared Willow for the passion she felt in Tom Worth's arms.

It was not until she was lying on top of her Indian bedspread, with his hands skilfully unbuttoning her white shirt, that her brain started to work again.

'Insp. . . Tom, really. This isn't suitable,' she said, her voice shaken by her passionately irregular breathing.

His strong hands stopped and, as he knelt over her, he burst into laughter.

'Suitable,' he repeated, still laughing. 'No, Will, it's not at all suitable. But that's just too bad. My God, I've needed you – ever since the beginning when I saw you sitting in front of me pretending to be so cool and spinsterish, while all the time you were positively pumping out physical attraction.'

Wanting to bury her head in his chest like one of her dottier heroines, Willow compromised.

'Really?' she said, frankly. 'I thought you loathed and despised me, and I was terrified of you.'

'Don't be asinine,' came his astringent reply. Then more gently he said, 'Will you let down your hair?'

Feeling as though she were really playing a part in one of her own books, she sat up a little way and tugged off the rubber band, shaking her head to let the luxuriant red hair fly about her face. Tom Worth gasped and, gently pushing her back against the pillows, kissed her again.

'God you're beautiful,' he said as his hands went back to the small pearl buttons on her shirt, and for once she accepted that statement as the truth.

In the terrifying, wildly exhilarating lovemaking that followed Willow's rational mind ceased entirely to operate. In bed with Richard she had always felt happy to know that she was giving him pleasure and sometimes felt the pleasure herself; she knew him well and liked him a lot; he was a gentle and considerate man, and she had always thought that making love with him was an excellent prelude to a good night's sleep. But in Tom Worth's arms the mixture of volcanic physical sensation and deep surging emotion left her gasping and afraid.

She turned her head on the pillow to look at him as he lay beside her and thought that she saw in his face emotions that mirrored her own. He lifted a hand and rubbed his dark eyes.

'I must be mad. Are you all right?' he asked.

'I have no idea,' she said honestly. 'Are you?'

'I hope so. I'm sorry. You must believe that I don't usually thrust myself on. . .'

'Murder suspects,' she suggested, feeling much happier as she regained some of her customary tartness. He, too, seemed to find it reassuring for he laughed a little.

'You know you're not that, Will. But I don't want you to think that you are one of a series. I have never, ever, slept with a woman in the course of an investigation. You just. . .' He broke off, turned his head and then with great gentleness stroked her thin face. 'You are just the most astonishing woman I have ever come across – and I think I've. . .'

At that a faint clarion call of danger sounded in Willow's mind and she laid one of her hands across his lips. His

198

eyes smiled at her over the barrier and, trusting him, she took her hand away.

'It's all right. I'm not going to throttle you with emotion,' he said. 'But I do find you unutterably desirable. And you got under my skin – through all my defences.'

'Well, that's all right,' said Willow, smiling back. 'You seem to have got through mine pretty effectively too.'

Before he left her shortly after six o'clock the next morning, she got up in her old towelling dressing gown, her hair cascading down her back, and cooked him breakfast. As they sat on opposite sides of the kitchen table eating and drinking coffee, he spoke:

'I said I wasn't going to throttle you with emotion, and I'm not. It's all right: you needn't look as though you were going to be sick. But will you promise me something?'

'What?' Willow asked, scooping a handful of hair behind her ear and looking exceedingly suspicious.

'Don't go for any more walks on dark commons, and don't ask too many questions.'

'Why not?' she asked rather crossly. 'Are you afraid I'll get to the solution before you?' Even as she spoke she realised what his reason was, but could not bring herself to admit it. He put down the cup and sat looking at her with a mixture of sadness and seriousness.

'No. It's not a race. It's a bloody important investigation into a vicious murder. I just don't want you to get yourself into any dangerous corners. I'm fairly convinced that this was a one-off, but it's dangerous to provoke anyone who has killed. I of all people know that. Whoever he is, I don't want you irritating him so much that he tries again. All right?'

She nodded, which was as far as her dignity would allow her to go.

'Why do you think it was a one-off?' she asked.

'You really are like a terrier; you just won't let go. Because of the state of the deceased's head. It had been hit inexpertly, a great many times, with something hard-edged, rectangular they think, about two or three inches by six or seven. It probably wouldn't have killed him at all, if some of the blows hadn't landed on his temple.'

'Not an actual weapon at all, then?'

He shook his dark head.

'So that seems to rule out hired desperadoes,' she suggested, refilling his mug.

'Not necessarily. It could have been done that way to make us think it was a random killing. But please lay off it all now. Haven't you enough to think about with your job at DOAP, your other life and your novels and, what was he called? Richard something. And. . .'

Willow waited for him to say 'and me', but he did not. Instead, he gulped down the rest of his coffee and stood up.

'It is not really adequate to say "thank you",' he said. 'But I do thank you, and I hope to God I haven't upset you too much.'

He had, of course, but he had not been alone when he did it and so Willow smiled a little and said: 'Or I you.'

'Bless you,' he said, leaned across the table to give her a quick, hard kiss.

'Before you go, Tom,' she said breathlessly and stood up to face him.

'Yes?' He stopped in the doorway of her shabby flat and her knees weakened as she looked at his dark eyes under their shaggy brows, his strong chin and endearingly broken nose. Forcing herself to concentrate on her mind and not her vitals, she said:

'Have you seen his will? Algy's will, I mean?'

'Yes,' he said, sighing. 'And you want to know who the beneficiaries are. Well I shouldn't tell you anything, but I'll give you the broad outlines if you can promise me discretion?'

Willow nodded.

200

'A considerable sum to Mrs Gripper. A smaller one to a girl called Gnatche who worked for him, small amounts to various charities and the residue to his party.'

'Nothing to the brother then?' she said, surprised and annoyed that her determination to discover the terms of the will had been unnecessary. 'You do know he had a brother, I suppose.'

Tom Worth nodded and just as Willow started to ask whether he had discovered the identity of the brother, left the flat. She could hear him bounding down the stairs and banging the front door behind him. But she could not be sure whether the urgency of his departure was caused by a desire to escape her questions or the emotions they had aroused in each other.

13

W HEN SHE reached her desk three hours later, Willow
sat down wondering how she was ever going to forget
what had happened. Nothing in either of her well-ordered
existences had prepared her for the rawness of such real
emotion. She found herself resenting Tom Worth as much
as she longed to be back in his arms. Telling herself that it
was no wonder she was feeling fragile since she had had
only about three hours' sleep, her head ached and her eyes
felt as though they had been rolled in old carpet, she tried
to concentrate on the idea of working.

There was a sharp, decisive rap on her door.

'Come in,' she said, hoping that the knock would
herald some crisis in which she could lose herself
and her exasperating emotions. 'Ah, Barbara. What is
it?'

'I just wondered if you had anything for me to do,
Willow,' said the Scottish girl. 'I've finished all that
redrafting and until it comes back typed, I'm stuck.'

'Yes, I'm sure there's plenty. Um, hang on,' said Willow
with such uncharacteristic indecision that Barbara looked
curiously at her. 'No, look: I'll sort something out for

you. But first, would you get me the personal files on the department's drivers.'

'Yes, of course. Why. . .?'

'Never mind now. Just fetch them – and don't go out of your way to tell anyone I've asked for them.'

'All right,' said Barbara, showing quite clearly that she thought her chief was mad. But she left the room and Willow was left to take two paracetamol tablets and try to wipe Inspector Worth out of her mind. Her continuing investigation into the possible suspects was a gesture of defiance that she hoped would exorcise him once and for all. She had quite dismissed Englewood from her mind as a conspirator to fraud, but there was no need to ignore the possibility of the fraud itself. Even if Englewood had not been employing Albert someone else might have – and whatever Tom Worth might believe, Willow was unconvinced by the driver's alibi.

It was quite a relief to think that at the end of the day she would be able to slip out of Willow King's life and character, rather like the species of lizard that can leave its tail behind to dupe pursuing predators. Cressida's luxuries, clothes, easy life and fantastic daydreams would absorb her once again and if they could not completely banish Inspector Worth at least they might help her to come to terms with what had happened to her.

Luckily for Willow her red telephone rang at that moment and, hearing the PUS's peevish tones, she was immediately absorbed into the machinations of the finance committee. He had just been told by Downing Street of the appointment of a new minister and wanted to enlist Willow's help in ensuring that the new incumbent would not disrupt the office's plans for the revised pensions structure. He also wanted Willow to accompany him and his PS to a meeting with the new minister in the House that afternoon.

'But why on earth?' Willow asked, surprised into uncharacteristic rudeness.

'Because it's that damned woman Elsie Trouville. She's eaten up with all this feminist nonsense and I want to show her that we're not "sexist pigs" in this office.'

'I see,' said Willow with considerable coolness.

'Yes,' agreed the PUS, not having picked up her emphasis. 'And I will say for you, Willow, you have never bored us with any of that kind of whining.'

'Thank you so much, PUS,' she said, cooler still. 'And what time should I present myself?'

'Meet us in the hall at two-thirty, would you, Willow? Good bye.'

He put down his receiver and Willow, in her own office, followed suit. If she was going to be out of the office for most of the afternoon, she would really have to get down to work. The urgency worked its usual trick with her concentration and she thought no more of the investigation until Barbara reappeared some time later with a heap of files. Even then Willow hardly looked up.

'Just put them on the side table, will you? I'll deal with them later. If you're still short of a job, will you persuade Roger to finish typing that report and check it carefully? You know how sloppy he can be about tabulated figures. Call them over with him, to double check, please.'

'All right, Willow,' said Barbara, in a resigned voice, and Willow hoped that this second unlikely instruction might make the girl think that both it and the previous one were merely designed to keep her busy so that she would refrain from commenting publicly on Willow's demand for the chauffeurs' files.

When her AT had gone, Willow nipped across her office to remove the file belonging to Albert and read it from beginning to end. There was very little in it that was any use to her except for the reference he had brought with him from the *Daily Mercury*.

It had been written by the personnel officer of the paper rather than Gripper himself and it struck Willow as being rather odd. Having explained that Albert had been an excellent driver, with a clean licence and no stain on his character, the writer went on to say that Albert's departure from the paper's employ was caused merely by a difference of opinion with Mr Gripper and ought in no way to reflect on his capabilities or honesty. Willow had never seen such a reference in her life and thought its bad reflection on Gripper must mean either that the personnel officer hated him and did not care who knew it or that Gripper himself had inspired it. Of the two she thought that the latter was the more likely and began to be very interested indeed in Mr Gripper.

That interest was reinforced when she suddenly remembered that she had not rung Cressida's answering machine to get any messages for days. Scrabbling in her bag for the remote control device, she dialled the number of the Chesham Place flat, knowing that at that hour Mrs Rusham would be out shopping, played the tape back and heard Nan Hambalt's voice saying that her friend on Gripper's Gripes, Jane Cleverholme, would be delighted to dine with Cressida and give her the low-down on gossip columns. Unless she heard to the contrary, Ms Cleverholme would meet Cressida in Chez Saint Simon in Walton Street at eight-thirty on Thursday evening.

Blessing her memory for having woken up in time, Willow checked her watch. One-fifteen. She would have to do without lunch and buckle to in order to dispose of the work strewn all over her desk before meeting the PUS at half-past two. She had lost almost all interest in Eustace Gripper since her encounter with Inspector Worth. He knew that Mrs Gripper had been Algy's mistress and he knew that Algy had left her a substantial sum of money in his will. That in itself suggested that for once Algy had been genuinely in love, as well as giving both Amanda Gripper and her unappealing husband two very obvious motives for murder. If Inspector Worth was still concentrating his investigation on the personnel of DOAP, that suggested he was satisfied that neither Gripper had been in a position to commit murder. Willow had enough respect for Worth's brains to accept his views on that.

There was, however, still the question of Albert. Obviously Worth was interested in him. It was still possible that Albert's dismissal from Gripper's employ had been a ruse and that the driver had been put into the department as a spy, so that when Gripper was finally maddened enough to want to kill the man who had cuckolded him, Albert was there to do the job for him.

'A little melodramatic, I think,' said Willow at her most dry and turned back to work.

Replacing Albert's file in the heap and pinning a note to the top file saying, 'Barbara, please return these to the filing department', she went back to her desk and got down to work.

Almost everything had been dealt with by twenty-past two, and Willow put the few things that still needed work on one side for Barbara, before washing her hands and dragging a moth-eaten hairbrush through her tangled hair. She twisted it up into its French plait again and then she ran for the lifts, jabbing at the button angrily when there was no sign of either lift appearing. By the time she reached the hall, the PUS and Bob were irritably looking at their watches.

'Two-thirty, I think you said, PUS,' said Willow, looking at her own.

'Yes, come on now. The traffic's frightful,' he said, leading the way out to the large black car that stood outside. Willow saw that the driver standing with his cap under his arm was Albert. Her spirits rose and she forgot both her breathlessness and her bad temper.

There was no opportunity to talk to him on the journey to Westminster, because Bob (as the most junior) was sitting beside the driver while Willow on the back seat tried to persuade the PUS of her undeviating loyalty. The traffic was not in fact too bad and they were calmly walking up the stairs to Elsie Trouville's office at five to three.

Willow had neither met her nor seen any photographs and realised that she had allowed the PUS's prejudices to infect her own mind. She had been expecting a harridan. What she was faced with was a shortish, slim, fair-haired woman in her mid forties, dressed with considerable style and wearing both make-up and jewellery.

The new minister shook hands impartially with all her three officials and began to win Willow's admiration with her intelligent questions and clear grasp of the business of DOAP. It rather amused Willow to see the increasing sourness of the PUS's expression, and from a small, half-hidden smile on Ms Trouville's face it seemed that she also found his attitude funny.

When she had exhausted her questions, she courteously asked them if they had any for her. The PUS demonstrated his old-fashioned manners by offering Willow the chance to speak first.

'None at all, Minister,' she said, smiling. 'But may I say what a pleasure it will be to work with you?'

'Thank you, Ms King,' she said without displaying either unseemly delight or arrogance at the prospect. She went up one more point in Willow's estimation.

'May I have a word with you in private, Mrs Trouville? There is something ra-ather sensitive we need to discuss,' said the PUS at his most pompous. 'Willow, do you mind?'

'Not at all, PUS,' said Willow, just managing not to smile as she caught the minister's eye. I'll wait for you in the car. Bob?'

As they walked down the stairs, through the lobby full of milling Members of Parliament, journalists, visitors, tourists, constituents and researchers, Willow tried to flog her brain into thinking of some way to get rid of Bob for a moment. She was just turning to suggest feebly that he went to have a cup of tea somewhere, when she saw his face light up.

'Charles!' he cried. 'Friend of mine from the Treasury,' he added more quietly to Willow. 'Will you excuse me for a moment? I ought to have a word with him.'

Willow merely nodded, and hurried out of the gloomy great building to talk to Albert.

He was leaning against the bonnet of the car, smoking and chatting to another uniformed driver. When he saw Willow, he straightened himself up with insulting slowness and eventually removed his cigarette.

'Oh, don't bother with putting that out,' she said, trying not to sound too ingratiating. 'You must need all the relaxing you can get with ghastly London traffic swilling all around you.'

'Thanks, mate,' he said and Willow was hard put to it not to tell him just what she thought of his manners.

'I hear you used to work in Fleet Street,' she said, smiling at him instead. 'Don't you miss all that glamour?'

He looked at her as though she was mad and so she tried again.

'You must have met so many interesting people. Doesn't DOAP seem very flat after that?'

'Perhaps a little,' he said, grinding out the end of his cigarette with his shoe.

'What made you join us?' asked Willow, shading her eyes against the sharp, low winter sun.

'Nearer to where I live,' he said. Feeling as though she were trying to coax a very canny spider down to the bath plug in order to wash it away, Willow thought of another question.

'Really? Are you a South Londoner, too? I've lived in Clapham for nearly twenty years.'

'Lived in Putney all me life, haven't I?' he said, and once again Willow wondered why on earth the elegant Algy should have wanted this truculent oaf as his personal driver. Perhaps Albert was one of those men who can behave politely only to other men.

'How nice,' she said. 'And what do you do to liven up the dullness of DOAP, Albert? Presumably you and the other drivers have ways of passing all the hanging-about time profitably.'

At that question, the only one so far to which she particularly wanted an answer, Albert narrowed his piggy eyes. His full mouth seemed to tighten and Willow noticed that his hands were twitching. His exaggerated reaction suggested that he definitely had something to hide. Willow was about to push him so that she could get nearer the confirmation of his guilt that she wanted when they both heard the peevish tones of the permanent secretary behind them:

'Where on earth is Bob?'

'He found a friend, PUS, in the lobby.'

'Fetch him, will you, Albert?' he said before turning to Willow to spit out imprecations on the prime minister for saddling him with Elsie Trouville as his minister.

Willow switched off, knowing that he would keep himself happily complaining without any intervention from her, and thought about Albert and who it might be who had enlisted him in a conspiracy – and how she could set about getting any proof.

When she got back to her office, she looked speculatively at Roger, virtuously typing at his desk.

'Roger, I want you for a moment. Come in, will you?' she said, smiling at him.

'What can I do for you, Miss King?' he said, as soon as he had shut the door behind them both.

'It's just an idle thought, Roger, but I'm a little curious. We've just been driven to the House by Albert – do you know him?'

'Faintly,' said Roger, looking put out.

'He was quite extraordinarily rude, and I wondered why. You know most things that go on in this office: do you know if he particularly dislikes me?'

'Oh I shouldn't think so, Miss King. He's got rather old-fashioned views about women: perhaps it was just that.'

'Then he must get on well with the PUS,' said Willow, laughing, and Roger joined in, but Willow thought that there was something strained – artificial almost – about his mirth. 'He told me that he lives in Putney. You do, too, don't you, Roger? D'you ever come across him there?'

'No,' said Roger very quickly. 'Can I go now?' Willow was astonished at the request and even more surprised to see that he was looking positively pale.

'Roger, what on earth is the matter?' she said. 'Have I upset you?'

'No,' he said, and his face seemed to crumple up. For one appalling moment, Willow thought he might be going to burst into tears. Making what was obviously a supreme effort, he said: 'I did once sort of meet him in a pub I sometimes go to. He was with some horribly rough friends and. . . and. . .'

'I'm very sorry, Roger,' said Willow gently, remembering both the vigilante incident she had read about and the various occasions when Roger had turned up in the office with a black eye or worse. 'Did they give you a bad time?'

'Well they did have a rather violent sense of what is funny,' he said, putting on his most camp voice. Willow rather admired his courage and let him go.

Just before he opened the door, she suddenly asked him:

'Whereabouts in Putney does he live?'

'Nanking Road, I think someone told me,' he said and then looked absolutely terrified again. 'But I'm probably wrong,' he added quickly as he escaped. Willow went back to work, trying quite hard not to look at the implications of Roger's oddity.

An hour-and-a-half later, irritable and hungry, she was fighting her way on to the Northern Line tube at Clapham Common and thinking that it really was time for Willow King to invest in a modest car. For once, she wondered whether Richard was right and she was mad to persist in Willow's old life for half of every week. If only she had stuck to Cressida's she would never have been involved in the investigation into Algy's murder, never be stuck in the foul, hot, crowded, dirty tube, and – most of all – she would never have met Inspector Worth or, forgetting all her principles, leaped into bed with him. Despite the heat and the bodies pressed all around her she shivered.

When she finally walked out into the fresh air again at Sloane Square with her hair and nails newly arranged, she took great gulping breaths of air to clean her lungs of the scented stuffiness of Gino's salon and her mind of the accumulated stresses and emotions. A peaceful bath, a cup of green tea, and a leisurely half-hour of dressing and make-up completed the cure, and by the time she got into the taxi to go to Walton Street, she was Cressida again, happy, self-indulgent, and without serious fears.

As she opened the restaurant door, she realised that Ms Cleverholme was before her. Sitting alone at a table on the left-hand side of the room was a young woman with wild orange hair, wearing an astonishing loose shirt apparently made of silk patches in clashing purples and greens. Like a moulting macaw, thought Willow disdainfully, before she remembered that she was Cressida once again and noticed the spectacular flamboyance of the colours and the glamorous droopiness of the shirt's lines.

'Jane Cleverholme?' Willow said civilly as she walked towards the table.

'Yes,' answered the apparition, holding out a well-shaped hand tipped with scarlet fingernails. 'And you must be the amazingly successful Cressida Woodruffe.'

'Well, Cressida Woodruffe, yes,' answered Willow, shaking the hand and then turning to give her coat to a hovering waiter. 'But I think amazingly lucky would be nearer the mark,' she went on, with an unmistakable laugh in her voice. Jane Cleverholme's face relaxed.

'You can't think what a relief you are,' she said in a lazy drawl. 'What shall we have to drink?'

'Anything you like. This dinner is on me. But why a relief?'

'I thought you were going to be one of those ultra-rich female novelists who take their "work" with the utmost seriousness.'

'Good God no!' said Willow, laughing aloud. 'It's not work at all, really. My life actually consists of other people paying me to sit and spin daydreams. Bliss!'

'Except that it must be work – at least sometimes. Or don't you suffer at all from the "Oh-God-I-can't-bear-the-thought-of-writing-another-word" syndrome?' Jane said with enormous emphasis.

'Oh that,' said Willow, theatrically casual. 'Yes, that has a slightly familiar sound. Actually, to be quite truthful, I find it gets worse with each book. But never mind now. What will you have to drink?'

'Whisky please,' said Jane, briskly. 'And how can I help? Sing for my supper? Nan said you were thinking of setting the next book in a gossip column like ours. It can be a pretty sleazy world, you know.'

'Well,' said Willow as soon as she had ordered the drinks, 'I thought I could have a sweet innocent getting somehow embroiled – a gentle English graduate perhaps. . .'

'The late twentieth-century equivalent of the nineteenth-century country virgin being picked up by a white slaver and tricked into the international brothel circuit?' Jane suggested sipping her whisky and water.

'That sort of thing, though perhaps not quite so dramatic. But what I really wanted from you was a sort of overview (vile word) to give me some idea of whether my vague plans for characters and emotions would fit. If you were to describe your office and the people in it from top to bottom as it were, that would be very helpful,' answered Willow, ignoring her glass of dry white wine.

'In fact you're inviting me to talk about myself. Dangerous! But irresistible. Do you think we ought to choose what we're going to eat before I start? Otherwise, you might not get any food until midnight.'

As they sat opposite each other, reading the tantalising menu, Willow thought to herself that despite looking like a moulting macaw, Jane Cleverholme was her sort of woman. She was about as far as possible from the sweet, gentle, over-privileged Emma Gnatche, and Willow thought that, whether or not the evening provided any insights into Algy's murderer, it would certainly be entertaining.

She was right. Jane had a caustic tone and an eye for the absurd, and her account of her own rise from provincial journalism to the semi-heights of 'Gripper's Gripes' was exceedingly amusing. She seemed to have no pretensions whatever and very few illusions, and she was the best company Willow had found in a long long time. In laughing at Jane's stories and listening for any hints about Gripper himself, Willow forgot both the horror of Algy's blood-splattered body and the terrifying abysses of emotion that Tom Worth had revealed to her.

As they were licking the last of the *crème brûlée* out of their teaspoons, as frankly greedy as a pair of schoolgirls, Willow said with what she hoped was the right degree of casual interest:

'Someone, I can't remember who, said they'd seen your Mr Gripper behaving in a most peculiar way at a private party last Monday week. It sounded weird when I first heard it, but from your description of him, I don't think it can possibly be true.'

'Oh, do tell me what it was. I love stories about the pig. But come to think of it, it can't be true, because last Monday week, he and the very beautiful Mrs Gripper were in a conspicuous box at Covent Garden pretending to enjoy *Don Carlos*,' said Jane.

'Pretending?' said Willow, sidetracked yet again.

'The pig couldn't possibly distinguish one note from another. He really is the most complete philistine. But he fancies himself as having achieved a certain prominence, and prominent people enjoy opera. . . *quod erat demonstrandum*.'

'Yes, I suppose so,' said Willow, looking sadly for any remaining scraps of *crème brûlée*. 'Does everyone on the paper hate him as much as you do?'

Jane laughed and the raucous sound brought back Willow's original thoughts about her macaw-like aspects. But what she said was useful.

'A lot of them hate him a damn sight more. He has nothing on me and I'm using him for the experience and the connections I can get working on the "Gripes". But some of the long-stay staffers would do anything to get rid of him – only there's nothing they can do while the "Gripes" sells the number of papers it does.'

'Does no one get the better of him?' Willow said, almost to herself, but Jane attempted an answer.

'Only one person ever has and that didn't last long,' she said, and her face closed into a kind of don't-ask-because-I'm-not-going-to-tell-you expression.

'Coffee?' suggested Willow, thinking back to her successful winkling of information out of Emma Gnatche.

'What?' said Jane, quite obviously disconcerted. 'Oh, yes. All right.'

'And a little brandy?'

'If you're trying to get me tight so that I tell you all my secrets, my dear Ms Woodruffe. . .'

'Don't be idiotic,' interrupted Willow. 'I'm excessively grateful for all the background you're giving me. And I realise how naive my views of Fleet Street have always been, but even they didn't ever lead me to think I could

214

loosen the tongue of a journalist with alcohol.' They both laughed, and Jane agreed to have some cognac. The order given, Willow went back on the attack.

'I had heard a story about an ex-chauffeur of Gripper's,' she said, not looking at Jane. There was such a long silence that in the end she did look up. Jane was looking at her with a hard expression in her green eyes; her full lips were tucked back and a crease ran on either side of her face from nostril to chin.

'Have I by any chance been led up the garden path and made an almighty fool of myself?' she said. 'You're not going to tell me that under some other name you write for someone else, are you?'

Startled, but she hoped not betraying it, Willow shook her head.

'No, I've never written except as Cressida Woodruffe, and I've never contributed to any newspaper, if that's what you mean. Why? Have I hit the nail on the head with the chauffeur?'

Before Jane could answer, Willow felt a draught on the back of her neck and looked round idly to see who had arrived so late at the restaurant. What she saw made her grip her lips together and turn straight back to her guest.

'Someone you know?' said Jane, clearly delighted to have a change of subject.

'Just someone making a rather childish point,' answered Willow, determined to ignore the new arrivals. But she was not allowed to do that. A hand on her shoulder and Richard's familiar voice interrupted her.

'Hello W. . . .' At that hint of danger, Willow turned round so fast that she almost pulled the table cloth with her.

'Hello Richard,' she said so sternly that he produced her public name.

'Cressida,' he said, and Willow saw that he had been deliberately teasing her. 'You remember Sarah Gnatche, don't you?'

'Yes, indeed. Good evening, Sarah. It was very sweet of you to let me come to your party last week,' she said. 'Jane, this is Sarah Gnatche and Richard Crescent. Jane Cleverholme.'

Jane smiled and waved her cigarette at the newcomers, who, perhaps driven away by the smoke, retreated to their own table at the other side of the restaurant.

'What was that all about?' asked Jane as the coffee cups were laid in front of them with her glass of brandy. The waiter left them alone and Willow shrugged.

'Just Richard punishing me for refusing to see him for the last few days. Over the last couple of years or so we've fallen into a routine of dining together a couple of times each week, but I've been a bit busy lately,' said Willow casually. She did not add that Richard was also in the habit of sharing her bed for most of the nights she spent in Chesham Place and might well have resented the interruption in his well-arranged life.

'The unfortunate female with him was part of his past before me,' Willow went on. 'She's now engaged to someone else. It's just a gesture showing me that Richard is quite capable of having a nice time without me. Doesn't matter at all. You were going to tell me about the chauffeur,' said Willow, not allowing Jane to escape. Jane managed to laugh, even though the sound was a trifle forced.

'If you ever decide that you want a job ferreting out gossip for a tabloid, let me know,' she said, giving in with considerable grace. 'You've put up a masterly performance and now I'm stuck with leaving you tantalised and likely to make all kinds of trouble finding out what was behind it or telling you the truth and hoping against hope I don't lose my job over it.'

'Why should you?' asked Willow.

'He's a very vindictive man is Gripper-the-pig; and if he got to know that I'd passed the story on, I'd be out of a job like a shot – and I could find it hard to get another,' said Jane with some bitterness. 'He gave us all the most tremendous warning only last week about talking to people about him or his private life. It had been sparked off by some red-headed snooper he had found outside his hou. . .' Her voice died and she stared across the table at Willow.

'It was you,' she said, very quietly but with absolute conviction.

'I find that very hard to believe,' said Willow, trying hard to ignore the look of horror on her guest's face and drag the conversation back. 'Surely the quality papers would never stoop to believe anything told them by a – what? – a pig? But in any case, he won't find out through me. I really am quite trustworthy.'

'It was you, wasn't it? Oh, shit,' said Jane, looking seriously frightened. Willow was appalled.

'Listen, Jane. It's pure coincidence, but I did run into him last Friday. I was walking down Graham Terrace and he almost grabbed me and issued some extremely exaggerated threats,' she said.

'And so you thought you'd get hold of me and find out about him,' said Jane. 'Christ, what a fool I am! Anyone would have thought I was your innocent virginal heroine – although,' she went on with a self-accusing laugh, 'I don't suppose for one minute you're intending to write a novel.'

'I am, in fact,' said Willow, filing away a determination to do just that to keep faith with this woman. 'But, come on, bite the bullet and tell me about the chauffeur. I have given you an assurance that I won't pass it on. And you can hardly put yourself in a more difficult position than you are now.'

'I can't imagine how you got on to it and I can only admire you,' Jane started, as though she recognised the truth of Willow's ruthless statement. 'It was all supposition and suggestion. . . circumstantial evidence at the most. But Gripper-the-pig got very paranoid a couple of years

217

ago that whenever we had a good lead on some really suppurating scandal in high life one or other of our rivals would get there first. We lost a lot of stories – and a lot of kudos at that stage.'

'But how on earth can A. . . a chauffeur have been implicated?' Willow asked, wanting to hurry Jane up for the first time that evening.

'Gripper decided – on no real evidence except his long-held dislike of his chauffeur, who had been a boxer and never quite kowtowed enough – that he must have listened to discussions that took place in the car and then sold the leads to rival papers,' said Jane.

'Well that sounds perfectly likely,' said Willow, who had come across Civil Service colleagues with (possibly apocryphal) stories of drivers collecting information which they used to make money in the city. 'I just can't imagine why he could have been so batty as to discuss secrets in a place where he could be overheard.'

'The theory is that the back of his flashy Rolls is soundproofed. Clever old Albert, or so the story goes, must have planted a small bug under the back seat, taped the stories and sold the tapes. Gripper was convinced that he had made a tidy little fortune out of the scam. Because Gripper couldn't prove anything to the satisfaction of his relatively powerful enemies on the paper, Albert was persuaded to leave with a nice little redundancy package. God knows where he is now – or what he's doing.'

Willow had actually opened her mouth before she remembered that as Cressida Woodruffe she could not possibly know the identity of drivers at the Department of Old Age Pensions. The temptation to display her superior knowledge was almost overmastering, but the shock of it brought her back to her senses, and she called for the bill instead. While she was waiting for it she wondered whether Albert could have been blackmailing the minister. If Albert had known so much about Gripper's business, he might well also have known about Mrs Gripper's infidelity and hoped to extract money from her lover. That at least would explain the otherwise unlikely coincidence of his having gone to work at DOAP.

'You've been splendid, Jane,' said Willow five minutes later as she signed the credit card slip. 'I hope it hasn't bored you too much?'

'Not remotely,' said Jane, who was beginning to recover her confidence. 'For part of the time I enjoyed myself, and I shall just have to trust you not to blow my cover.'

Having decided to like Jane, Willow was tempted to exchange a confidence for a confidence and blow her own, but her deeply engrained sense of self-preservation stopped her just in time. They left the restaurant together and stood on the pavement outside the restaurant until a free taxi appeared.

'Shall we share it?' said Willow. 'I'm going to Chesham Place.'

'Opposite direction,' said Jane. 'I've just moved to Fulham from Putney. You take it.'

Willow signalled the taxi, but when it had drawn up, she did not get in for a moment.

'Putney?' she said, looking at Jane, who was searching the middle distance for another orange taxi light. 'Everyone seems to live there now. No, it's all right, I know you said you'd moved. But I was talking to someone the other day who'd just bought a house in Nanking Road,' she went on, trying to get some idea of the kind of people who lived there. Did you know it?'

'You've rich friends, Cressida,' said Jane, smiling. 'Half a million at least now. They're vast houses, with immense gardens.'

'You want a cab or not, lady?' came a raucously Cockney voice from the taxi.

'Yes, please,' said Willow getting in at last. She pulled down the window, thanked Jane again for all her information, and they parted on a note of restrained friendliness.

Sitting back in the taxi as it sped through the quiet streets, just sprinkled with the first snow, Willow thought from what she had heard that Gripper was unlikely to have engineered Albert's employment at DOAP for the purpose of shadowing and then murdering Algy Endelsham. Private enterprise on Albert's part seemed far more likely, and if Albert really had been clever and unprincipled enough to carry off the scam described by Jane, it was even possible that he himself was running a fraud similar to the one Willow had imagined for Michael Englewood. And if Albert's house had really cost half a million, he would have to have some source of money beyond his wages. Unless, of course, having lived in Putney all his life he had inherited it. . . . But that seemed just as unlikely. Willow concentrated hard on the memory of his personal file, and was almost certain that the address he had given had been quite different from Nanking Road, which would suggest that the house was a new acquisition.

Could Algy have stumbled on whatever nefarious things his driver had been doing? Willow asked herself. Or was there after all some foundation for the story she had heard at DOAP the previous week? It was the executive officer from registry who had suggested that Algy was being blackmailed and had got himself murdered when he had refused to pay any more to the blackmailer.

The more Willow thought about that the less she could believe it. Surely Algy was too powerful – and confident – ever to allow himself to be blackmailed. She much preferred the idea that he had uncovered some corruption.

'And got himself murdered?' said Willow aloud at her most self-derisive. The cabby looked at her in his mirror in considerable surprise and Willow smiled placatingly at his reflection. 'It's just near the corner with Lowndes Place,' she said to him and watched his face relax.

It would have to be a really enormously profitable bit of corruption, she thought, for Albert to have gone to such lengths. Could he possibly have organised a fraud as labour-intensive and wide-ranging as the one she had invented? And even if he had, how could Algy of all people have discovered it?

Willow's cogitations were brought to a halt with the taxi. Paying the driver and tipping him, she walked up the steps of her home and had a moment's violent irritation with the ground-floor lessee, who yet again had left the front-door unlocked, and climbed slowly up the stairs towards her bath and bed.

14

MUTTERING to herself, 'We'll have a burglary if they go on bloody leaving the front door open,' Willow stalked upstairs. She was just feeling in her bag for her keys when she noticed that the door to her flat was standing about four inches open.

Slowly straightening up, with her keys in her hand, Willow stood looking at that gap. It was perfectly clear what had happened, but her mind tried out various other possibilities for her: Mrs Rusham might have left the door open; the lock might have failed; there might have been a small earth tremor that had shaken the bolts out. At last, even her imagination ran out of ideas and she was left alone to face the reality that her flat had been burgled.

She was physically terrified, and when she caught a whiff of cold tobacco smoke, sweat and cheap aftershave she nearly vomited.

Trying to control herself, Willow listed the various feelings that were churning around her: she was afraid of what might be done to her if the burglars were still inside her home; she was sickened by the thoughts of the damage and filth she might find inside her door; she was outraged by the invasion; she was desperate at the knowledge that what had seemed to be her sanctuary was safe no longer. She was also ashamed of the naivety that had allowed her to believe that one locked door would keep her safe from marauders.

Dizziness threatened to overcome her; tears rose in her eyes. She stood alone, shaking like a piece of wastepaper blown on to barbed wire in a storm.

But Willow did not faint, or cry, or throw up. She put her finger on the bell and kept it there until any burglars would have thrown themselves out of the window or at least come thundering through the front door. Then she gathered herself together, pushed the door wide open and walked into what had once been her home.

The tiny square hall was just as it had always been; even the blue-and-white bowl of pot-pourri on the little oak chest was untouched. Wondering whether to feel relieved or not, she went on and walked into the drawing room. There she saw what the invaders had done.

Her once-glorious Turner was a mess of ripped coloured paper, gilt wood and glass, all lying in a heap on the floor. At the opposite side of the room the Chippendale looking-glass was a pile of glittering shards, pointed up by the glossy black pieces of the Ming vases. They were smashed beyond repair, and the flowers and water they had held had been flung against the pannelling, staining the pale greenish-blue paint. Someone had obviously tried his knife on the silk rug, but it must have been too tough to cut, for only one edge had any marks.

Perhaps because he had failed there, he had taken his knife to the walnut bureau-bookcase and scored the veneer in a dozen places. Someone had kicked over the mahogany Pembroke table and stamped on the telephone answering machine, too. Its entrails and highly coloured wires were spread around, mixed with the brass feet of the table and the smashed and splintered wood. The sofa cushions had been slashed and over everything lay the white feathers that had escaped.

Willow stood just inside the doorway, feeling utterly bereft. Never had she been so alone; never had she minded solitude so much. Her handbag dropped to the floor and she brought both hands up to her eyes as though to contain the tears that started to spurt out of her eyes. The room she had loved so much more than any person in her life lay ravaged before her; none of its pretty things had escaped. The cruel malice that had driven the burglars in their orgy of wreckage seemed to have infected the very air. Willow gagged suddenly and stumbled across the ruins of her dream to fling open the windows.

Breathing in the icy wind, she felt her teeth aching and her throat cringing, but at least the cold seemed to dry up her tears and give her back some power of thought. Once again she looked around the lost treasures of her kingdom, but this time with more objectivity, and she saw a letter addressed in competent typing to 'Cressida Woodruffe'. Picking her way more delicately across the ruins, she went to fetch it and, using only her fingertips as though she was afraid of picking up some infection from the paper, she opened the envelope. The note inside was roughly typed on completely plain paper. It read:

Keep your trap shut and your long nose out of other people's business. Curiosity killed the cat. If I were you I wouldn't want to find out what it would do to a bitch – or her friends.

The risible, television-gangster wording did not dilute the violent menace of the warning.

Then the feebleness and misery alike were drummed out of her mind by rage at what had been done to her flat – and by the penetration of her disguise. She slammed her fists against the panelling again and again until she raised such bruises on her hands that she had

224

to stop. Then she stood, looking down at her hands, the fingers slightly curled upwards as though in supplication, wondering what on earth to do.

'Police, obviously,' she said to herself. But there would be little any policeman could do: she had no evidence as to the identity of the men or women she had so frightened by her 'curiosity'; they had certainly worn gloves and so there would be no fingerprints amid the viciously destroyed furniture and pictures.

'But I must tell someone,' she said aloud, feeling slow and somehow stupid, almost as though she were coming round after a general anaesthetic or a blow to her head.

She knew that at some time when she was feeling stronger, she would have to tackle her insurance company and she would need a police reference number for any claim; and, of course, there was her civic duty to consider: no crime ought to go unreported, particularly no violent crime and there had been violence in that room, even if there were no human victim.

Suddenly as though a missing piece of her brain had slotted back into place, she thought of what the knife-wielding invaders had written. She could not understand why she had not worked it out before. This wreckage of all the things she had most cared about was the result of her investigation into Algy's murder. Pushing the hair out of her eyes, she knew then whom she had to telephone.

With shaking hands and trembling knees, she walked out into the small hall where she thought she must have dropped her handbag. It was still there. She opened it, saw her wallet with all its credit cards and money intact, and rifled through its contents until she found his card. Then she went back into the devastated room to telephone. At the sight of the heap of crunched black plastic and multi-coloured wires, she swore in a torrent of wild, furious words.

It was a good ten minutes before she could regain enough control to force herself away from the scene of

225

destruction and find one of the other telephones. Then, sitting bolt upright on the edge of her bed, she tapped in his number. The telephone rang five, six times and she was about to replace the receiver in despair when he answered.

'Worth,' he said and for once his voice carried with it the possibility of comfort.

'It's Will. . . , no Cressida Woodruffe here. You know. Sorry, Willow King,' she blurted out, not knowing where to begin, what to say or whether he, too, regretted their encounter and wanted to avoid speaking to her ever again.

'Sh, sh, sh, sh,' he said, as though calming a panicking child. 'Take a deep breath. I'm here. Now, tell me.'

Gathering up all her scattered self-discipline and gripping the telephone receiver as though it were the only lifeline in a tempestuous sea, she tried.

'My flat's been broken into; they've wrecked it. . .the drawing room. With a knife, I think, and boots. They've left a letter, telling me to stop interfering – no, nosing around. . . . Something like that.'

'All right,' he said in an especially calm voice. 'All right. They've gone, have they?'

'Yes.'

'Are the locks on the front door still intact?'

'No, I don't think so.'

'Go and check them. I'll hold on. Then come back. All right, Will?'

'All right,' she said and did as she was told. When she came back, she noticed that the receiver of her telephone was covered in sweat. She wiped her hand on her skirt and then picked up the receiver again.

'There's only the bolts, which we hardly ever used to use. They're okay. The locks are smashed now,' she said, not wanting to name him for some reason.

'All right. Now, I'm going to ring off and come straight round. I want you to make yourself something hot to drink and if possible eat something sweet. Don't have anything alcoholic; don't answer the door to anyone except me; and don't be afraid. I'll arrange to get new locks put on. All right?'

'Yes,' she said, breathing deeply and deliberately. Then she spoilt the effect for herself, by adding like a six-year-old, 'Will you be long?'

'No, not long. I'll be as quick as I can. I'm not far from Abbeville Road,' he said and Willow only just managed to make her mind work enough to say:

'No. No, I'm at home. In Chesham Place.'

'Ah,' he said. 'Good thing you told me. What's the number?' Willow gave it, and Tom's last words before he put down his telephone were: 'Keep warm, Willow.'

She did as he said, and his intervention had been so successful in dealing with the effects of shock that she even managed to be amused at her own lack of resentment at his orders. It was a very long time since anyone had given orders to her, and she was surprised to feel the comfort that obeying them gave her.

By the time he arrived she was enough in command of herself to greet him politely and thank him for coming out so late. He looked at her in silence for a moment or two and she could not understand the weird mixture of expressions that crossed his rugged face. She had forgotten that he had known her only as Willow. Just as the silence was beginning to frighten her, Tom Worth took two steps towards her and enfolded her in his arms. At first she stiffened; it felt almost insulting that he should have seen through her façade. But then as the strength of his body made itself felt, and the warmth of his affection and care, she relaxed against him. Still he did not speak, but she felt one of his large hands gently stroking her hair, again and again.

'Now, Will, do you feel strong enough to show me? Or would you rather go and lie down while I look?' he asked at last. She pulled herself out of his arms, braced to deal with whatever had to be done.

'No,' she said. 'I'll show you. I have to look at it again some time, and it'll probably help if I have you there while I do it.'

'*En avant*, then,' he said, and together they walked into her drawing room.

Despite her bracing up, she still stopped on the threshold and gagged at the sight in front of her. Each treasure that the man with the knife had scored or smashed had represented a bulwark against the real world that she had inhabited for so long in such cold, grey lack of happiness. After the first couple of years as Cressida Woodruffe, Willow had felt untouchable and safe, surrounded by the material comforts that her dreams had won for her. After that evening she would never be able to feel the same, even if the insurance company came up trumps and she managed to replace each ruined picture and piece of furniture.

Longing for comfort, she yet hoped that Tom Worth would not touch her again. When he had made love to her, he had smashed the last illusions of Willow's self-sufficiency just as surely as the knifeman had broken her pretty toys. Either Tom Worth understood her unexpressed shrinking or he had had no intention of touching her again, because he left her in the doorway and picked his way through the mess with extraordinary delicacy for so large a man. She watched him peer and examine and note. When he had searched his way across the room to the two big windows, he turned and smiled at her.

'Well, it could have been a lot worse,' he said.

'Thanks a bunch,' she said, regaining some of her normal astringency. 'How?'

'They could have had a go at you.' In the split second it took for his tone to get through to her brain she thought of a scene in *Gaudy Night* and a most inappropriate smile flashed across her pale face.

228

'What's so funny?' Tom asked, justifiably annoyed both with himself for allowing some of his feelings to show and with her for laughing at them.

'I was just remembering when Harriet Vane's Chinese chess set had been smashed with a poker and for the first time in their lives she wept over Peter Wimsey,' she said, assuming that he would know precisely what she was talking about. When she saw that he did not, she tried to explain. 'It's in a detective story by Dorothy L. Sayers. I find that it helps to tie vile things in one's own life to books, but you probably find that irresponsible. I'm sorry.'

She did not even notice that she had broken her rule about never apologising; all she knew was that she had to take the hurt look out of his dark eyes. In that she succeeded. He did not even laugh at her. Instead he said quite gently:

'If it helps, there's nothing irresponsible about it. But I seem to remember your saying that using your analytical talents helped too. So, what do you make of all this?'

'Well,' she said, taking a deep breath and standing up straighter, 'it must have been caused by questions I've been asking. I should have told you sooner, but last week I was afraid that someone had got into the flat and searched it.'

'My God, Willow,' said Tom, clearly furious. 'Why didn't you tell me? Or at least your local CID?'

'Well I wasn't certain,' she said. 'Nothing had been broken; nothing stolen. No locks had been broken. Mrs Rusham – my housekeeper – must have let them in, thinking they were bona fide inspectors of some kind. I haven't seen her yet to ask about it. And, besides, I felt a fool.'

'At least you needn't feel that any more,' he said, and there was something in his comforting voice which told her that he understood precisely how much she hated being thought foolish.

She watched him pick his way back to her and then felt one of his hands under her elbow.

'Come on; I've seen enough for the moment. Let's go and sit somewhere else and thrash it out.'

'Is the kitchen all right for you?' Willow asked a little anxiously; she very much did not want him in her bedroom. 'It's warm there by the Aga.'

'The kitchen's fine,' he answered, ushering her out of the door. She looked back and up into his face to see whether he had understood, but there was no expression in his eyes to bother her. She was too accustomed to knowing more about everyone else than they knew about her to feel completely comfortable with the idea that he understood her.

'You must have had fun,' he said looking round her kitchen.

'What, designing this?' she said, turning from the Aga, where she was starting to make a pot of tea. 'Yes, it was terrific fun; the idea of having enough money to have whatever I wanted in the way of cookers, pots and pans was one of the earliest delights.'

'That too,' he answered, watching her with a smile in his eyes. 'But I really meant shuttling between Abbeville Road and this, knowing that no one who knew you in one life had any idea of the other – except whatsisname.'

Willow picked up the heavy kettle and poured boiling water on the Lapsang Souchong tea leaves, before attempting to answer. This man with his dangerously attractive character and the strength of his large body had understood her far better in a few days than Richard had done in three years.

'His name is Richard,' she said crisply, and poured out the tea. Then in a quite different voice added: 'but I don't think he is the only one who knows.'

'No,' agreed Worth. 'Clearly this bloke knows, too. Have you decided yet who it is?'

Willow drank some tea, swallowed and then said:

230

'I think it must be Albert – the minister's driver.'

'Now why?' asked Worth. There was no antagonism in his voice, but he was clearly doubtful. 'I know you've suspected him, and I know you don't like him, but you must accept that he has been cleared of all suspicion of the murder.'

'Are you sure?' said Willow. Then she shook her red head: 'I'm sorry; that sounds as though I think you're stupid and I don't think that at all.' He drank some tea and laughed.

'Thanks for the testimonial,' he said. 'Yes, we are sure: apart from several other witnesses, there is a woman whose ground-floor flat overlooks that corner of Cedar's Road. She was so surprised to see such a large, opulent car parked outside her building that she watched it for nearly two hours – hoping, I suspect, for the sight of some glamorous celebrity.'

'But. . .' said Willow. Worth put a large hand over hers as it lay on the table.

'Wait, Willow,' he said. 'At nine-fifteen when Albert decided that there was something wrong, he saw the light in the old girl's flat, rang her bell and asked to use the telephone to call us. She has positively identified him – and he was still in her flat when our men got there to talk to him.'

'Oh,' said Willow inadequately, thinking once again how unfair was the advantage that he and his men had over an amateur like herself.

'But,' he went on, 'that's not to say he couldn't have done this. Even if there is a connection with the murder, I'd stake my job on the fact that whoever's wrecked your flat is not the same person who beat Endelsham to death.'

'Tell me why not,' she said, and felt interest pricking the fears out of her mind.

'The men who did this are the sort to put the boot in – it was rough, straightforward and efficient violence.

231

Endelsham was killed by someone in a panic and a hurry.'

'Did the wounds tell you that?' Willow asked, and Tom Worth was relieved to see that her eyes were slowly returning to normal, the pupils shrinking again and the lids blinking in normal time.

'Yes. They were all over the place – some on the head, some across the eyes, some on the cheeks and chin,' he said and Willow felt sick all over again. Determined to keep her brain going, she decided to ask something that had been teasing at the back of her mind.

'But, Tom,' she said and his head lifted at the sound of his name.

'Yes, Will?' His voice was very kind.

'If it was as frenzied as that, surely Algy must have got some blows in. He was a tall man and if not as strong as you, certainly as heavy. I cannot believe that he'd have stood quietly by, while some thug or lunatic did that to him.'

Worth sipped his tea and put the mug down on the table, wondering how much she could take. After all, he thought, she had been fairly close to the man even if she had denied him what everyone seemed to want of her.

'No, we're sure he didn't.'

'In that case, wasn't there something on his hands or under his nails that could identify the killer for you? Wouldn't he at least have scratched whoever did that to him? And if he did, couldn't you have got some tissue out from under his nails that would allow you to do that DNA fingerprinting business?'

'If he had we probably could have. But whatever he did to defend himself, seems not to have broken the skin. That's why we haven't been examining all the suspects for surface cuts and abrasions.'

Then that definitely puts Roger in the clear, thought Willow relieved but not very surprised.

'The only blood we've identified on the corpse belonged to it,' went on Tom, 'and all we've got from under his nails was the usual mixture of London dirt, sweat and minute bits of whatever he had for lunch. We've some hairs on his clothes – both male and female, but they haven't been identified yet, and in any case probably got there quite innocently.'

'I see,' said Willow, glad of the confirmation that Roger's scratches had had nothing to do with the murder on the common. 'So we're back with motive. Are you quite certain that it couldn't have been random louts like the ones I was afraid of on the common last week? Or the vigilantes?'

'I think that's highly unlikely. The so-called vigilantes are a bunch of youths full of sound and fury, happy to bash up a pub or two, scratch broken bottles down the sides of expensive cars and throw dogs' excrement about; but they're not into real violence – thank the Lord.'

Willow got up and walked across to the Aga. Standing with her back to it, she leaned against its warmth, clasping her porcelain mug of tea in both hands.

'It's all so horrible,' she said naively. 'I never knew that there was so much violence and hate about.' Then she made herself laugh a little. 'That must sound idiotic to someone like you: SAS and the police – violence and hate are what you're there for, aren't they?'

'Will you tell me why you think that Albert could have done this?' he said, ignoring her outburst.

Willow left the Aga's warmth and walked slowly across the quarry-tiled floor.

'Listen, Tom,' she said, her face taut and somehow professional looking, as though she had forgotten both her fear and her disgust. 'I think that Albert is running some kind of scam at the department.'

Tom's face creased into a tolerant smile, which annoyed Willow, but as she expounded her theory of the pension

233

fraud, his expression changed: the tolerance and the amusement were overtaken by curiosity.

'Don't pensioners have to collect in person and show some form of identification?' he said as she finished.

'Of course not, Tom. You must know that. Think how many pensioners are in wheelchairs, arthritic, unable to go themselves, without transport if they live in the country, or being cared for in homes or hospitals. It simply would not be possible to insist on personal collections. Albert and whoever he has recruited could have the money posted or they could go and collect from selected post offices.

'And as for the department's checks,' she went on warming to her story, 'what happens is that a letter is sent to the pensioner's registered address asking if they're still alive. Albert and his troops would merely reply in the affirmative and everything would go on as before. I don't see that Albert could do enough of it on his own to make all that much money, but if he's subborned one or more of the clerks and uses other drivers to do the collecting of the books in the first place, he could get a nice little earner going.'

'It sounds feasible,' said Tom, betraying none of the excitement Willow had felt when she had invented the scheme and merely sounding very tired. 'It'll have to be investigated – although you have no evidence at all. It may be no more than your novelist's brain inventing the improbable.'

'It's entirely supposition,' she agreed, responding to his rational objection without even thinking about it. 'I've always been doubtful about whether Albert has the brains to organize anything like it, but you could find out fairly easily, I imagine. You'd need to know whether Albert has any friend, mistress, relation – or even blackmailee – in the lower ranks of the clerical officers. Your best bet would be the under secretary (estabs)'s secretary, Valerie,

234

I imagine – or you could try my CO – Roger. He knows everything.'

'Okay,' said Worth. 'But I'd need a bit more solid evidence before I diverted manpower away from the murder just at the moment.'

'Well,' said Willow, seeing the force of his objection. 'There are one or two clues to support the idea that something is going on at the department.'

'Such as?'

'On the Thursday after the murder when I left DOAP to come here, I was convinced someone was following me – although I couldn't actually see anyone doing it. Nearly a week ago as I told you – someone searched this flat. Then, when I got back to DOAP, I realised that the same person had been through my office there.'

'How?'

'I don't know,' she said crossly. 'How do people normally search offices?' At that Tom laughed and the sound made Willow feel almost as warm as the Aga had done.

'No, idiot,' he said kindly. 'How do you know it was the same person?'

'There was a smell,' she said and even at the memory all the warmth drained out of her. She shivered in disgust. Tom did not press her to tell him anything more. Willow tried to pull herself together.

'Now this afternoon, I had a chance to interrogate Albert, and I asked him whether he and the other drivers had found any profitable ways of using all the time they have to spend hanging about waiting for us. . . .'

'Oh, my God,' said Worth, running both hands through his thick, dark hair. 'Never mind now. Tell me how Albert could have known you were interested in him before this afternoon's indiscretion.'

'Damn,' said Willow briefly. She had been too taken up with other things even to consider that. 'No wait,' she went on after a few minutes' silent thought, 'I do know. On the day after Algy's murder, Albert overheard me cracking a joke with a man who works in the registry department. I was suggesting – frivolously – that the minister might have been blackmailing the registry staff because he had discovered some nefarious goings-on there. It was just a joke, to try to make him and the rest of them stop speculating so wildly about what Algy might have been doing to get himself killed. But Albert must have thought. . .'

'Hmmmm,' murmured Worth. 'It's fairly far-fetched – and wholly circumstantial. But we'll have to look into it. Damn.'

'Why the curse?' she asked, getting up again to refill the teapot. Her mouth felt furred with tannin, but she was too restless simply to sit doing nothing.

'Because,' said Worth, still sitting in his chair, 'I've enough on my plate trying to prove who murdered your minister.' As she came back to the table with the teapot, he held out his mug for more tea. Her eyes widened.

'That sounds as though you think you know who did it,' she said. He could hear the tightness in her voice, but he could not know that she felt suddenly faint. She sat down heavily on a chair opposite him, nursing the hot teapot in her lap. At last noticing the heat against her thighs, she put the pot back on the table.

'Yes,' he said. 'I think so. We usually do know who, but it's far more difficult getting proof to satisfy a court of law.' He paused and then said quite gently: 'And you know, too, don't you, Willow?'

'No,' she said more emphatically than she should have done. Worth simply looked at her.

'I don't believe it,' she added rather pathetically. 'There's no real motive. I think it's far more likely to have been the vigilantes.'

Worth sat across the table from her, his eyebrows meeting across his misshapen nose. Despite his obvious strength and the brains of which she was so well aware, he seemed vulnerable then and desperately tired. Quite against her better judgment, she said abruptly:

'Have you talked to the tramp at Clapham Junction yet?'

'Tramp? What tramp?'

'There's an old man – homeless presumably – who hangs about the station there, who told me that on the night of Algy's murder he saw a man washing in the gents'. It may mean nothing, but the washing was obviously fairly extensive, because otherwise he'd never have told me about it: I'd asked him, you see, if he had seen anything unusual that night.'

'And trains to Surbiton stop at Clapham Junction,' said Worth meditatively.

'And a vast number of other places,' Willow snapped back at him.

'I know, my dear,' he said, and then looked down at his watch. 'You ought to be in bed. Will you promise me something?'

Willow neither moved nor spoke.

'Promise you won't ask any more questions,' he said. 'You've made someone bloody angry and they've already had a go at your flat. I don't want them getting their hands on you.'

'I thought the police were far more exercised about crimes against property than against the person,' said Willow nastily, because his concern for her moved her and she did not want him to know it.

'Willow, two nights ago we made love to each other; you slept in my arms. Did it mean so little that you think I wouldn't care what happened to you?'

'No,' she said with such emphasis that she shocked herself. 'I mean . . . you . . . It meant a lot. Please don't think that. It's just . . . I'm just all shaken up. I'm sorry.

237

You were angelic to come to the rescue tonight, and to worry about me.'

'You've had a bad shock,' he said, raising his head at last and smiling at her so kindly that she almost burst into tears again. He hugged her before he left, but he did not even try to kiss her as though he had understood her reluctance to be touched.

15

W HEN TOM had left her, promising to file a report and get someone to ring her with the reference number for her insurance claim, Willow was too over-stimulated to think of sleep. It was partly all the tea and coffee she had drunk, partly the adrenalin that had flooded through her body as she was forced to assess the assault on her possessions, and partly the excitement – or fear – generated by talking once more to a man whose brain moved as swiftly as her own.

Whatever the ingredients, she knew that their effect would be to make her toss and turn sleepless in bed and so she decided to tackle the mess instead of trying to sleep. At last taking off her high heels, she bound her hair back out of her eyes, put on a pair of rubber gloves and raided Mrs Rusham's cupboards for a bundle of plastic bin bags. Then with heavily-repressed regret twisting at her, she piled the remains of the Turner and the vases into bags, twisted closures about their wrung necks and stacked them up to await the loss adjuster.

The spilled feathers billowed around her whenever she moved, and the dust they raised caught at her throat, but as she gradually reduced the mess to some kind of order she found a certain peace. At last with all the debris stowed away, she fetched a dampened cloth and wiped the mess of flower stalks and water from the walls and stood back to see the skeleton of her favourite room laid bare in front of her.

It would not take all that long to reflesh it, she told herself, and it was even possible that some skilled cabinet-maker could repair the once-lovely walnut bureau. As Tom had said, the warning-off could have been infinitely worse. Happier, physically tired out at last and soothed by what she had achieved, she went to bed and in the end she slept.

The next morning, she was still heavily asleep when Mrs Rusham arrived for her day's work. Noticing that her employer was still in bed, the housekeeper moved with careful quietness about her tasks and Willow slept on until woken by the ring of the telephone beside her bed. Groggy with sleep, she reached for the receiver.

'Hello, Tom,' she said in an indistinct, thickened voice.

'Willow, my dear?'

'Ah, Richard!' she exclaimed, wide awake at last and hoping that the disappointment did not sound too clearly in her voice. 'How are you?'

'Full of apologies, Willow, for last night. It was stupid. I'd been wanting to ring you for days, but I've had a simply frightful deal. . . . Meetings until the small hours every morning. And then when I rang Mrs R. last night, she told me you'd be at that restaurant, and so I. . .'

'Let's forget it, Richard,' said Willow, determined not to cap his apology with one of her own. 'How's the deal now?'

'We've completed now, thank God.'

'Good. I hope you won, Richard,' said Willow, wanting him to get off the telephone in case Tom was trying to get through and yet not wanting to upset Richard. After all, he had said sorry and she had been rather cavalier with his sensibilities when they had last met.

'Yes we did. And the fees will be correspondingly enormous. The clients had ghastly doubts half-way through, which added to our problems. But at least now they think we're miracle workers. And they're set to make a lot out of it, so I don't see why we shouldn't.'

'No, indeed,' said Willow, although she rather disapproved of his bank's methods of billing according to the wealth of their clients rather than simply to the hours worked.

'So,' he said, as though she had not spoken, 'I thought we might celebrate. Both my deal and the end of our separation.'

'Richard, hold on. We haven't had a separation. I know that it's been a week, but I've been horribly busy as well. What. . . ?'

'It's all right, Willow,' he said interrupting. She could hear the smile in his voice. 'Manner of speaking only. Will you come out to dinner with me this evening? Please, Willow?'

'I'd love to, Richard,' she answered, suppressing an internal caveat that if Tom Worth wanted to talk to her, he would take precedence. They settled that Richard would pick her up at half-past eight, and then she got out of bed to dress and see what Mrs Rusham had provided for her breakfast.

Willow had finished her second cup of coffee before she realised that she had been thinking exclusively of Inspector Worth and how he might be progressing with the dual investigations at DOAP. She still hoped desperately that they were both wrong in their suspicions of Algy's murderer, but she was becoming more and more afraid that they were not.

Trying to stop her mind dwelling on the consequences of her intervention, Willow thought instead about Algy, and about whether he could be said to have borne any responsibility for what had been done to him. There was no longer any doubt in her mind that he had perpetrated some dreadful cruelties, and probably enjoyed them too. She frowned and put down her coffee cup.

During his early days at DOAP, Willow had prided herself on being one of the very few Civil Servants who could keep up with him and occasionally get the better of him in arguments. She had even been pleased at times to think that they were rather alike. But it had recently begun to dawn on her that she had been in danger of sharing several of Algy Endelsham's less desirable qualities as well as his wits and drive. Like him, she had often watched in cool contempt as other people wasted their energies in rage, or desire or fear, and had prided herself on not being at the mercy of her feelings as they were.

Unlike Algy, though, Willow had never enjoyed the sight of their weakness and turmoil. Indeed, other people's strong emotions had often frightened her just as much as the prospect of her own. But it was true that she had stayed calmly apart from the rest of the world, and only now could she see how dangerous and how destructive that could be.

If it had not been for Tom Worth, Willow thought, she might never have understood that. She was not ready to admit him into either of her lives, and she still shuddered to remember the terrifying possibilities of feeling he had aroused in her, but she was grateful to him for showing her what she had been doing. His kindness to her the previous night, his unconditional warmth and support, had given her something she had not even known that she lacked. And his lovemaking had shown her what it felt like to be submerged by passion, to give up all self-control and to allow another person to have enough power over her to damage her if he were to misuse it.

Willow knew quite well that Tom – and the feelings he had aroused in her – could destroy her carefully balanced existence if she let him, but perhaps when she knew him a little better she could explain herself to him and come to some kind of arrangement with him.

242

She laughed at herself then because she knew that Tom Worth could never play the kind of part in her life that Richard Crescent played; but she also knew that whatever happened, she could trust Tom Worth with anything.

Willow went back to her novel after breakfast, rather glad to have the option of retreating into the old unfeeling fantasy life for a time. The investigation was over as far as she was concerned: the police no longer suspected her – if they ever had done – and mercifully it was their job to bring the investigation to its inevitable end. If the murderer did turn out to be Albert, she would be relieved. But if. . . her mind shied away from the other likely possibility and she forced herself to concentrate on her work.

The writing went quite well that day and Willow got her heroine safely into the deadly drama from which the hero would eventually rescue her, before leaving the word processor to bathe and change. When Richard arrived at half-past eight, he bore an immense bunch of white roses and a hopeful, gentle smile. Willow smiled to think of the easy, happy arrangement they had achieved and she kissed him warmly.

'Richard, darling,' she said, 'you look as though you expected me to hit you. Surely I haven't been that beastly?'

'No, my dear, you haven't at all. What an idea! It just is awfully nice to see you after such a hellish week. Here, take these.'

He thrust the five dozen roses at her and she looked at them a little helplessly, wishing that Mrs Rusham had not left.

'Put them in a sinkful of water,' said Richard, 'and let Mrs R. see to them tomorrow.' Willow was about to compliment him on his unwonted perspicacity when he added, 'It would take far too long to arrange them now.'

Ah well, she said to herself as she carried her trophies

into the kitchen and ran cold water into one of the sinks for them, perhaps it is for the protection of his lack of understanding that I keep Richard by me. She returned to him with a smile on her face. He took her mink from her and draped it round her shoulders.

The dinner was so good, Richard's conversation so unworrying and his smile so charming that Willow acceded to his request to take her home. When the Audi drew up outside her front door, they turned to each other and Richard asked a silent question. Willow smiled and nodded. As she opened her door to get out on to the pavement she looked up at her front door. In the shadows of the fat white pillars stood a man. Seeing the car he moved forward a little into the light. Willow stiffened. She felt one of Richard's hands on her arm and heard his urgent whisper:

'Stay there, darling. I'll see him off.' Willow gripped his wrist with her free hand.

'No, Richard. You can't, I'm afraid. It's the police. Ah, good evening, Inspector Worth. Have you met Richard Crescent? Richard, this is Inspector Worth of the Metropolitan Police.'

'Good evening, Inspector,' said Richard and Tom answered simply, 'Sir.' Then he turned to Willow.

'I need a word with you, Miss King. Alone.' Before Willow could answer, or even decide what she was going to say, Richard stepped between them.

'Inspector, I think I ought to sit in on your interview. Miss King has no legal representative available, but she ought to have someone to advise her and after all I am her alibi.'

Thinking ungratefully that she was not his chattel and he had no authority over her, Willow forced herself to speak with reasonable politeness.

'There's no need for that, Richard,' she said. 'If the inspector had come to arrest me he would have had a woman police officer with him. Isn't that right, Inspector Worth?'

'That's right, Miss,' he answered, making his voice even blanker than usual. 'I'll say goodnight then, Sir.'

'Yes, do go on, Richard,' said Willow. 'I'll see to this and ring you tomorrow.'

'Are you sure you'll be all right?' he asked, peering at her in the dull light and quite ignoring the policeman. 'Won't you let me come in and . . .'

'Protect me?' she said a little mockingly. 'I don't need protection, my dear. Thank you for my lovely dinner. Don't look so anxious. There's always another day.'

It was not in his nature to make a scene in front of someone else and so he took his departure with dignity intact. But he showed his feelings in the viciousness with which he slammed the car into gear. Willow watched the car pull away and then turned back to the inspector, her front door key in her hand.

'Come on up, Tom,' she said. 'Drink?'

'No thanks,' he said. I just came to bring you this.' He held out to her one of the familiar brown envelopes in which internal communications were passed about DOAP. Surprised, she took it from him and ripped open the envelope. Inside was a single sheet of A4 paper covered in handwriting she recognised as Roger's.

Dear Miss King,
    You will probably know by now what has happened, but I wanted to write to explain that I couldn't help it.
    I have a friend in registry, and Albert made him work for them by threatening me. At first he refused, but when some of Albert's men beat me up, he didn't have an option really. And when I tried to stop it, they did the same to him. We had to go along with them, Miss King. It wasn't safe not to. They said if we told the police they'd kill one of us.
    After Albert heard you talking about corruption in registry, he thought I'd told you what had been going on. He

245

said he'd wreck my friend's life – break his back so that he'd be paralysed. I had to give him something to stop him. I promise I didn't tell him you are Cressida Woodruffe; but I did say that he might get something if he followed you one Thursday evening. I had to. The police told me what he'd done to your flat. I'm so sorry, Miss King, so terribly sorry. But I couldn't let them break his back.

I'm sorry.
Yours, Roger

Shocked by what she had read, Willow could hardly make her voice work. Eventually, without looking at Tom Worth, she asked:

'Do you know what's in it?'

'No,' he said, his voice as unemotional as when she had first heard it. 'But I can imagine. I had him in for an interview first thing this morning and he came across with the whole story. You were right about Albert and the fraud, you see.'

'Roger just told you,' said Willow, looking up at last. Her eyes seemed dazed, as though she could not understand. 'But in this he writes that he was too frightened. . .'

'Presumably I frightened him even more than Albert,' said Worth. There was something in his voice that cut through the fog in Willow's mind. He sounded disgusted with himself.

'What's the matter?' she asked, not altogether sympathetically.

'It's a talent I have – frightening people,' he said. 'I loathe it, but it is too useful to ignore.'

'Not physically?' whispered Willow, genuinely appalled. Worth laughed, a short bitter explosion of sound.

'Of course not,' he said. 'But just as effective it seems.'

'You've presumably arrested Albert,' she said when she had recovered some of her equilibrium. 'Are you charging him with the murder?'

'No, Willow. Don't you remember, he has a cast-iron alibi for that?' said Worth patiently.

'Oh yes, so you told me,' she said vaguely. 'And Roger? Does he get arrested too?'

Worth nodded. At the sight of her face, white and tense, he said:

'He may well not be charged, my dear. It's obvious that he played the most peripheral part in it all and was clearly forced to do that much. But it doesn't rest with me; the case'll go to the Director of Public Prosecutions now. Don't look like that, Willow,' he said sadly.

She shook her head and then tucked the thick red hair behind her ears.

'It's not you,' she said. 'It's me. You realise that this means that Roger – whom I have always rather despised for his silliness and indiscretion – has known about "Cressida Woodruffe" for years and kept it to himself. . . and that I. . .'

Tom Worth shrugged. 'It can't be helped, my dear,' he said before she could finish whatever she had been going to say. 'He's a victim – but not of yours.'

'I don't know,' said Willow, turning away to look out of the window down into the dark street, where the snow was just beginning to lie. 'Don't you see that if I hadn't made that silly, unnecessary joke, Albert would never have thought that I'd discovered what was going on. . . . None of this need have happened.'

'Stop that, Willow,' said Worth. There was tremendous authority in his voice, and when he came to stand behind her she could feel his strength, although he only laid one hand on her shoulder.

'If none of this had happened, Albert would still be running his conspiracy and threatening your clerk and his friend. However horrible, it's better that it's ended.'

'You're right, of course,' she said, turning round to face him. 'Thank you. If there's anything I can do for Roger,

247

will you let me know? A lawyer, or a character testimonial or anything?' Worth nodded.

'Thanks,' said Willow, hating herself. As a distraction she asked: 'And what about the other investigation? How's it going?'

'Hard to say precisely,' he said. 'We've still got your tramp at the station. Don't look like that, my dear: he's warm, well fed, full of good strong tea. They've been taking him through a series of photographs, hoping for a firm identification, all day, but he's either being deliberately uncooperative or else he really can't identify anyone.'

'I see,' said Willow. 'Tom, I think I need. . .'

'I know,' he said, moving away from her. 'I'll get out of your way now. Try to sleep, Will, and don't worry too much.'

'Tom?' Her voice was urgent.

'I can't help it, my dear,' he said, easily understanding what she meant. But he was implacable. 'If he did it, it's better that he should be charged and dealt with. . . .'

'Prison?' said Willow, thinking of all the articles she had read and all the television documentaries she had watched of the wretched conditions in overcrowded prisons: of three men cooped up in a cell built for one for twenty-three hours a day; of inadequate sanitary facilities and 'slopping out', of drug abuse and worse; of the effects of a long sentence on the mental health of prisoners.

'It's better than hanging,' said Worth without any discernible expression.

'Yes,' she answered. 'I know. Will you tell me what happens?'

He nodded, touched her face lightly and then looked at her carefully, as though he was trying to make up his mind about something. Eventually he did say:

'You told me yesterday that you didn't think Albert had the wits to run a scam like that on his own.'

'Yes,' agreed Willow, her eyes sharpening and her voice lifting slightly as her mind welcomed the distraction. 'It always seemed more likely that he was employed by someone cleverer.'

'He was,' answered Tom, still standing very close to her. 'Your friend Algy.'

'What?' exclaimed Willow, genuinely flabbergasted.

'That's what Albert claims,' said Tom. 'He says that very soon after he got the job at DOAP Algy put the proposition to him. . .'

'I wonder,' said Willow interrupting without ceremony.

'What?'

'Whether I was right that Albert wanted to work for Algy in order to blackmail him about Mrs Gripper. You see,' she went on, getting more excited about the idea, 'Albert is about as subtle as a steam-roller and he would probably have plunged straight in with his demands without waiting to find the best way of putting them. Algy, past-master as he was at manipulating people, would have seen at once that the best way of deflecting Albert would be to suggest that they'd both make more money with the pensions scam. Thick as he is, Albert would have thought that a terrific idea, and then Algy would have had him exactly where he needed him. Any more threats of exposing Algy's private life could have been countered with the threat of exposing Albert's fraud. . . . Algy would of course have ensured that there was no evidence of his involvement at all.'

'Isn't all that a little over-subtle?' asked Worth, the scepticism blatant in his eyes and voice.

'I don't think so,' said Willow shaking her head and trying to keep a certain admiration out of her mind. 'Algy was subtle – and clever – and very much enjoyed having people make fools of themselves. How he must have laughed at us all!'

'No wonder your books are so successful!' said Worth, smiling. When Willow looked surprised, he amplified his compliment a little: 'Somewhere in that famously cool analytical brain of yours is an excessively vivid imagination. Well, my dear, I'd better leave you to it. I'll be in touch.'

Almost as soon as he had gone the lightness and amusement Willow had achieved as she described Algy's possible involvement in the fraud disappeared. She was left with the guilt and regret about Roger's involvement and her fears about Algy's probable murderer. Telling herself that opportunity, anger, unhappiness and a certain intensity of character were not enough to prove a man's guilt, she still could not put them out of her mind; but nor could she imagine any motive that seemed genuinely convincing.

Dredging up the remains of her self-discipline, she put the problem from her and went to bed, where, despite taking two yellow sleeping pills, she had a disturbed night. In the morning, with her head aching and her eyes feeling burnt and sore, she went straight to her writing room after breakfast and tried to write.

Not surprisingly both inspiration and professionalism failed her and she turned instead to the perennial task of tidying up the room. It was the one place in the flat where she did not allow Mrs Rusham to work, and rough paper, notes, typescripts and proofs tended to pile up unmanageably.

The sorting and filing and throwing-away did soothe Willow after a time and she even began to enjoy watching the surface of her large desk becoming clearer. By the time she started to file the miscellaneous correspondence, she had achieved a reasonable degree of serenity. But as she reached for the file, which always hung at the back of the filing drawer, she noticed a rolled photograph jammed behind it.

Willow sat back, surprised, and carefully unrolled the long picture on her desk.

'Why did I ever bring it here?' she asked herself aloud,

for it was the one official photograph of the senior staff of DOAP that had ever been taken during her time. There had been some reason for it, which she could not now remember, and it had been taken soon after the arrival of Algernon Endelsham as minister.

It was posed like an old-fashioned school photograph, with the minister and the permanent secretary in the middle – on chairs – and the rest of the Civil Servants arranged in order of rank around them. The deputy and under secretaries stood in groups on either side of the minister and the perm., with the assistant secretaries flanking them, with the principals sitting on the floor in front like new bugs at a prep school.

Algy stood out, as he would have done in any gathering, for his height and his splendid shoulders and his features: the big grey eyes, the straight nose and dominating chin. Even his lips looked generous, thought Willow, knowing that she would never again believe those novelists who wrote that character could be read from a person's features. She looked along the lines of dark-suited men and the few women until she came to the man she suspected of the murder.

As she peered at his likeness on the stiff, glossy paper in front of her, she was visited by an extraordinary idea: an idea unlikely in the abstract and yet so obvious with the evidence in front of her that she wondered that she had never even considered it.

She pulled the telephone towards her and pressed in the number of the department. When one of the girls at the switchboard answered she asked to be put through to Valerie, the establishments officer's secretary.

'I'll put you throu-ough,' sang the telephonist and a moment later Willow heard Valerie's voice, saying:

'Can I help you?'

'Valerie, it's Willow King here,' she said. 'Is the under secretary still closeted with the police or could I have a word with him?'

'I'm afraid he is still with Inspector Worth, Miss King,' said Valerie. 'Is it very urgent? I know that they will be breaking for lunch at twelve today. Could I get him to call you then? Oh, but your aunt isn't on the telephone, is she? Well you could ring back.'

'I'm not with her today,' said Willow, pleased to notice that Roger's indiscretion and Albert's discovery had not yet reached their colleagues. She improvised quickly: 'I've had to get a neighbour in to see to her while I come up to London today. But I must see Mr Englewood. Look, will you tell him that I shall be in Selina's wine bar – where he and I had a drink the other day – from twelve onwards. Can you ask him to join me if it's humanly possible?'

'Of course, Miss King. I'll tell him,' said Valerie, sounding as though she was enjoying the hint of drama. Willow thanked her and put down the receiver. She went to change into her noncommittal jeans, called out to Mrs Rusham that she would be out for the rest of the day and left for Abbeville Road.

The temperature was even lower than it had been the previous few days and the new snow was lying thickly on the pavements. As she walked towards the tube station, Willow kept sliding and nearly lost her balance more than once.

But she reached Clapham at about ten to twelve and made her way as carefully as she could to the wine bar. There she ordered a jug of mulled wine, two helpings of hot *pâté en croûte*, and settled down to read the newspaper she had brought with her. It was only a few minutes before she was interrupted.

'Willow, my dear,' came Englewood's voice, sharp and anxious. 'Are you all right? What has happened?'

'Michael,' she said, flinging down the paper. 'Thank you for coming. Sit down and have a glass of wine.'

'But what is it? Valerie told me you sounded distraught on the telephone,' he said, and her conscience pricked as she saw how worn he looked and how the lines

252

on his face had deepened since the beginning of the investigation.

'I'm afraid she must have been investing a perfectly ordinary message with drama, Michael,' she said unfairly. 'Roger is for ever doing it. But I did badly want to see you.'

'Why?'

'Have some wine,' she said, pouring him a glassful. 'And some *pâté*.'

'Why did you want to see me, Willow?' he asked, and there was a quite different note in his voice. For the first time since she had decided to talk to him she remembered her promise to Tom Worth, but despite the promise and her sudden fear, she did not consider abandoning her task. As though the sound of his voice had stiffened her resolve, she sat up straighter, looked at him directly and said:

'Michael, I cannot believe that you intended to kill your brother. I am quite sure it must have been an accident. But you can't really have expected to keep it secret for ever, can you?'

At that he did pull out the chair opposite hers and sat down heavily. His shoulders drooped and he breathed deeply several times.

'How did you find out?' he asked at last in a voice that expressed no more than a mild interest.

'About your relationship?' asked Willow. He nodded. 'I can't think why I never realised it before,' she went on. 'But today I was looking at that photograph that was taken of us all and I saw how alike you are to him. Take away the moustache, and your faces are exactly the same shape. Take away his arrogance and the drawl, and your voices are – were – the same. Your hands, too, now I come to think of it.'

He snatched them off the table and stuffed them between his knees. But he did not speak.

'What horribly bad luck that he turned up at DOAP,' she said with some genuine sympathy. 'Having changed your name and got away from him, you must have thought that you were safe.'

'The change was no choice of mine,' he said, and again she heard that faint echo of Algy's voice. 'He was still at Cambridge when I left my humble red-brick university, and he was already making a name for himself. He told me that I was to call myself something different because he did not want his future to be messed up by any embarrassing connection made with me.'

'God, he was a shit!' said Willow, her own voice warm with anger. Englewood made his usual half-bow in acknowledgement of her sympathy.

'Yes,' he said as he expelled a deep breath. 'You obviously know rather more about us both than I had realised and so I won't need to give you the background of our childhood.' He laughed and curiously there was little bitterness in the sound. 'You're right about his shit-like character, but I was pleased enough to do what he wanted then. I made him a deal: I would change my name, never communicate with him, never tell anyone I was related to him however wonderfully successful he became, on condition that he never approached, spoke to, or searched for me again.'

'But it went wrong,' said Willow. 'How did he meet your wife?'

'Just as I told you,' he answered. 'I do truly think that that one was a coincidence. He wouldn't have recognised the name, you see, because he had no way of knowing what I'd decided to call myself. I changed my name by statutory declaration so that there would be no record. But I ought to have known that I'd never be safe. It may have been just damnable luck that Algy met my wife like that and was taken with her. She was exceedingly pretty – and susceptible: thrilled, I suspect, by his glamour.' He fell silent and when Willow refilled his glass he drank the warm wine down in one gulp.

'She invited him to dinner with us unexpectedly or I'd have stopped it. You should have seen his delight when she introduced us! I could see straight away what he was going to do. You see, Willow, that was one of the ghastly things: I had to watch the seduction every step of the way and there was nothing I could do to stop it, although I tried. And even while Algy was reducing her to a state of desperate desire, he was watching me to see how I was taking it. In a way it was a kind of relief when she finally said that she was leaving me to go to him.'

Willow found herself quite unable to eat, but she too drank the stickily cooling wine and held up the empty jug to signal to the waitress for more.

'But of course, Algy didn't want her. As soon as he had got her away from me, he dumped her,' said Englewood, staring down into the bottom of his empty glass. Willow looked at him in speculation.

'And wouldn't you have her back?' she asked at last. At that his face began to redden and his moustache quiver with the anger that she now knew lay just below the placid surface of his character.

'I begged her to come back,' he said, and Willow almost shivered at the sound of his voice. 'But as I said before, she could not bear the thought of living with someone who had witnessed the whole of her humiliation.' His face had reverted to its normal pallidity and Willow saw that he was chewing at his bottom lip. She waited.

'That's why I was so afraid for you, Willow,' he said. She shifted uncomfortably under the intensity of his stare. 'When I saw that you were not going to be taken in, I knew that he would be furious and I wondered what he would try next. He wouldn't have been able to leave you the winner like that. Somehow he was going to have to humiliate you. . . as he did everyone in the end.'

'But he didn't, Michael,' said Willow gently. 'It was months since he had understood that I would not sleep with him, and he was still perfectly friendly.' The new jug of wine was brought to their table and Englewood absent-mindedly poured them each a glassful.

'I suspect he would have done,' he said sadly. 'It was simply not possible for him to leave anyone else in a position superior to his own. That's why he was so successful always. He was driven to it.'

Englewood had been so absorbed in his story that he had never looked round when the door opened and new customers came in to find tables around them. As he produced his last indictment, the door opened once again and Willow looked up to see Inspector Worth flanked by two uniformed policemen come into the small wine bar.

Worth caught her eye and she knew that she had never seen him so angry. Checking that Englewood's attention was still deflected, she looked back at Tom Worth, shook her head very slightly and gestured towards an empty table. Much to her relief he took it and made his officers sit there with him. When they were settled, Willow poured out more wine and said softly:

'How did it happen Michael?'

He put down his glass and covered his face with both hands. Gently she put her hands on his wrists and pulled them away from his face.

'Michael,' she said. He sighed

'You know,' he said at last, 'I've been longing to talk to you about it. I nearly told you that other time we were here.'

'I know you did,' said Willow. 'Tell me now.'

'All right. As you probably know, Algy couldn't help tormenting me. I'd done all right in the Civil Service. Under secretary (establishments) in DOAP isn't the most thrilling peak of a man's career, but it's all right.'

'Of course it is, Michael.'

'But Algy wanted me to know how pathetic he thought it – and then more: he wanted to show me that I couldn't even do that properly; and went out of his way to cause trouble and difficulty whenever he was bored.'

Suppressing the thought that poor Michael Englewood must have become paranoid about his brother, Willow sat and listened in silence; as did Inspector Worth and his men sitting at the next table.

'Between that and what he was trying to do to you,' said Englewood, 'I realised that I had to stop him or I'd have no self-respect for the rest of my life. I asked him to come to my office that evening to tell him that the worm had turned, that if he didn't lay off I'd blow his cover.'

'How?' asked Willow involuntarily. Englewood shrugged his tweed-covered shoulders.

'Oh, by telling the tabloids about him: the mistresses, the persecutions, forcing me to change my name – even my poor wife. And then he'd be exposed to the world for what he actually was: cruel, mischievous, power-crazy and damned dangerous.'

Willow caught sight of Inspector Worth gesturing to one of his men, who opened a notebook and took a pencil from his tunic pocket.

'So what happened, Michael?' she asked.

'He told me we'd have to talk about it and asked me to walk across the common with him to his car so that we could get it all said without inquisitive people listening to us. I heard him ring Albert and tell him to wait at the top of Cedar's Road, and then we set off.

'At about half-way over, while he was talking and I was answering back for once, he suddenly grabbed me by my neck.' As he said that, Englewood pulled the cravat he wore away from his neck and Willow saw the fading remains of ferocious bruises on either side of his jugular.

'As you probably know,' he went on while she tried to deal with the effects of shock in herself, 'he was immensely strong and I panicked. All I had to defend myself was. . .'

'Your chess computer,' said Willow suddenly. 'That's what it was, wasn't it?' Englewood nodded. 'And I suppose you just hit him and hit him and hit him until he let go,' she said. He nodded again.

'And by then he was dead,' he said.

'You needn't tell me the rest,' she said. 'I know that you must have wiped the blood off your face and hands with something, put your reversible coat on the other way about so that the stains didn't show on the outside, and walked to Clapham Junction station. There you washed the remaining blood off your face and hands and neck in the gents' lavatory, and took a train to Surbiton – later than the six-fifteen from Waterloo, despite what you told me.'

'Yes, that's right,' he agreed. 'I should have known that someone would find out, but I never thought it would be you.'

'And I suppose you got rid of the chess computer somewhere,' Willow went on, trying not to hear the pain in that statement.

'Yes,' he said again. 'And all the clothes I'd been wearing. That night when I met you outside the building, I was on my way to buy more. And when I got back to Surbiton that night, I soaked all the bloodstained stuff in a huge basin of surgical spirit to get the blood out and then in the middle of the night took it to the river, weighted it with a couple of bricks and chucked it in. I don't think anyone saw me.'

Willow saw Tom Worth standing up, but before he could cross the small strip of floor between their two tables, Englewood said:

'I'd better go and find Worth now.' He smiled at Willow and she tried to think that there was a new look of peace in his face, but she could not quite manage it. 'I suppose I always knew that I wouldn't get away with it in the end,' he said. 'And I was always prepared to confess if they accused one of the staff.'

'I realised that that was why you sat in on all the interviews,' said Willow. 'I am sorry, Michael.'

'Yes, Algy wasn't worth going to prison for,' he said and turned to face the police.

Epilogue

THAT EVENING at about half-past nine Willow's front
door bell buzzed. She got up from the silk rug in front
of the drawing-room fire and picked up the entry-phone.

'Yes?' she said, hoping that it would not be Richard.

'Willow, it's Tom. May I come up?'

'Please,' she said simply and pressed the buzzer. When
he reached her flat, she let him in. He no longer looked
as angry as he had in the wine bar, but there was an
expression in his eyes that worried her.

'Drink?' she said as she had said the night before.

'Whisky please,' he said shortly and then went and sat
down on one of the bedroom chairs she had put in the
drawing room until she could replace the damaged sofas.
She went to pour him some of what little Emma had told
her the Sloanes called Leapfrog whisky. Handing him the
glass, she said:

'Are you still angry with me?' He took a deep swallow of
the peaty whisky and shuddered as it went down.

'No,' he said, looking at her with a slight smile. 'But I was
when I discovered what you were up to. Willow, it was so
damned dangerous: how could you have taken such a risk?'

Remembering that she had promised him that she would drop her investigation and ask no more questions that might inflame people, she tried to explain.

'After Roger's bombshell, I couldn't just let it go. I'd been so wrong about Roger that I thought perhaps I was wrong about Englewood too. I was fairly certain that it was he whom you suspected, as I did, and I had to make sure. That's all.'

'How did you discover that he was Algy's brother?' said Tom.

'That was chance, but I can't think why I never suspected it before. I was sitting looking at an old office photograph and realised how alike they were; then I remembered that poor Roger had once overheard them quarrelling and been unable to distinguish which one of them was talking – their voices were extraordinarily similar you know, except that in normal speech Algy drawled. And then it all just fell into place. I'd heard a lot about the brothers when they were at prep school and Michael Englewood really did seem to be the kind of man that pathetic Endelsham Ma. might have grown into. What'll happen now?'

'Well, what he said to you is not admissible evidence, unfortunately, but we did finally get an identification from the tramp,' said Worth.

'Are you telling me that Englewood hasn't confessed formally?' said Willow, astonished. 'But that was what he was going to do.'

'I know,' said Worth. 'But I reminded him of his right to have a solicitor present during our interview.' He fell silent and sat turning the heavy glass tumbler round and round in his strong hands.

'Ah,' said Willow, thinking both that she now understood the odd expression in Worth's eyes and that he was going to be immensely unpopular with his superiors for effectively silencing a confession. 'But you have your identification.'

'Yes, we have,' agreed Worth. 'But whether your tramp'll identify Englewood in court and whether he'd withstand a good cross-examination, I don't know.'

'Why? D'you think he was drunk?' At that Tom looked up at last and even smiled.

'It helps to talk to someone intelligent,' he said. 'Yes, and not only drunk but the kind of ill-washed homeless man who travels the tubes and trains and frightens other passengers into changing carriages; no jury is going to send a man down for life on his evidence. There's no harm in him at all and he has perfectly good eye sight and plenty of intelligence. But not a good witness.'

'No,' agreed Willow, 'but whatever his solicitor has done so far, I think Michael might plead guilty when it comes to court.'

'Perhaps,' said Tom. 'And perhaps they will get him off on self-defence.'

'Surely not all the way off,' protested Willow, actually shocked, although a moment earlier she had been appalled by the prospect of life imprisonment that Michael Englewood faced.

'Shouldn't have thought so. Manslaughter, probably. But it'll be a horrible case: there's the public view of Algernon Endelsham, you know, and the judge and jury will have to be convinced by the defence that he wasn't at all like that before they'll even begin to understand that pathetic man.'

Willow stood, looking down at the bowed head of Tom Worth, hardly even aware that she was thinking of his really remarkable charity: surely most investigating officers would be so pleased to have unmasked their murderer that they would hardly spare a thought for the poor chances of his defence, particularly if the Sunday paper's article was right and Tom had been put on the case because it was thought to be insoluble. Forgetting Michael Englewood for the moment, all Willow could think of was that she minded very much that Tom Worth was feeling unhappy.

262

He lifted his head and looked up at her for a long, silent moment.

'What'll you do?' he asked heavily at last. 'Will you go on at DOAP?'

'Oh, I think so,' said Willow. 'For the moment anyway; I've had a lot of shocks one way and another just recently, and I need to get back into my old routine before I can absorb them and decide what to do about them.' She tried to smile at him.

'Am I one of them?' he asked gently and when she nodded silently, he added: 'Well you don't have to worry about me. I meant it all, including the fact that I don't plan to smother you with emotion.' He stopped there and she could not think what to say next.

'Thank you,' she said at last and from the way he smiled at her thought that he had understood her fears and her reservations.

'Could I have some more whisky?' he said. Willow got up and poured them both more. She sat, sipping her drink, thinking about the two unhappy Endelsham brothers, and all the people who had been hurt by Algy's games: Michael Englewood, who had been driven to kill and now faced years in gaol; Amanda Gripper, desperately unhappy and stuck with her dreadful husband, who would probably resent her inheritance from Algy's estate even more than he had resented their love affair; little Emma Gnatche who had loved him too; even Richard, whose schooldays he had made miserable; and all the people who had ever worked for him and been alternately exalted and humiliated to suit his capricious pleasures. Perhaps he was better dead, she thought a little desperately.

'Willow,' said Tom quietly. She looked up obediently and saw that he was smiling again. He raised his glass to her. She wondered what he would say and arranged her mind to accept some declaration with becoming gratitude and without betraying too many of her fears.

263

'I'd still like to strangle you, Cressida Woodruffe,' he said, and her tense features relaxed. 'But I had to come to see you. I meant what I said about not stifling you with emotion, but I needed you tonight.'

With a feeling of quite unprecedented emotion, Willow walked across the carpet to his chair. She knelt down on the floor (not even thinking that whenever Richard was in her flat any kneeling was done by him), took Tom's glass away from him and took his rugged face between her cool hands.

'And I needed you, too,' she confessed and kissed him.

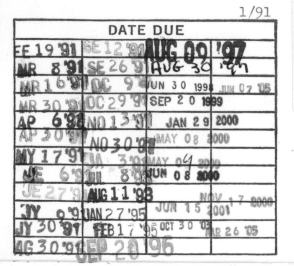